MW00714872

RETURN
OF THE JAGUAR

RETURN
OF THE JAGUAR

A Novel

NORM CUDDY

Return of the Jaguar
Copyright © 2017 by Rose Cuddy

First paperback edition published in December 2017

www.returnofthejaguar.ca

ISBN 978–0–9958689–0–8 (paperback)
ISBN 978–0–9958689–1–5 (eBook)

Front cover photo © anankkml
Author photo © Rose Cuddy

Editing by Maureen Phillips (www.lifeandwords.com)
Cover and interior design by Jan Westendorp (www.katodesignandphoto.com)
Production by Behind the Book (www.behindthebook.ca)

Printed and bound in Canada by Friesens

MIX
Paper from
responsible sources
FSC
www.fsc.org   FSC® C016245

This book is dedicated by me, Rose Cuddy, to my husband Norm, who wrote it. Norm did not live to see his novel published. After working on it for many years, he finally finished this version in January of 2016. Norm died five months later.

Norm, I am so very proud of you. Words cannot say how much I respect your courage in pursuing this novel, and I'm truly amazed at how you evolved as a writer over the years.

I'm not sure you wanted your novel published, but . . . here it is!

I'll love you forever.

Rose

PROLOGUE

Norm Cuddy, sadly, didn't live to see *Return of the Jaguar* published. His wife, Rose, soul mate and love of his life, was surprised to find a memory stick in Norm's desk drawer after he died of cancer in the summer of 2016. On the memory stick was Norm's manuscript. In a scene from the novel, Ted Somerville, the main protagonist, witnesses the celebrations for the Day of the Dead in Acteal, Mexico. Norm writes, "Life was transitory, death inevitable. To die was simply to move from one dimension to another." With these words, Norm seems to have prophesied his own demise.

It's a great gift to Norm that Rose has taken this work of historical fiction and published it for the enjoyment of others. And what a tale it is. Set against the backdrop of the Zapatista Revolution that took place in the mid 90's, Norm's book is not only a love story but an engrossing tale of intrigue and mystery that shines a light on the massacre of forty-five people in the small village of Acteal, Mexico, on December 22, 1997. This is a mystical story, both troubling and difficult at times, but it is also a celebration of the freedom that ultimately came to the people of Acteal and the Zapatista revolutionaries.

It's heartening to know that in next year's 2018 election in Mexico, for the first time ever, a Mayan Indian—and a woman at that—will run as a candidate with the support of the Zapatista Army of National Liberation. Rose's timing in bringing this book to light is fitting. Or was it Norm who gently directed her from "another dimension"?

Maureen Phillips

Editor

"Long ago, before the conquistadors, the jaguar lived in Chiapas. He was the lord of the jungle and the god of my ancestors. He controlled the sun in the sky and ruled the animals in the forest. His name was El Jaguar, and this was his land. And the land was free."

—Abelardo in *Return of the Jaguar*

On December 22, 1997, a band of gunmen charged into a mountain village in Chiapas, spraying rifle fire and swinging machetes. The Red Cross said that forty-five Mayan Indians were killed, including fifteen children.

Subcomandante Marcos, the leader of the Zapatista rebels, claimed that government-sponsored paramilitaries were responsible for the attack.

The killings in Acteal capped an outburst of violence in which more than three hundred opponents of the government have been killed. Tensions continue to simmer because the government has refused to make peace with the Zapatista guerrillas, whose strongholds are in the region.

The Zapatistas are demanding freedom for the Mayans, more land to farm, equal justice, and autonomous political power. Their anti-government cause has gained widespread support throughout rural Mexico.

CHAPTER 1

Sandy mountains stretched to the horizon—craggy hills, expanses of waste land. None of the pretty postcard hues, no majestic cacti—just mud colours under a white-hot sky.

Ted leaned against the bus' window sill. He put his head on the glass so the cold blast of the air conditioner would take away the ache behind his eyes. He had been forced on this trip—a ridiculous notion—go to a spa, get well. And then everything would be okay. Like hell it would.

"Is this your first time?"

It took a moment for him to focus. The woman next to him was of indeterminate age—she could have been anywhere between forty-five and seventy. Her skin had the waxy tightness left by plastic surgery.

"My first time?" he asked. "What do you mean?"

"Your first time to the spa?"

"Oh, the spa. Yes, it is," he said, and turned his attention out the window.

"This is my fourth time. I'm from Phoenix. How about you?"

"Canada . . . Vancouver."

"Oh? Where is . . . "

"North of Seattle."

"Oh, yes, I know where that is. My name's Mary . . . So what's yours?"

"My name?" He sighed and half turned in his seat to face her. "Ted, Ted Somerville."

"You're travelling alone?"

"Alone? . . . That's for sure."

"Have you heard about the things they have been doing with green grapes? They are the new wonder cure for every . . . " Mary droned on while Ted hunched lower in his seat.

He glanced listlessly at his travelling companions—typical tourists bound for Mexico—a mixed group, mostly single, a few couples, some younger men, obviously gay. Frizzy hair and face-lifts making inane conversation. Nothing here to interest him.

A perky tour guide was explaining the protocol at the border. "Usually we stay on the bus. But today we must go inside. There has been trouble with the Zapatistas. It is nothing to worry about, just sign your forms and . . . "

Who or what was a Zapatista? Not that he cared. He knew next to nothing about Mexico and had no interest in learning.

He first noticed the woman when she introduced herself to her seatmate. She sat directly in front of him, one row up. He could not see her face, only a fall of dark hair. "Barbara . . . Barbara Jones. I'm in brokerage . . . a . . . bookkeeper."

Something in her tone attracted him. Flat and listless—just like his mood—making small talk but wanting to be somewhere else. Maybe he had something in common with at least one other person. He began to eavesdrop.

The woman next to her was telling the story of her life, all the while chewing bubble gum.

"I'm from LA. Where you from? This is my third trip to the spa. I'm a fitness instructor, you know. How about you?"

"This is my first time."

"The classes are great. Have you ever done a Pilates workout?"

"No," Barbara replied, in a voice as far away as the mountains.

"Oh, but it's great for toning. You'll have to try it."

The bus passed a group of migrant farmers tending a parched field, working with shovels and hoes around a few spindly plants. Dark eyes visible beneath broad, beaten hats, skin baked black by the sun.

"Wetbacks," the fitness instructor said, "shiftless and lazy. Sneak across the border whenever they can. We should do something about the problem, but the . . . "

Barbara turned in her seat and looked directly past him out the window. He guessed her to be in her early thirties, with regular features—dark hair with fair skin. Something about those eyes, silver-grey crystalline—he looked away.

It was as if a cloud had blocked the sun and a chill touched him. He felt she was staring directly into his head. Her lips moved—he heard her voice as a whisper—in Spanish, most of which he did not understand. Just the phrase "*es muertos.*" He lost the rest in the road noise.

She turned back in her seat.

"Ever been to Mexico before?" said the fitness instructor, examining her nails.

Barbara answered so softly he could hardly hear. "Once. A long time ago."

"You don't say," said the fitness instructor, snapping her gum. "Wait till you get to the spa. They do a dynamite massage."

Barbara turned back to the window. She fiddled with a loose strand of hair. "Excuse me, I have a headache." She reclined her seat and closed her eyes.

Fifteen minutes later, around a bend in the road, the crossing came into sight—a clutch of cement block buildings. No trees. No greenery. Just the sprawl of a dirty border town in the background.

"Look, we're here." The fitness instructor nudged Barbara's arm. "Those hills over there, that's Mexico."

He watched as her shoulders stiffened. Her right hand seemed to dig into the hair behind her ear and then dropped to her neck—she was pressing so tightly the flesh on her fingers turned white. Her gaze seemed fixed on something in the distance. He looked in the same direction, but there was nothing there to see.

Looking back at her, he was riveted, unable to tear his eyes from her hand, fingers now almost imbedded in her neck. He had a sense of déjà vu. Did he know her from somewhere? Surely not. But the hairs on his neck were tingling. The countryside that had seemed so uninviting before now promised . . . he wished he knew what. His eyes swept the horizon but came back to settle on what he could see of the woman's head as her forehead pressed against the window. He clenched his hands, conscious of the moisture on his palms. He failed to notice the bus had stopped.

The passengers filed off the bus into the customs office. Barbara pulled her jacket around her shoulders and rose from her seat. Ted followed at a distance, not letting her out of his sight.

CHAPTER 2

"*Atención!*" THE GUARD ANNOUNCED. "Have your papers ready."

The checkpoint was a one-story building with a flat roof, its windows coated with dust. The words "Welcome to Mexico" were faded and covered with graffiti. The interior reminded Ted of something from an old Hollywood movie, with props from central casting, battered desks, ancient file cabinets, an old ceiling fan turning slowly. Flies buzzed on the window.

The bus passengers lined up along the front of the room. The day was sweltering, the building an airless oven. The others began to fidget and loosen their clothing. Ted hung back and completed his form. He hated lineups.

The lone customs guard was a big man in a uniform that looked too tight. He seemed oblivious to the heat, taking his time and smoking cheap cigarettes. Ashes spotted his jacket and papers. An attractive young woman sat in front of him.

"What is the reason for your visit to Mexico?"

"I . . . I'm going to the spa."

"Is that for business or for pleasure?" The guard was staring at her breasts.

Ted felt a rivulet of sweat run down his neck into his collar. He wanted out of here.

"Pleasure . . . Yes, it's for pleasure." The woman blushed.

"Ah, yes, pleasure." The guard stamped her passport and looked up. The woman escaped back to her friends.

"Next!"

Barbara took a seat in front of the guard. She clasped her handbag close to her chest. She was dressed all in black—her jacket was large on her and too warm for the weather.

She handed the officer her immigration form. The guard glanced at the document and looked up.

"Take off your sunglasses," he said.

She removed them and put them on the desk. Too quickly, Ted thought.

"You have not filled in this form correctly. There is only one name. Go back in the line. You must fill in all the spaces."

"Sir, I have filled it out. Bailey is my full name."

"I do not think so, señorita. Everyone has at least two names—unless you are some famous movie star like Madonna, eh?" The guard rose to his feet and came around the desk. He looked her up and down. His hand trailed across the back of her chair. Her shoulders narrowed.

"You do not look like a movie star."

The ticking of the clock grew loud in Ted's ears. What the hell? Her name was Bailey? On the bus she had called herself Barbara—he was sure of it.

Perspiration beaded on her brow. "Really, sir, I only have one name."

"Do not fool with me! Maybe you are trying to sneak into Mexico. The capitán will speak to you." He took two steps towards the back office and gestured to the guard inside.

"Please, it's true," she called after him. "I'll miss my bus. Look at my passport." She opened the booklet to a page filled with American currency.

The guard stopped and turned, but before he could see her hand, Ted moved between them. He covered the money with one hand and thrust it in his pant pocket. He put his other hand on Bailey's shoulder.

"There you are, dear. I told you to wait for me."

"Qué? Who are you?" the guard demanded.

"Any problems, officer? Ted Somerville is my name." He slid his passport and documentation across the desk. "Bailey and I are off to the spa for a week."

For a moment Ted thought it would not work. The guard hesitated, picked up one passport and then the other, examined the photographs and rifled through a rolodex. He gave Bailey a last appraising look and stamped the documents.

"Next."

Ted held her tightly by the arm until they were out of the building.

As soon as they were alone she pulled sharply away. "What the hell did you think you were doing?"

"Sorry, I just thought you needed some help."

"I didn't need your help. He would have taken the money."

Ted pointed to the sign outside the shed. "Don't you read?"

The sign stood in contrast to everything about the customs post. It was bright and new.

ANYONE CAUGHT BRIBING
GOVERNMENT OFFICIALS
WILL BE PROSECUTED.
HAVE A NICE STAY IN MEXICO.

"Yeah! You'll see." She turned, and got onto the bus.

CHAPTER 3

Bailey avoided conversation for the rest of the trip. The fitness instructor found someone more receptive to her prattle and left her alone. On arriving at the spa, she exited the bus quickly and caught a cab outside the gate.

"Back to town," she told the cabbie.

She checked into a budget hotel on the main street of Tecate. It was a dingy place with spotted sheets and plastic curtains. She changed into jeans and a khaki shirt.

She picked the smallest of the many pawnshops. The store boasted a large selection of firearms, from silver-plated derringers to assault weapons. A hand-lettered sign advised that purchases were cash only and in American dollars. She stood in front of a glass case full of handguns.

"May I help you, señorita?" The clerk asked.

"I want a pistol."

"We have many kinds as you can see. What do you want it for? Sport? Marksmanship? Protection perhaps?"

"It's for sport," she said. "I'll take the Smith and Wesson thirty calibre, the black one. And a box of hollow-nosed bullets."

"Hollow-nosed? That is not the ammunition for target practice, you need . . . "

"Just wrap them up, okay? I have the cash." She paid the clerk and slipped the weapon into her pack.

Back in her room she took out an old copy of *Newsweek* and opened it to a dog-eared page. The photo showed a handsome olive-skinned army officer, late thirties or early forties, with his hat cocked at a jaunty angle. He held a large cigar, and on his face was a self-satisfied smile. The caption read

"Mexican Army Wins Battle with Rebels." She spread the magazine on the pillow, took the pistol and the box of bullets, and lay on her side. Her face was level with the magazine.

"So, Hernandez," she whispered to the photograph, "I have a surprise for you. I'm back. And I'll be coming. Can't wait to see you." She caressed each bullet as she loaded the pistol.

She lay awake for a long time, fully clothed on top of the sheets with her eyes open. Even so, she could not stop the memories that played in a continuous loop across her mind.

Bailey wipes her brow and sets her knapsack on the ground. She has been climbing all day on an endless road through a stunted jungle. She arrives in a little village, the houses neat and freshly painted. She calls to a house across a picket fence.

"Hello! Is anyone there?"

A dark face appears at a window. "There is no need to shout. My hearing is very good. What do you want?"

"I'm looking for the village of Acteal," she said in Spanish. Is this it? I'm from Farm Relief. I'm to be working here. I was told to ask for Rosa."

"This is Acteal, and I am Rosa," the woman answers. "We were expecting someone much older." Her round face formed into a half smile. "So what does a child like you know about farming?"

"You're Rosa? Good! No, great! There's so much to plan. I saw your fields on my way here. Those fruit trees by the road, they're not doing well. They need some fertilizer. I know something that will work; we will collect the chicken droppings. And the beans should have less water. We can build a trench, and the water the beans don't need we can use to grow more tomatoes. We should get started right away, the rains will be coming and then—"

Rosa shook her head and smiled. "Slow down, everything in good time. Now you must eat. You must be hungry. We have been waiting for you. Here are my children. Pedro! Jose! Manuela! Come meet our guest!"

A clutch of villagers converges on her. A man takes her knapsack and escorts her to a table set with many places. Somewhere a guitar begins to play.

CHAPTER 4

TED HARDLY NOTICED THE BORDER TOWN they passed—it could have been a town anywhere, just poorer. More boarded up windows and false fronts. What had he been thinking? Butting in to help some stranger. For all he knew she might be a criminal. And then she just brushed him off like he was trying to pick her up. He burned with embarrassment. He was such a fool.

The spa was just outside the border town. The bus drove through a security gate and up a driveway lined in flowers, the first bit of colour since leaving San Diego. The tourists lined up in the elegant rotunda of the reception centre. He looked for Bailey among the bobbing heads but could not spot her.

His reservation was processed by a young Mexican woman. She asked a series of questions, ranging from his physical fitness level to his fondness for soy products. "We need to know these things for our records."

"Age?"

"Forty-two."

"Occupation?"

"Attorney."

"Oh, we get many attorneys here."

"Lucky you . . . Sorry, just a long day."

"Is okay. Next of kin?"

"None."

"That's all for now. Anything you like, you call us," she said and smiled.

"One more thing," he said. "I have a friend staying here, name of Bailey. Could you give me her room number?"

"Sorry, señor, there is no one staying here with that name."

"How about Jones, Barbara Jones?"

The clerk checked her files and then shook her head.

He settled into a hacienda set slightly apart from the other buildings. He told himself to look on the bright side. He was here for a week, may as well make the best of it. At least the accommodations were nice. His front window looked out over a ravine; a river ran as a ribbon far below. Maybe this would do him some good.

Where was she?

His good intentions did not get him through the first day. He went for a morning hike, breakfasted in the common room, attended a lecture on nutrition—and then quit. He could not take the idle conversations. The "Hi-how-are-you-I'm-Sally" chatter made him want to scream. And he spent every minute scanning the crowd for Bailey—and hating himself for it.

He retreated to his hacienda and a book but ended up sitting on his piazza with his book unopened. He couldn't read. His mind kept churning. Bad decisions, bad marriage, no future. He tried to focus on the sunlight playing on the nearby hills. But he could not stop the thoughts. And they kept coming back to the same thing. His life was a mess and this place was not the answer. He needed a drink.

He called the front desk. "This is Ted Somerville in 40G. Something has come up. I have to leave early." He threw his clothes in a suitcase. Maybe he could find a beach hotel that served scotch.

He paced the floor, waiting for the porter. Where was this damned service they promised? Finally a knock came on his door. "A minute!" he called and zipped his suitcase shut.

The knock came again, but louder.

He pulled the door open. "I said I'd be right . . . "

Bailey stood under the light. She was dressed in denim, with her hair pulled back. Her lips formed a straight line, as though her jaw was clenched too tight.

"This is a surprise," he said. "I thought it was the . . . Come in."

She walked right past him, and he closed the door.

"Sit down," he said. "Can I offer you—"

"This isn't a social call," she said. "I need your help. Someone is following me."

"What?" This made no sense. The spa was fenced and guarded.

"I'm staying in town. In a hotel," she said. "They are watching my room. I can't go back there."

Bailey sat on the edge of the bed. She pulled a piece of paper from her shirt pocket. Her hands trembled as she unwrapped it. "This was left in my room."

The message was in a scrawled hand. "GREETINGS BAILEY. WELCOME TO MEXICO."

"Have you called the police?"

Her look told him he was an idiot for asking. "Look, this is Mexico. The police probably sent this."

Too fast. He was trying to make sense of this. Why would the police follow her? And if they were, why should he get involved? This was trouble. His instincts told him to avoid all complications.

But he felt it coursing through his body—the same high he had felt at the border. In spite of himself he had been looking for her for two days, and now she was in his room. And she needed his help.

"I need to get my stuff from my room, but I can't go back there. They don't know you. If you could just go in and get it for me . . . "

"Let's go," he said, trying to sound more assured than he felt.

Ten minutes later they were in a cab, heading out the gates towards town.

Darkness was falling when he entered the lobby of a budget hotel, a flophouse with thin walls and noisy air conditioners. The desk clerk did not look up from his newspaper when Ted rang the bell.

"Ten dollars," the clerk said.

"For what?"

"Ten dollars an hour and no questions. No parties or rough trade. No receipts."

Ted pulled the newspaper away from the clerk's face. "I have a friend staying here. I need her key and her passport."

The clerk put his cigarette down. "Look we don't . . . "

Ted pushed a hundred dollar bill across the desk. "Her name is Barbara Jones."

The clerk slid the money into a drawer. He pulled a key off the wall behind him. "2B, top of the stairs, turn right." He shrugged. "But no passport."

Ted pulled out his wallet and peeled off more bills.

"Not that," the clerk said, looking wistfully at the money, "the policía took it—this morning. They do that sometimes. They check it against their computers and then give it back. I get it for you in a day or two."

He slipped the clerk another twenty and went up to the room.

He turned the key and opened the door. The room was in semi-darkness, lit only by a neon fixture in the street below. He groped for the wall switch. The lights went on before he found it.

"Good evening, señor," said the policeman sitting in the chair beside the wall.

He turned for the door, but another uniformed officer blocked his escape.

"So, how do you know this woman?" the first policeman asked.

CHAPTER 5

TED OPENED HIS EYES TO A BRICK WALL, inches from his face. He shook his head and pulled himself to a sitting position on the bunk. He sensed something touch his foot and kicked it away in disgust.

He had been here since late last night. They interrogated him for hours, threatening him with deportation and a prison sentence. He had told them nothing—he had nothing to tell. They already knew her name was Bailey. He said they were strangers and he was doing her a favour. They did not believe him. They kept asking questions about Zapatistas and what he knew of a place called Acteal. The questions meant nothing to him.

Now the long hot afternoon seemed to go on forever. Ted sat on the steel bunk staring at the ray of sunlight filtering through the bars. How long would they keep him here? Were they serious about prison? He had done nothing wrong. But did that matter? Who was this woman, and why were the police so interested in her? He could not stop the thoughts. He kept coming back to the same thing. He was in trouble.

His life? The thought made him wince. *What a joke.* What life did he have anyhow? Forty-two years of age, no wife, no kids, probably no job. Who would have thought it would turn out like this. Butting into customs inquiries, bribing desk clerks—who did he think he was, James Bond?

Small black bugs were swarming over his uneaten food. He made no effort to brush them away. He lay back on his bunk and stared at the ceiling.

Night fell and the cell slipped into gloom. The only illumination came from a light standard on the main street. From further away he could hear music from a cantina. Somewhere people were laughing. He tossed uncomfortably.

He heard tapping at the barred window. At first he ignored it, but it was repeated. There was someone outside. He got up and stood by the opening.

A whisper, a husky female voice. "Ted. Ted, are you in there?"

"Who's there?"

"It's Bailey. I'm going to get you out."

"How? The police are looking for you."

"Never mind that. Tomorrow, when the guard tells you to go, do as he says. I'll be waiting."

"But how?"

"Got to go. See you."

"No, wait . . . " But he heard only retreating footsteps in reply.

He lay awake for most of the night while a rodent made noises in the wall beside his head. He would doze momentarily and then start with a sound, imagining something just outside his cell.

Now breaking out of jail! Ted Somerville, you are right out of your mind!

It was mid-afternoon. Ted had been on the edge of his bunk all day—waiting for something, anything to happen. Finally, someone was coming. He heard the guard approaching, keys jangling on their ring. *What now?* The guard stopped at the cell door and with a large key turned the lock.

"Señor Somerville, I am going for my afternoon siesta." The guard touched a forefinger to his temple in a kind of salute and shambled down the hallway to the outer office.

What was going on? Was this it? Was he supposed to escape now? Bailey told him to follow the guard's instructions. But the man had said nothing. He looked out the cell window into the hallway. Nothing moved.

He took a deep breath and pushed on the cell door. The hinges squealed. He stopped and listened. The hallway was empty. He stepped out of the cell and walked out of the police station with his eyes straight ahead. There was a clerk typing at a desk, but he did not look up.

He opened the door onto the front street. The street was empty. The shop shutters were down, and there were no vehicles on the road. He took a few steps and broke into a run.

A truck was bearing down on him. Ted looked for a doorway to hide in. Too late—he had been seen. The truck slowed. It stopped beside him. The passenger door was thrown open from inside.

"Get in!" the driver yelled.

He peered into the vehicle. "Bailey! What are. . . ?"

"Shut up and get in!"

He obeyed. She shifted noisily into gear and paused before letting out the clutch.

"Sit up and act calm," she said. "We'll go nice and slow until we're out of town."

They drove down the main street, stopping at the red lights and driving well under the limit. A police car passed them going the other way, but took no notice. They were soon out of the town and on a deserted road.

Once they left town Bailey gunned the engine and the truck picked up speed. They were now racing down a gravel road, the vehicle's suspension chattering across the uneven surface. Bailey clutched the wheel, eyes fixed on the road ahead, her hair whipping in the wind.

"What's going on?" Ted shouted over the truck's roar. "How did you get me out? Where are we going?"

Bailey waved her hand, gesturing that it was too noisy to talk.

Minutes later she brought the truck to a halt. They were on a dirt road in the midst of barren, rock-strewn hills. Only cacti and stunted trees broke the monotony of the desert.

———

The sun was still high in the sky and the desert was a cauldron, the white rocks holding and reflecting the heat. Ted immediately began to drip with perspiration.

"I wish I could have got you out sooner," she said. "They give you a rough time?"

"No. I'm all right. But they had lots of questions about you. Tell me how you did it. Last night I couldn't imagine how you could get me out."

She smiled. The gesture was sudden and unexpected. It was a lovely smile, but sad at the same time. The corners of her eyes failed to turn up with the rest of her face. He momentarily lost track of her words.

"Here's a primer on Mexico. Everything is for sale—drugs, guns, justice, you name it. If you've got the money, someone will sell it to you. I paid the guard two hundred American dollars to take a walk, and the rest was up to you."

"The truck?" Ted could hear his voice was thick.

"I stole it," she said, in a matter-of-fact tone.

"You stole it? You mean just stole it off the street?" Ted mentally added car theft to the crimes for which he would spend the rest of his life in jail.

In response she smiled again. *What was it about that smile? And why was it affecting him this way? Could she see the colour he felt growing on his face?*

"We've been heading due north," she said, pointing up the dirt track. "The American border is about a five-mile hike."

"Then let's go," he said.

"I'm not leaving Mexico," she said.

"What? But you said . . . "

"You go on if you like. I'm going the other way. With a bit of luck, the federales won't catch you, and the Americans will let you in."

"Why wouldn't they let me in? I'm a Canadian. I'll ask for asylum or something."

"Maybe," she said. "Or the US authorities could decide that you are a fugitive who broke out of jail and stole a vehicle, and just turn you over to the Mexicans."

Ted's optimism drained away. He had thought for a moment he was going home.

"Don't worry, I have a plan," Bailey said. She laid her hand on his forearm. Ted felt his skin tingle where she touched him, and he was aware of a sudden warmth on his face. *Was he blushing?*

"Maybe we can give them something to think about." She took out a road map and folded it to show their location. She marked a line leading to the American border and placed the map on the floor of the truck.

His mind had drifted off. He should be scared out of his wits, but all he could think about was the way her hand had felt on his arm and wonder about the way it had made him feel and whether she would do it again.

Bailey was twenty paces away, already climbing the first hills. "Are you coming?" she called.

He started after her and was already out of breath by the time he caught up. They hiked up a steep incline, Bailey in the lead, not looking back. She climbed with an effortless long-legged stride. He plodded, his steps feeling heavy and awkward. He was no match for her pace or the small mountain. Within minutes his breath was coming fast and hard. He tried to control his breathing and kept going without complaint.

Bailey stopped and waited for him at the top of a small outcropping. They were several hundred feet above the road, their truck sat almost directly beneath them. By now Ted could barely breathe. His pulse pounded in his temples and his mouth felt caked with dust. He sat heavily onto the nearest rock. Bailey shrugged out of her knapsack and passed him a water bottle. He gulped at the liquid.

"Not too much. It'll make you sick."

It was some time before Ted could put words together. "That . . . was . . . some . . . climb."

"You better get used to it. There's more of the same ahead."

After a minute his pulse slowed. "Now how about some answers," he said. "Who are you? Why are the police so interested?"

"I'm not answering any more questions."

"What?"

"You heard me. I got you out of jail—we're even." She pulled a pair of binoculars from her pack and panned the horizon. Her lips formed a grim line.

"Hey, I'm not trying to interrogate you," he said, "but since I'm here hiding in the desert with you, shouldn't you at least tell me what is going on?"

Bailey put her binoculars down but continued to stare off into the distance. A minute went by.

"Let's start again. My name is Ted Somerville and your real name is. . . ?

Come on," he said, trying to engage her with a smile. "This is the part where you answer."

Her features softened, she turned to face him. "Okay. My name really is Bailey, just Bailey. And before you ask, that really is the only name I have. And as you've probably guessed"—she exhaled a long breath—"I wasn't going to the spa. The bus was just a way to slip into Mexico. They usually don't even check it at the border. I got unlucky. And why did you help me? It was none of your business."

Ted had asked himself that question about a hundred times without a good answer. "I'm not sure. I guess I didn't like what was happening, and I thought you needed some help. It's not really my style. I hope I don't live to regret it."

She smiled again, and he liked that. "Well, thanks. If they'd held me it wouldn't have taken them long to figure out . . . "

They were interrupted by the noise of straining motors and squealing brakes. Bailey raised a finger to her lips, and crouched behind the rocks. Two police vehicles pulled to a stop on the road below. Half a dozen brown-uniformed men dismounted and searched their stolen truck. After a few minutes they huddled in conference and set out in a loose formation heading north.

"They're buying it," Bailey said. "They think we've tried to make our way to the border."

"Now what?" he asked.

"We stay put. Just keep your head down."

An hour later the men returned and drove away, taking their stolen truck with them. They watched from their perch until the convoy faded to black specks in the distance.

With the soldiers gone, everything became deafeningly quiet. Even the afternoon breeze had stopped. She was facing away as if she had forgotten about his existence. A chasm had grown between them.

"You were about to tell me what the guard would have figured out," he said.

"Was I?" Bailey seemed uninterested.

"Yes. You were about to tell me what you were doing on that bus and why you were sneaking into Mexico."

"Let's leave it."

"Why were the police asking me about Zapatistas?" he said. "Are you one of them, whatever they are?"

Ted realized his mistake. Bailey's face tightened in anger.

"If you don't like it, you can leave. The soldiers have gone. The danger's over. The border is that way. Take the water bottle." There was no longer any trace of her sad smile.

"No, wait, that's not what I meant. I just want some answers."

"This is as far as we go. I shouldn't have said as much as I did." Her face was expressionless. "The less you know about me, the better off you'll be. I'm trouble, and you don't want any part of it."

Ted knew he should have said something. Something, anything, just to ease the tension. But he had never been very good at that sort of thing. He sat there dumbly and his silence only added fuel to her anger.

"What do you want from me?" she said. "If I told you I'm off to join the Zapatistas would that satisfy you? Or maybe you'd like to hear that I fell in love with you at the border and couldn't live without you. How about that? Or how about we just both shut up and try to get a good night's sleep." She walked several paces away and busied herself removing items from her pack. She remained standing with her back towards him.

"I'll find my own way in the morning," Ted said.

"Fine. You do that."

———

A pink glow spread across the western sky. The fading light silhouetted rocky hills, huge boulders glowed orange in the last rays of the sunset. Darkness came quickly, and within minutes the first dim stars appeared.

With nightfall came the desert chill. The ground was hard but Ted was too exhausted to mind. He huddled on a shelf between two large rocks. The last thing he saw before closing his eyes was Bailey seated on the cliff's edge, staring into the deepening dark.

CHAPTER 6

Bailey finds success beyond her dreams. She teaches the villagers how to add fish-meal and dried chicken droppings to the fragile jungle soil. Orchards that stood abandoned on her arrival now produce harvests. For the first time in years the village has enough to eat. The people begin to treat her like a saint. "Ella que da vida," *they call her—"she who gives life." She has friends. And laughter. And for once she's making a difference in people's lives. She has never been so happy.*

She is at the market, in front of a carver's stall. The miniatures of birds are exquisite. They seem to be alive. She is holding a carved bird to the light, as if waiting for it to fly away.

"Buenos dias. *May I help you, señorita?*"

She looks up into the face of a young man. He has large brown eyes set in smooth olive skin, glossy black hair, and a brilliant smile.

"My name is Ernesto. Do you like the carving?"

"Yes, very much. I must have it. How much is it?"

"For you, señorita, there is no charge. It is a gift. In return I ask only that you have tea with me this afternoon."

CHAPTER 7

TED SLEPT SOUNDLY BUT AWOKE shivering with cold. His arms were cramped and he shook them to restore feeling. He stood and stretched.

"Good morning," Bailey said. "How do you feel?"

Ted groaned as he touched his cramped muscles.

"Don't worry, you'll get used to it. The rocks are not so hard after the first night." She was cheerful, as if their argument had never happened.

Ted was unsure of what to do. Was this the point at which he asked for directions and went on his way?

"Let's start again," she said. "I'm prepared to get you out of here. Just don't keep trying to figure me out. Is that a deal?"

The night before he had been angry, ready to strike out on his own. Now he realized the futility of his plan. The terrain all looked the same, mile after mile of rocky wasteland. Bailey seemed to know where they were, while he was totally lost. And to hike to the border? The way he felt right now, he was not sure he could make the crest of the next hill.

He smiled. "Okay, no more questions."

In response, he saw once again the suggestion of that sad smile. He would like to see it again.

Around noon they found a village. In the middle of a sun-scorched plain, a tiny settlement appeared. From a distance it looked like a mirage—miniature houses shimmering in the heat. It was inhabited. Smoke curled from the chimneys, and somewhere a dog was barking.

Ted waited behind while Bailey walked into the village. She returned fifteen minutes later.

"It's safe," she said. "There are no police. It's patrolled by pistoleros, but none have been seen for several days."

"Pistoleros? Sounds like the bad guys from an old Western."

"It's nothing to laugh about. They're hired mercenaries," she said, "armed and extremely dangerous. They work for the large land holdings called haciendas. They keep the campesinos under control and off the hacendados' land. They do the dirty work for the police and army."

"That sounds ominous."

"You don't know the half of it. But we have nothing to worry about today—this village is sympathetic to the Zapatistas. The people will warn us if there's danger." She slung her pack over a shoulder. "Let's go."

The main street was a dirt track. The houses were rough shacks, most with tin roofs and pieces of plastic serving as windows. Duct tape seemed a favoured building material. Black smoke wafted from tin stove pipes, and no power lines connected the dwellings.

"There are no phones here," Bailey said, "but at least we'll find something to eat."

She knocked on the door of a dwelling built out of discarded billboards. One exterior wall advertised "Lucky Strike Cigarettes." Nearby two urchins were playing with dolls in the dirt. The little girls covered their faces to share whispers.

The door opened halfway. A heavy-set Mexican woman wearing a faded print dress filled the doorway. A pork pie hat was perched on her head. Bailey delivered a greeting in fluent Spanish. The woman's response was suspicious, and she began to close the door.

Bailey spoke sharply. Ted caught the word "federales."

The woman stopped and ventured a question. For several minutes she and Bailey engaged in a conversation punctuated by hand gestures. Finally the woman opened the door and stood back to allow them in.

The interior of the building was furnished with rough-hewn furniture, and religious paintings adorned the walls. Cooking smells filled the air.

"What was that about?" Ted asked.

"She thought we were from the haciendas," Bailey said. "A man called the Cacique heads the haciendas. He's like a feudal baron. The campesinos hate him."

"She seems friendly enough now. We got lucky coming here." He smiled at the woman and gave her an appreciative nod.

"No, not really. Hospitality is part of the campesinos' way of life," she said, taking the seat nearest the window. "We would have received the same reception in any house in the village."

In the corner of the main room was a white porcelain toilet. It stood out from the wall with no apparent connections to plumbing. As they watched, the woman lifted the lid from the tank and pulled out an armload of tomatoes and peppers.

Bailey shook her head. "The foreign aid people have been here. That's one of their favourite tricks—give everyone in a village without running water an 'American Standard' toilet. Makes the world free for democracy and lets us all sleep soundly knowing we're helping the underprivileged. Not to mention, they make very nice vegetable bins."

Ted found her small wry smile oddly charming. "So how do you know so much about foreign aid?" he asked.

"Something I just picked up."

Bailey and the Mexican woman carried on a conversation in Spanish. Bailey pointed towards the hills and then to Ted, providing a running translation for his benefit.

"*Bastardos!*" The woman smacked her fist into her palm. Bailey did not translate.

The woman bustled about her tiny kitchen, clattering dishes and gathering utensils, producing bowls of steaming chilli and a stack of fresh corn tortillas. She set a pitcher of homemade beer on the table. The liquid frothed with brown foam.

They finished their meal and said their goodbyes. Bailey drew a few bills from her shirt pocket and offered them to the woman.

The woman waved her hands in protest. "*No dineros, no dineros.*"

Bailey smiled. "*Gracias,*" she said, with Ted joining in with his own muttered "*Gracias.*" His first attempt at Spanish earned him a look of approval from Bailey.

Outside in the yard, one of the little girls presented Bailey with a small bouquet of wild flowers.

Bailey smiled. "*Gracias,*" she said. "*La muñeca es bonita.* Let me see it?" She pointed to the girl's rag doll.

The girl handed her the doll. Bailey slipped a twenty-dollar bill under the dress.

"Now go show your *muñeca* to your mama." With a quick wave, the girl ran into the house, and Ted and Bailey set off walking towards the centre of the village on the same dirt track they'd come into town on.

"So what now?" Ted asked.

"Are you up for a little more bus travel?"

"The truth? I never want to ride another bus in my life."

"Too bad, but we have no choice. The bus is used only by the campesinos to get to market. It's slow going, but the police don't give it much notice."

"Where are we going?" Ted asked.

"I think our best plan is to go east. You can cross the border into Texas. We'll travel to Chihuahua and then head north," she said.

"How far is it?"

"Chihuahua is probably a thousand miles."

Ted stopped in his tracks. "Forget it. I'm not travelling a thousand miles on a bloody bus. There has to be another way."

Fire flashed in Bailey's eyes. "Sure, here's a better idea. We could steal a couple of mules and ride there. Or, let's see, we could walk up to the nearest Hertz counter, tell them you've lost your licence, that your friend is a terrorist with only one name. I don't have the time to argue. You can either come with me or find your own way."

"Okay. I'm sorry. When do we leave?"

"Whenever. Just follow me, and keep your mouth shut." She marched up the road with Ted following behind.

The bus was dirty orange in colour, not that there was much paint remaining—it was covered in years of grime and rust. The interior was visible through holes in the side panels, the seats removed in favour of wooden benches.

Ted groaned.

"Get ready for a new experience," Bailey said, her anger gone. "Travel here is nothing at all like at home. There are no schedules, and the bus only goes to the next town. The next town is about thirty miles, far enough to get us clear of the federales. We'll probably stay there for a couple of days."

His mouth must have been hanging open. She patted his arm. "Don't worry, you'll survive."

———

A group of about twenty dark-skinned men and women were waiting to board. They were dressed alike in worn dungarees and broad-brimmed hats.

"Mexican Indians. They don't speak English, so we can talk freely," Bailey said. "They are travelling to work for the hacendados. When there's no work, they come home to their villages."

"Why don't they work closer to home?" asked Ted.

"It's the way the hacendado controls them. They spend their lives as migrant workers. That way there's less chance of them starting farms of their own."

"Was that what you were doing in Mexico? Helping the peasants break away from the hacendados?"

Her grey eyes bored into his. "How do you know about that?"

He broke off eye contact. "I . . . I don't. I just put two and two together. Problems in the rain forest, the Zapatistas, things like that. I just thought . . . "

"You think too much!"

"No, I . . . not really . . . "

"I thought I made it clear." She jammed her finger into the middle of his chest. "You mind your own damned business and I'll mind mine!"

Bailey turned abruptly and boarded the bus. She passed by several open benches and sat beside a young woman. Ted was forced to take a seat two rows farther back. She looked away as he passed.

There was no cargo bay and the luggage was carried up top. Lumber, pottery, market produce, and cardboard suitcases tied with twine were all secured to the roof with rope. A pulley hoisted a crate of chickens, squawking loudly. Feathers floated in the air.

When the bus was fully loaded, it contained about thirty men, a handful of women, a goat and a small pig. The Mexicans chattered in a local dialect and from their glances were curious about the newcomers. The man sitting beside Ted offered him a brown pear.

"*Gracias.*" It occurred to Ted that this was the second time in his life he had spoken in Spanish. And all in one day.

The man opened his mouth in a gap-toothed smile.

The bus lurched forward with the grinding of gears. It noisily picked up speed, bouncing on the pot-holed road. In close quarters the passengers exuded the earthy aroma that came from hard work. The smell was at first offensive, but Ted quickly accommodated. The Mexicans kept up non-stop conversations with finger pointing, back slapping, and laughter. Despite having just been told off by Bailey, Ted was intrigued by the scene around him. To these Mexicans a bus trip was not something to be endured but was welcomed as an opportunity to share news and tell stories. A guitar was produced and the people sang badly and out of key, but with gusto.

Ted surprised himself by enjoying the ride. The warm afternoon breeze blew on his face through the missing windows. The desert hills were eye-catching. The blues and the greys mixed together in straight lines that looked too perfect to be real. And no one tried to bore him with a discussion of soy products or green grapes. He sat contentedly munching on his brown pear. For the first time in ages, Ted felt strangely at peace.

Ahead of him, Bailey was engaged in conversation with a young Mexican woman. Bailey's thick brown hair tumbled across her bare shoulders. Her arms were lightly bronzed, and sunlight illuminated the wispy down. Her skin looked buttery smooth, as if it might melt in the warm sun. Ted had an urge to touch it, to brush his fingers along her arm. He drifted in pleasant daydreams.

Two hours later they reached their destination, more houses made of clap-board with tin roofs, baking on a barren plain. It looked no different from the village they had just left.

Bailey motioned for him to come and meet her companion from the bus. Her anger had vanished like a passing cloud.

"Ted, this is Maria."

"Pleased I meet you," said the young Mexican girl. "Forgive my mistakes. I am learning better English. Me and my father. We are both learning."

"Maria's father owns a café in the town. She says he will find us a place to stay."

"Thank you," said Ted. "I think that is 'mucho gracias.'"

Maria smiled, but didn't correct him. "Maybe tomorrow we help each other."

"Come on," Bailey said. "It's just down the street."

They walked towards a small building on the main street. Its painted wooden sign read "Café Antonio."

They passed a row of refrigerators sitting just off the main street. Some were still in their cardboard shipping crates. "Look, American aid again," Bailey said. "These guys kill me. Now they're sending appliances to villages without electricity. What will they think of next?"

The refrigerators were being used to house chickens. The doors to the appliances were propped open, and the chickens passed freely in and out. Rows of hens perched on the wire racks. A flock of them surrounded the crates, pecking at the ground.

"So what do you think of using a fridge as a henhouse?" Bailey asked.

"If you're asking my professional opinion," he said, "I think this use probably voids the warranties."

Bailey touched his arm and laughed. "Only a lawyer would come up with that. I was wondering if they shut the doors at night to keep out the foxes."

They entered a small café that smelled deliciously of roasting coffee. Maria made introductions to an elderly Mexican standing behind the bar. "Buenos dias . . . Welcome . . . My name is Antonio." He seated them at a table and poured coffee.

Antonio returned behind the bar to feed pieces of wood into his cookstove. Ted leaned across the table to Bailey. "Tell me, do all the criminals work for the government, and the nice folks live in the villages, or is that just a first impression?"

"No, I think that you've got it about right."

There was that smile again. He was finding it worth the effort to be pleasant.

The sun had set and kerosene lanterns lit the café. Antonio served them a simple meal and then showed them to a storeroom at the back of the building. Bags of vegetables took up most of the space. They made up two large stacks of burlap, creating beds that were soft but scratchy. Bailey closed the door. A lantern provided the only light.

"Ready?" she asked.

"Sure, you can turn it off," Ted said, settling into his palette.

She blew out the flame, plunging the room into darkness. Fabric rustled as Bailey slipped into the other bed.

Time passed slowly. Ted was unable to sleep. As usual, his mind was turning over, only this night was different from most. His thoughts were on the woman sleeping next to him. Bailey was a mystery. Attractive, bright. But there was something very wrong about her. He was acutely aware of her presence only inches away. He could hear her regular breathing. He thought she must be asleep.

An hour later, Ted was still awake. Bailey began making small sounds deep within her chest. At first he took the noises for talking in her sleep. Then she took a deep breath and sobbed as she exhaled. He heard sniffling sounds, and ragged breathing. She was crying. She had to be awake.

Ted felt in the dark and touched her shoulder. "Bailey, what's wrong?"

She brushed his hand away. "Don't touch me! It's none of your business." She blew her nose. He could hear her rustle in the burlap and imagined she was sitting up straight and facing him. "And remember this, Ted Somerville. This is the last time I'll tell you. Never touch me again. I don't want to be touched. Not by you, not by anyone. Do you understand?"

"No, I don't understand, not a bit of it."

"That's your problem. Just leave me alone."

Bailey makes love to Ernesto the day they meet. It happens so fast that it takes her breath away. They are walking in the fields, under the fruit trees at night. And suddenly . . . She has never been with a man like this. There are no complications. He loves her, and she wants him.

Ernesto awakens a passion in Bailey she does not know existed. She is savage in her desire. She wants him constantly. She reaches for him every morning, searches for him at midday, and holds him inside her in the tropical nights. The steamy jungle is the perfect setting. Is this love or merely lust? Bailey does not care. She wants it to go on forever.

Bailey was up brewing coffee when he entered the cantina. Her hair was neatly pinned up.

"Good morning," Ted said.

"It's about time. I've been up for hours," she said. "Another fifteen minutes and I was going to send in one of the dogs to get you up."

"About last night," he said. "I didn't mean to . . . "

"Forget it. We've got things to do. First thing is to get you cleaned up. Take a look."

Ted caught his reflection in the mirror behind the bar. He was unshaven, his face covered with yellow-brown bruises. His clothes were creased and sweat-stained and he needed no reminders about his aroma.

"No argument," he said. "Is there a shower anywhere handy?"

"No, but there's a stream about half a mile from here. I bought you a razor and a toothbrush. You can clean up there."

"Thanks, but you can't go on supporting me. I need to find a phone so I can get some money."

"It doesn't matter," she said. "I've got enough money to get us where we're going. We're here for another day at least. The next bus leaves tomorrow." She tossed him a towel. "Let's go."

The stream ran deep and cold, fed by the mountains to the west. The day was sticky hot. Ted was perspiring from the hike, his clothes matted to his body. Even Bailey seemed affected by the heat. A damp spot had appeared on the back of her shirt. Again, he was struggling to keep up to her. By the time they reached the point where the stream broadened into a large pool and the current slowed, Bailey was twenty yards ahead.

"This looks great," she called back.

Ted caught a fleeting look of her kicking off her boots and unbuttoning her shirt. In a fluid movement she stripped off her jeans. When he arrived at the pool, Bailey was poised on a boulder, clad only in panties. She raised her arms above her head and paused before diving in. For a moment, she was silhouetted against the rock face. Ted's breath caught in his throat. It was as if he had stumbled upon a naked wood nymph. His eyes took in her small rounded breasts and muscled buttocks. Her entry into the water caused barely a splash.

Was he supposed to have seen this? Was this for his benefit?

Her head surfaced in the middle of the pool. She was looking directly at him. "Hope you got a good look. You've been staring at me for days." She backstroked away, her body a flash of white skin below the water's surface.

Ted stripped carefully to his shorts and waded in. He remained close to the shore, leaving Bailey to swim further out. He concentrated on rinsing his hair, not looking in her direction. After a few minutes, he waded to the edge of the pool and pulled his shirt from the bank. He swished it around in the water, and spread it on a rock to dry. He dressed except for his shirt and waited for Bailey in the shade of a tree. When she joined him she was fully clothed. He clenched his stomach muscles.

"How was it?" he asked.

"Great." Her eyes held him captive. "Did I embarrass you?"

"No . . . Er, yes, a bit. I just wasn't expecting you to . . . "

"Good," she said. "You've been staring at me. I don't like it. I do whatever I want, whenever I want. And don't get any ideas. Understand?"

"Sure. Go ahead. Take off your clothes whenever you want. I don't mind."

She threw his towel at him. "Come on. We should be getting back."

All the way back to the village Ted was smiling inwardly, replaying the image of Bailey diving into the pool.

They arrived at Antonio's café in time for a plate of beans and a cool glass of beer.

"How do I tell him that I would like another one?" Ted asked.

"*Otra cerveza, por favor,*" Bailey said.

Ted tried it. Antonio appeared to understand and nodded brightly, but before he could respond there was a commotion in the street. Antonio's daughter ran into the café. She spoke in rapid Spanish first to her father and then to Bailey.

"Pistoleros! Come, we have to hide," Bailey said.

They hurried out the back entrance and across the lane. They found a spot amongst some scrub trees where they could watch but not be seen.

A pickup truck drove slowly down the main street and stopped in front of Antonio's café. Two men got out. They were tall and well-muscled, bigger and lighter skinned than the local farmers, and armed with machine guns. Bandoliers of bullets criss-crossed their chests. The pistoleros swaggered as they walked, cigarettes hanging carelessly from their mouths. One of them entered the building and returned with a six-pack of beer. The men lounged against their truck drinking beer, their eyes scanning the village. The street was deserted. Even the children had disappeared.

Ted could sense the villagers huddled in their dwellings, peering out their windows, waiting for the danger to pass. The minutes crept by.

Fifteen minutes later the pistoleros had finished the beer, the last of the tins thrown into the street. One of the men walked to the back of the truck, opened his pants, and began to urinate. He glared at the houses, as if daring anyone to challenge him. In reply the village was deathly silent. The man zipped his jeans, and retrieved his machine gun. He pointed it into the air and pulled the trigger, releasing a long blast of automatic fire.

The shots were louder for being unexpected. The reports echoed from the hills. Ted pressed his body into the ground. He felt the pistoleros knew he was there and were staging this performance for his benefit.

The men threw a last contemptuous look at the village, and drove away, their truck spinning its tires and spitting gravel. Racing across the desert, the vehicle faded to a speck, clouds of dust billowing behind.

"What was that all about?" Ted brushed the dust from his clothes. "Were they looking for us?"

"No, not likely," Bailey said. "That was just a social call. The pistoleros do it to scare the locals. It keeps them in line."

"It certainly worked for me. They got my attention."

Entering Antonio's cantina they found him leaning on his counter placidly smoking a cigarette. He wore a bemused expression as if something funny had just occurred, a joke that only he understood.

"Are you all right, Antonio?" asked Ted.

"I am fine, señor. I enjoy our little visits from the soldiers of the hacendados. They are always welcome here. They should come more often. They are necessary."

Antonio acknowledged the question on Ted's face. "You wonder why? You see, señor, we are poor people, very poor. It is hard to be poor and sometimes hungry, but it is difficult to be angry. These men, these pistoleros!"—he spat on the floor, his expression darkening—"These men we can hate! They remind us why we are poor. Without these reminders and their visits, we would no longer struggle for our freedom. Let us drink to our friends. Drink with me, señor. To them, and to the Revolution." He raised his glass, but he did not smile.

CHAPTER 8

AFTER ONE MORE NIGHT IN ANTONIO's storeroom, they set off. They caught another old bus to another town. There was another storeroom, more plates of beans, and then they were on the road again. The days quickly fell into a pattern. They travelled for several hours each day, sometimes walking or hitching rides.

Travel was agonizingly slow, and as Bailey had warned, there were no schedules. Departure dates were governed by the whims of the local farmers—when enough people wanted to go to the next village transportation was arranged. From time to time the journey was interrupted because the driver was ill, or one of his children had a birthday. No warnings were given—the trip was just cancelled.

The buses broke down often, and took hours to fix. While waiting, the Mexicans would stage impromptu picnics by the side of the road. Guitars would be produced and the people would sing. The Mexicans played games of chance to pass the time.

Bailey had continued to help Ted with his Spanish and he was now able to carry on simple conversations.

"Which one you choose, señor?"

"Which one?" Ted asked. "What do you mean?"

"The roosters, señor. The man pointed to two crates, each with a rooster inside. They fight. You bet. Which one? Fifty pesos."

"Take the black one," Bailey pointed. "He looks mean."

"The black one—*el negro*," Ted said. Bailey counted out the money.

The roosters were uncrated and set upon each other. Shiny metal talons were attached to their legs. Amidst great shouting, the two birds flew at each other. They tore at each other in a fury, feathers and blood flying. Ted was both revolted and compelled—here were two living creatures locked in mortal combat. The campesinos cheered and shouted for their favourite. It was over in seconds. The black cock lay sliced apart and inert. A reddish-brown rooster strutted away. A few pesos changed hands amidst smiles and backslaps.

"It looks like we didn't win," Ted said.

"It could be worse," Bailey said. "Have you ever plucked a chicken? You're about to learn."

After their clashes of the first few days, they had reached an understanding. Anything about the here and now was fair game. Bailey seemed delighted to teach him Spanish and to explain the local customs.

"*Burrito*," she said. "Bu-ree-to. Try it."

"Bur-r-e-o," Ted said, mangling the consonants.

"Very good, except instead of ordering a meal, you just ordered a donkey. Let's try it again." On a good day, Bailey smiled her words.

The past and the future remained out of bounds. At any mention of her past, Bailey became instantly withdrawn. She gave no hint of her future plans. Ted had stopped asking pointed questions and let his imagination fill in the gaps. Why was she slogging her way across northern Mexico? What awaited her in Chihuahua?

After the first night in Antonio's village, Ted avoided touching her and worked at maintaining physical distance even while jostling on a swaying bus. He tried not to even let his hand brush hers. It struck him as odd that Bailey showed no similar restraint. She talked with her hands. Ted lost track of the times she touched his arm to direct his attention or to make a point.

They formed a close but uneasy friendship. She was still wary and could be prickly, but for the most part they were getting along. Ted had not complained. He was enjoying her company—a lot.

A week into their travels they found a telephone. After three attempts Ted managed to place a collect call to his law firm in Vancouver. He reached Bill Turcotte.

"Bill, it's Ted. I'm calling from Mexico."

"Yes, I know who this is. I just accepted the charges, didn't I? What the hell is going on down there?"

Ted had a sick feeling—Bill never swore. "What do you mean?"

"Don't play games, Ted, I was visited by the RCMP this week. What's this about you assaulting a guard and breaking out of jail? They say that you were trafficking in drugs."

"I'm in trouble, but it has nothing to do with drugs," Ted said. He told Turcotte of his encounter with the police.

"It's worse than you think. There's an international warrant out for your arrest."

"A warrant?"

"It's something to do with the crackdown on drugs. If you're arrested anywhere, you can be extradited back to Mexico."

Ted held the receiver away from his mouth. He felt lightheaded.

"Ted, Ted, are you still there?"

"Yes, I'm here," Ted said, working at keeping the emotion out of his voice.

"I'm sorry, I feel like this is my fault. You were in no shape to be going anywhere. I should have made you see a doctor."

"Don't blame yourself. Anyhow, I think that this may turn out all right. When I get far enough east, I'll cross the border into Texas. No one will be looking for me there."

"You don't sound very convincing. Can I do something to help? Should I come down there?"

"No really, I'll be fine. Really I will. All you can do for me is send some money. But thanks. I appreciate your offer."

They made arrangements to wire funds to Chihuahua. Ted reassured Turcotte again that everything would be fine, promised to phone him again when he could, and said goodbye.

"So how'd it go?" asked Bailey.

"Fine, everything's fine. Come on, we have a bus to catch."

CHAPTER 9

SEVERAL DAYS LATER THEY BOARDED a bus from one anonymous town on their way to yet another unknown destination. They were nearing the province of Chihuahua, although none of the local people seemed to know or care where the boundary lay. The passengers were the usual assortment of farmers and travelling artisans, all dressed in similar dusty attire.

One passenger stood out from the rest, a tall man with a big beard. Ted noticed him walking up the aisle. His head was up, back straight, yellow-green eyes watchful. Catching the attention of another passenger, he made a subtle gesture of closing his fist and raising it slightly.

Bailey nudged Ted's arm. "That man, I'm pretty sure he is a Zapatista. That's their sign," she whispered. "We'll wait until the next town and then speak to him."

Ted studied the man out of the corner of his eye. He had heard of the rebels, glowing stories of idealism and heroics. This one looked harmless enough. He was looking forward to meeting him.

The bus bounced along through the bleak and deserted landscape. There was nothing out of the ordinary. They passed endless miles of hills and scrub, inhabited by scrawny cattle.

As if from out of nowhere, a black pickup was racing alongside. One of its occupants brandished a machine gun, gesturing for the bus to stop. The speeding vehicle cut into the bus' path, forcing it onto the shoulder.

"Pistoleros!" Bailey said. "Be careful. Don't antagonize them. Avoid eye contact." She gave his arm a squeeze. "And please, Ted, no matter what happens, don't do anything stupid. I'm a big girl. I can look after myself," she said.

Two men in paramilitary uniforms sprang from the truck. They burst through the doorway, grabbed the driver by the collar, and threw him into the roadway. The pistoleros pointed machine guns at the startled passengers.

"Out! Everyone, now! *Prisa! Prisa!*" Hurry! A pistolero stood at the doorway, slapping at the people with his hat as they passed.

The passengers were lined up on the roadside. The Zapatista was standing next to Ted. The pistoleros walked slowly past, looking into each man's face.

The taller of the two, a big man with a jagged white scar across his cheek, seemed to be in command. He growled more than spoke. Seeing something in a farmer's expression, he lashed out with a back-handed blow that drove the man into the side of the bus. He kicked him as he lay on the ground, and walked on.

The pistolero stopped at Bailey and gave her a long look. He raised his hand to her face. He stroked her cheek until she turned away, then seized her cheeks between his fingers, pulling her near.

"What is a pretty white woman like you doing on a bus like this? Eh?" he asked in English.

Bailey kept her eyes averted and did not answer.

"What? You do not like me already? Later, señorita, you and I will have some fun, eh?" He grabbed his crotch with his free hand. Bailey tried to turn her face away. He released her, trailing his hand across her breasts.

Ted seethed with impotent fury. He took a deep breath. *Don't do it. Keep your mouth shut. Look at the ground.* The pistoleros moved on, mocking him with their eyes. The message was there—we can have your woman, if we choose. Stop us if you dare.

The gunmen reached the Zapatista. The leader looked closely at the man's face, his features narrowing into a scowl. The Zapatista returned the glare, showing no sign of fear.

"Who are you? What is your business here?" the pistolero demanded.

The Zapatista spat on the ground.

With the speed of a rattlesnake, the pistolero drove the butt of his weapon into the Zapatista's stomach. The man doubled up. The pistolero smashed the barrel against his face. A sickening thud of metal against skin, and the

Zapatista dropped to the ground. The remaining campesinos shrank out of the way.

"Look, all of you!" the pistolero shouted. "This is how we deal with disrespect!" He drove his boot into the side of the Zapatista's head. The man grunted once and lay still.

The smaller pistolero unshouldered his weapon. He worked the action and pointed it at the Zapatista. "*Adios, amigo.*"

Ted held his breath, waiting for the explosion of bullets.

"Stop! Hold it right there! Drop the gun!"

Ted whirled. Beside him, Bailey's arms were extended, holding a pistol pointed at the pistoleros.

The pistolero with the machine gun made a snorting noise. "So, the señorita, she likes to play with guns." He swung his weapon in a lazy arch.

"No!" Ted shouted. He lunged at him.

The shot was like the crack of a whip. The air was parted past his head.

A small red hole appeared above the pistolero's ear. A puzzled look flitted across his face. He dropped his weapon and clasped a hand to his head. He opened his mouth as if about to speak, but in that instant his eyes rolled back in their sockets. He collapsed like a broken marionette.

Ted was already halfway to where the man had been standing. He hit the remaining pistolero with a flying tackle and they went down together. He hit the man as hard and as fast as he could, his fists pummelling, knees driving. He butted him with his head and heard a grunt. *Was he winning?*

The pistolero threw him off as if he were a child. Ted was on the bottom as the pistolero grabbed him by the shirt.

"Fuck you, gringo! You die now!"

The fist hit him like a hammer, and for an instant everything went black. The man grasped his throat and slammed Ted's head repeatedly against the ground. Ted tasted blood in his mouth. His vision dimmed.

The beating stopped. Ted lay on his back looking at the sky. The pistolero released his grip and rose from his chest. What was going on? Ted looked into a forest of dark faces. They were all around him. Staring down.

"*Merdre!*" the pistolero said. He lunged for his machine gun.

A booted foot kicked the weapon away.

A group of campesinos circled the pistolero, machetes out and ready in their hands. The men were silent; their eyes spoke of hate. The pistolero ran to one side, then the other, trying vainly to escape the circling blades. The campesinos closed in on the pistolero—metal flashed. The pistolero shrieked only once, and then all was still. The campesinos sheathed their weapons and turned away from the body lying bloody in the dirt.

Ted rose to unsteady feet. The pistoleros lay prone by the side of the road. Blood was pooled in the dust and splattered the side of the bus. The campesinos were attending to the Zapatista.

Bailey still held the pistol, the barrel pointing at the ground. Her eyes were blank. Ted heard the muttered words. "I never meant to shoot anybody. I bought the gun at the border. I never thought I would use it. Not like this."

He ran to her and opened his arms. She recoiled. She held her hands defensively in front of her.

"Stay away!"

"Bailey, it's okay. It's okay."

"Don't touch me."

"He would have killed that man," Ted said. "And me too. You had to do it."

Her face was white, her cheeks streaked with tears.

"I'm going to be sick." She wretched by the roadside until she made only dry heaving sounds. Ted stood by her, not knowing what to do.

The bus driver had taken charge. He directed the campesinos to drag the bodies into a nearby ditch. They covered them roughly with rocks and loose scrub. The bus chugged back into life, and the passengers climbed aboard.

The bus driver stopped Ted at the doorway. "Señor, this is very big trouble. You must get out of here. These men have friends who will come looking for them."

"Take their truck," the bus driver said. "We can't leave it here, and you will travel faster. Their friends may find the bodies. And this man, you must take him, too. He will be killed if he is found. I will tell you of a place where you can go. It is in Chihuahua. There will be friends there. You will be safe." He handed Ted a slip of paper.

The campesinos helped the Zapatista into the pickup. Ted stood looking both ways up and down the roadway. This was all they needed, an injured terrorist in the back of a stolen truck. He didn't like it at all. No matter, there was nothing to be done. He slid into the driver's seat.

His pulse was still racing. He was driving dangerously fast, his only goal putting distance between themselves and the scene they left behind.

Bailey was slumped head down in her seat, her face wet with tears. Ted slowed to a reasonable speed, reached over and took her hand. For once she did not resist—her hand lay limp in his.

"There was no choice," he said. "What you did was very brave. You saved that man's life."

It took her time to answer. "I've never done anything like this. I fired a gun at a person. I killed a man."

"There was nothing else you could have done."

"You don't understand anything, Ted. None of this had to happen!"

"That's not true. If not for you, I'd be rotting in jail."

"No, you shouldn't even be here . . . I lied to you about crossing the border."

He brought the truck to a halt, the wheels skidding as it stopped in the middle of the road. "What did you say? You lied to me?"

"You're a Canadian. They might have held you for a while, but they wouldn't have sent you back to the Mexicans."

"Why did you do it?"

"You helped me and I couldn't leave you in jail . . . But it was more than that . . . I needed someone . . . a travelling companion. A woman on her own raises questions. I was using you . . . After a while I stopped thinking about it. You were always there, and . . . Well, you know we were getting along. I feel stupid saying this now, but I was . . . I liked being with you . . . There could never be anything between us, I'm way too screwed up, but . . . I was going to tell you the truth, but I kept putting it off."

Did he hear that right? She liked being with him?

"When were you going to tell me?" he asked.

"When we arrived in Chihuahua. I was going to take you to the border and send you home. But I can't do that now. It's all ruined."

Ted sat quietly for a moment. Surprisingly he felt no anger. Betrayal was the bane of his existence and usually drove him into one of his rages. He had been double-crossed by everyone he knew—Suzanne, Crandle, now Bailey. But her declaration served to cancel out his other emotions. For the moment his fear was gone; her words made him almost giddy.

Today he had done something he had never done before. His last fist fight had been in grade three—he considered himself a coward. Now he was driving a stolen truck with an injured revolutionary in the back, and a woman with a gun had just told him . . . What exactly did she say? He shook his head in disbelief. He was elated—they had finally connected.

Ted started the truck and shifted it into gear. Bailey sat hunched in her seat. She cried softly to herself and said nothing more.

Ernesto attends a gathering in the hills and seems troubled on his return. He sits at the supper table picking at his food. Bailey asks why he is suddenly so quiet.

"The Zapatistas are organizing here. They want me to be their leader," he says.

"Don't do it. It's too dangerous," she takes his hand. "I don't want you to. There will be trouble."

"Don't worry. No one takes notice of what happens in a tiny place like Acteal. I have decided to accept."

The men begin to call themselves Zapatistas and to dress in black dungarees. Ernesto grows increasingly open in his criticism of the government.

A large crowd gathers in the village square. "We must have more land!" Ernesto cries. "If the governor does not agree, we will break away and form our own state here in Chiapas! The government will be run for the people!"

Men wave guns in the air. Shots are fired. "Land and liberty! Down with the governor. Viva Zapata!"

CHAPTER 10

THEY ENTERED THE CITY OF Chihuahua at dusk. It had no discernible skyline and few structures taller than about five stories. Church spires poked above adobe houses. They were quickly engulfed in the city. Chihuahua seemed to be a series of villages, one flowing into the next, each centred on its own small market and church. The streets were narrow and mostly unpaved.

Ted drove their vehicle into an unlit alley. He pulled over and turned off the motor, killing the lights. The sudden silence was oppressive. Bailey had said nothing in hours. The Zapatista had not moved since they left the bus behind. When the truck crunched to a stop, he sat up and groaned. His bushy beard was splattered with blood.

He spoke in English. "Who are you? Where am I?" He held his hand over the top of his head. "Why am I in this truck? I was on the bus." His eyes cleared and he stared at Bailey. "I know you. From before. You were there also. On the bus."

"Do you know why those men tried to kill you?" Ted asked.

The Zapatista screwed shut his eyes as if trying to remember. "You saved me, is this true? I remember shooting. I thought at first I was dead. And now it is over and I am in this truck. Are you the ones who helped me? Why did you do this thing? You are gringos, yes? This is none of your affair."

"We'll talk later," Ted said. "We have to get out of here. This address, do you know how to get there?" He unfolded the slip of paper from his pocket.

"Si, it is not far from here. But you are right. The pistoleros will be looking for their truck."

Ted left the keys in the ignition, and they walked away from the vehicle. A clutch of idlers edged towards the truck before they turned the first corner.

They ventured deeper into the city, passing markets and stores. Although only early evening, they met few people. The buildings were shabby, mostly run down and neglected. Few of the streetlights were working and as the light waned, the three walked mostly in the dark. In the distance a siren wailed.

The Zapatista led them through the dark streets without difficulty. He walked without assistance, his gait a fluid stride in which his feet seemed to barely touch the ground. Like a cat, Ted thought. He kept up a steady conversation.

"Killing a man with your hands is hard work," the Zapatista said. "Pistoleros are vicious but they are lazy. They would never do anything difficult if they could settle it by using one of their guns. May the devil take their souls." He spat on the ground.

"See over there, the 'palace of justice.'" He pointed at a nondescript brick adobe building. "What a name, eh? No palace, and certainly no justice."

"Chihuahua you know was the birthplace of Pancho Villa. He was a Zapatista too, one of the first."

They had a street address, but there were no street signs. The buildings bore no numbers. They walked through a deserted market, and down an adjoining alley.

It was now fully dark; the only light was on the street corners. From a cantina the sounds of music and laughter spilled into the street.

"So, my friends, should we stop for a meal or do you suppose the police are on our trail?" the Zapatista asked. Delicious cooking smells wafted from a restaurant. "Do you suppose that a man covered in blood would be cause for comment?"

The wail of another siren could be heard in the far distance.

"Don't worry, they will not catch me. I have more lives than a cat," said the Zapatista. The sirens seemed to be drawing closer by the second. The Zapatista's eyes widened ever so slightly. "Yes, perhaps you are right. We will send for food later."

They pushed on, hurrying after the Zapatista's long strides.

They came finally to a nondescript clay building backing onto an unlit alley. There was no number on the house. The Zapatista gave a quick rap on the door, and two soft whistles. After a moment the door opened a crack and there was an answering two-note call. The Zapatista spoke rapidly in Spanish, Ted making out only the words "Marcos" and "*amigos*." The door opened fully and they ducked into the dwelling.

They were in a small house with white-washed walls and a low, beamed ceiling. The only occupant was a handsome young man with blue-black hair and a mouthful of shiny white teeth. A smile seemed his constant expression. The Zapatista and the young man embraced, clapping each other on the back.

"Ricardo."

"Marcos."

"I hope we are in time for supper," the Zapatista said. "Meet our new friends."

"My name is Ricardo," the young man said. "You must be the gringos who saved our comandante. We have been told that you were coming. Welcome. Welcome. We must drink to your safe arrival." Ricardo spoke in perfect English with barely an accent.

Comandante? Heard we were coming? What was this? The incident with the pistoleros was only hours past. Ted turned to Bailey, looking for help, but her face remained blank. She was starting to worry him.

The Zapatista walked from room to room and returned, seemingly satisfied that they were alone. He spoke now in cultured English, dropping his rough accent. "I have not properly introduced myself. My name is Marcos. Some call me the Subcomandante. And I have not properly thanked you. I owe you my life."

Subcomandante Marcos. Ted's mind went into overload. He knew of Marcos, of course. It was impossible to be anywhere in Mexico and not know the name. The stories were whispered in every village. Around the campfires in the evening the campesinos could talk of little else. A legend in his own time, known as the Subcomandante among his troops, he had been the spokesman for the Zapatista rebels since the fighting began.

The stories were improbable. He was said to be highly educated and fluent in four languages, yet he lived as a commando in the jungle. He was reputedly not Mayan, but for some unknown reason he had adopted their cause. He was known for a sense of showmanship and an eye for young women.

"I think I will have that drink now," Ted said.

45

CHAPTER 11

UP CLOSE, MARCOS WAS A BEAR of a man, heavily bearded with huge yellow-green eyes. They were his most striking feature—unblinking, piercing, like those of a large cat. He spoke in halting but perfect English. Education showed in his speech.

"Sit, my friends, sit," he said. Marcos gestured to wooden chairs set around a round table. It was the only furniture in the room. "Ricardo, bring the glasses."

"I know you," Bailey said. "I have seen you before. In Chiapas, many years ago. You were wearing a mask."

Ted had heard that Marcos always appeared in a trademark balaclava. For years, the government had tried to discover his identity, yet the man remained a mystery.

"Ah, yes. Now you have seen my face, I will have to kill you."

Ted's mouth went dry—for a fleeting second he thought Marcos was serious. But the Subcomandante's mouth twisted with amusement.

"If I wear the mask here, I should just wear a sign—here is a terrorist. But you have nothing to fear from me. We are compadres. Marcos does not forget the man and woman who saved his life."

"Why are you in Chihuahua? Why were you on the bus today?" asked Bailey, her eyes intent on Marcos. "You're a long way from Chiapas."

Marcos' presence filled the small room. He took one of Bailey's hands in his. "I have been in the north, meeting with Zapatistas here. I have found in the past that it is much safer to travel alone. Groups attract attention."

He stared steadily into Bailey's eyes—he looked about to devour her. "The Revolution has gone well. The government has changed. They are tired of fighting us and want to make peace, to talk. But the army and the pistoleros like you saw today, these men do not want to stop the war. Some of their leaders are bad men. We meet to decide how to end this."

Bailey and Marcos remained touching. A smile came to her face.

"Excuse me, I need to freshen up." Bailey pushed away from the table and walked to the adjoining room. Ted's eyes followed her. She had been acting strangely ever since Marcos had announced himself. Now there was an uncharacteristic sway to her walk.

Marcos lifted the drapes, looked out the window, and returned to the table. "Tell me," he said to Ted, "Bailey and you, you are together?"

Something about Marcos' directness affected Ted's answer. "Yes . . . Well, no."

"Do not misunderstand. Man to man, Bailey and you, you are not intimate? Am I right? You do not touch."

"We're just travelling together. Just friends."

"Thank you, compadre." Marcos patted Ted on the shoulder. "Ricardo, bring the tequila."

Conversation stopped as Bailey re-entered the room. In the short time away, she had transformed her appearance. Her long hair shone from brushing and hung in waves to her shoulders. Instead of her usual denim shirt, she wore a white silk blouse, open at the neck. Makeup emphasized her smoke-grey eyes. Her lips were glossy red.

Marcos started to his feet and pulled a chair from the table. She smiled and laid her hand on his arm.

Ted felt his cheeks burn.

"Isn't this Zapatista rebellion just Communism under another name?" Ted asked, more loudly than was necessary. Marcos turned his attention from Bailey. He gave Ted an appraising look.

The room turned ominously silent.

"Careful, señor," Ricardo touched Ted's arm. "It is a dangerous thing to ask the Subcomandante such questions." He paused before breaking into a wide smile. "For if you get him talking of politics you are in for a very long evening."

The tension eased. Marcos cuffed Ricardo on the ear. "Yes and watch for this one. I think that he joined the Revolution just so he could shoot a gun."

"*Si*, Subcomandante, and so I could hide in the jungle and eat snakes."

"Make yourself useful, Ricardo. Fetch us some food and more tequila."

Marcos filled their glasses. "I take no offence. You make a good point. At one time I was a Communist. But the campesinos told me they were not interested in Marx or Lenin. Their heroes were Mexicans—Pancho Villa and Emiliano Zapata. A leader must reflect his people, so I became a Zapatista. This is not a Communist Revolution—it is a Mexican Revolution. There is a difference.

"Our demands are few—land, food, schools, hospitals. These things have been denied us by the hacendados, the government, the pistoleros. The campesinos have fought for their liberties since the conquistadors. It is not Communism—it is just the Mexican way. Our war cry is *Tierra y Libertad*. In English that means 'Land and Freedom.'"

"You spoke of the army leaders," Bailey said. "The ones who want to keep fighting. What will you do about them? Will you have them killed?"

"Bailey, what are you talking about?" asked Ted.

"Stay out of this Ted. This is between Marcos and me. Marcos, I have a little proposition to discuss with you." Her hand returned to his arm.

Marcos looked puzzled, as if he recognized something in her voice.

"This Revolution is all about killing, isn't it?" Ted said. "There's killing on both sides. Someone gets in your way, you kill him. That's about it. Don't try to justify it with fine words."

"Ted, stay out of this."

Marcos ignored him and spoke to Bailey. "Death is all around us. Sometimes it is necessary to kill. You know how it happens. That pistolero today, you did not set out to kill him. It was forced upon you, just as violence is forced upon the Zapatistas. Often there is no other choice."

Marcos' voice was hypnotic—Bailey leaned closer.

Ted grabbed her arm. "I'm not putting up with any more of this. Come on, Bailey, we're getting out of here."

Bailey brushed his hand away without looking up.

"In any case, it is too late, señor." Ricardo was standing behind Ted, holding a bag of food. "The police have found the truck and they are searching every-where." He put the bag on the table and pulled out a bottle. "Have another drink, señor. Marcos, tell them of the struggle of the downtrodden people. That is my favourite part."

Marcos laughed. "This one has a special job in our army. He is to make sure that I do not take myself too seriously. Come, señor. Let us be friends."

"I need to know," said Bailey, "among these army officers, is there one by the name of Hernandez?"

"Later, little one. We will talk of it later."

———

The conversation became a three-sided duel. Bailey asked repeatedly about Hernandez. Marcos refused to respond directly, preferring to wax poetic about the Revolution. Meanwhile Ted continued to challenge Marcos. At another level it was a mating dance, and one that Ted was losing.

"When the land barons are gone, there will be food enough for everyone. Mexico is not a poor country—it is only the government that keeps the people poor. It is a system that favours only the rich. When that changes, we will have won," said Marcos.

"But won what?" demanded Ted. "You are not even one of them. What is in this for you?"

"Why to be *el presidente*, of course." Marcos' expression was unreadable.

He was at one moment the impassioned defender of the people, the next a philosopher. He told funny stories. "I was discussing strategy with old Manuel when a wild boar suddenly attacked us. My rifle was out of reach, and so I had to run up a tree. 'Manuel, my friend,' I said, 'it is very difficult to lead a revolution with any dignity while hanging from the branch of a tree. I don't think that pig is a Zapatista.'" He slapped his knee and laughed.

———

Ted had all but given up. Bailey was ignoring him. Marcos refused to react to his barbs, deflecting his petulance with easy good humour.

"Marcos, I need to talk to you." Bailey's voice had dropped a full octave. "Alone. You know what I mean."

Marcos bid Ted and Ricardo good night. He extended his hand to Bailey. She took it and began to follow him from the room.

Ted rose from the table. "Bailey! What the hell do you think you're doing?"

"What I came for," she said. "This is none of your affair."

She left without giving him another glance. Marcos shut the door to the bedroom behind them.

Ted was left standing in the middle of the room, staring at the closed bedroom door. He clenched and unclenched his fists.

Ricardo tossed back his drink. "The Subcomandante, he is a wonder with women. Someday, I hope to be like him. Good night, amigo."

Ted felt as foolish as he could ever remember. How could he have got her so wrong? Only today she had said . . . Said what? She liked him . . . Wasn't that it? And damn it, he had to admit Marcos had spark. He was hard to dislike even while stealing his woman.

His woman? Whatever had he been thinking? He poured more tequila.

The bedroom was a small whitewashed chamber containing a narrow bed, a single chair and a night table. A bare bulb filled the room with harsh white light.

Marcos placed his finger under Bailey's chin, raising her face to meet his. His huge eyes sparkled; a smile curved his full lips. "Now what is this all about?"

Bailey undid the top button of her blouse. "I think you know. You want something from me. I want something from you. Hernandez—I want you to kill him for me."

"That is not such a bad bargain," he said. "I am sure we can work something out." He pulled her into his arms. He was surprisingly gentle for a big man.

Bailey placed her arms around Marcos' shoulders. Her eyes were closed, lips slightly parted.

"So, what is your interest in Hernandez?"

She opened her eyes as Marcos stepped back a pace. "After all, I am not an assassin. If I am to kill someone, I would like to know why."

"Acteal."

His mouth tightened. "I should have known. It was Acteal where we met."

He sat on the edge of the bed and patted the spot beside him. "Sit down, we must talk."

"Just talk?"

He sighed. "Yes, just talk. It has come back to me. I know who you are. You are the American woman who was in Acteal. I am right?"

Bailey continued to unbutton her blouse. "Yes, Marcos, I am that woman. And now you understand I will do anything to see Hernandez dead. Anything."

Marcos reached up and took her hand. "Stop. Enough of this. We must talk. Would you really trade love for a man's death?"

"Yes."

"I have killed before. But I would be less of a man to kill for the pleasure of a woman's body. Let us remake our bargain."

"What do you mean?"

He tugged at her hand until she sat beside him. "Bailey, what you ask is not right. I know some of what you have been through, but I know also hatred can destroy you."

"I didn't come here for a lecture. What do you want from me in return?"

"You must come back to Chiapas," Marcos said.

Bailey's eyes met his. "Do you know what you're asking? I can never go back there. Never. You know that. I came here to kill a man. I need your help. Are you going to help me or not?"

"I owe you my life, and Hernandez is an evil man. I will do what I can. But sex is not the price. You are needed in the mountains as much as ever. I know what you did for the people of Acteal. You could be of service again. Come back to Chiapas with me. That is my price. Then we will see what we can do about Hernandez."

"No, Marcos, anything but that." She twisted away from him.

"Rest now, we'll talk more of this in the morning. Take the bed. I am used to chairs." Marcos turned out the light and left her alone.

In the dim light before dawn, a rooster crowed. Bailey tossed in her sleep and opened her eyes. She was fully clothed. Across the room, Marcos was sleeping upright in the only chair. He snored gently, a small smile on his lips, as if he were enjoying a pleasant dream.

It came back to her. Marcos wanted her to return to Chiapas. Impossible.

She drifted back to sleep, dreaming of a time in the past.

Bailey goes with the other women to the orchard in the early morning. It is warm and sunny. The fruit trees are in bloom, promising a fine harvest. She is enjoying the heat on her arms and the satisfaction of physical labour.

At midday Ernesto appears. He takes Bailey's hand and leads her away. The women smile behind cupped hands.

Alone in her hacienda, she and Ernesto embrace. He undresses her; his mouth presses hungrily to her bare flesh. His fingers are like fire on her skin.

"Touch me," she murmurs.

She is consumed by the touch of his hands, the scalding heat of his lips. The hacienda is an oven, she is melting, her blood feels about to boil.

He lowers her to the bed.

Her skin flows with perspiration, filling the nape of her neck, the hollow of her belly, running between her breasts. Ernesto licks the sweat from her skin. Their bodies move wetly together.

"You are so beautiful."

"Touch me, Ernesto. Don't stop. Never stop."

She imagines herself as one of Ernesto's carvings, taking shape under the touch of his hands and the brush of his lips. Her skin glows like the sheen of freshly cut mahogany.

Afterwards Bailey lies on her back, while Ernesto wipes her skin with a cool, wet cloth. She drifts with the sensation, tracing patterns with her fingers on his now soft penis.

Hammering on the front door startles them. "Open up! Open up!" a voice demands.

Bailey leaps from the bed. Through the window she sees soldiers armed with machine guns. Behind them waits an open truck. In the back, men are bound in chains.

Ernesto grabs for his clothing.

"Do not be afraid. It is me they are after, not you. You will not be harmed. Wait for me. I will hide in the hills." He kisses her once and races for the rear entrance. She stumbles to the bed.

The front door collapses in splinters. Soldiers rush into the room. They tackle Ernesto and hold him as he struggles.

"What is the meaning of this? Let me go!"

An officer strolls into the room. He is sallow-faced with a pencil-thin moustache and an aquiline nose. He is wearing polished knee-high boots and a wide leather belt. His lips are set in a tight smile. Ernesto is naked, being held by two soldiers, while Bailey covers herself with the bedclothes.

"So," the officer pokes Ernesto's belly with his riding crop, "not only is our friend preaching rebellion, he thinks he is good enough to sleep with a white woman."

The officer looks about the room, touching pieces of clothing. "Perhaps I am wrong. Maybe she is just a whore." He does not look again at Ernesto. "Take him away."

Ernesto is dragged through the doorway.

"If you hurt her, I'll kill you!" he shouts.

"How noble," the officer says.

The officer turns to Bailey. His tone is mocking. "Señorita, my name is Capitán Hernandez. I must inform you that your presence in Mexico is no longer permitted. My men will escort you to the airport where you will board the next airplane to America." He smiles again, an expression devoid of any warmth. "If you return, you will be shot. Do you understand?"

"You pig—"

Hernandez slaps her hard across the face. Her face explodes in pain. Blood wells from the corner of her mouth.

"You yanquis, who do you think you are? You think that you can come to our country with your fine ideas and your money!" Saliva forms on his lip. "You think that we should all bow down and kiss your feet. Your friends out there. See them now! They thought they could defy the governor and that you would help them. They will pay for their crimes."

"You won't get away with this! You can't come into my home and assault me. I'm

going to the police. I'll complain to the American consulate."

Hernandez' eyes narrow. "The police? The American consulate? And you, you are nothing but a whore!"

Hernandez puts his hand in Bailey's hair and hauls her from the bed as she clutches the bedclothes. She screams, but stops when he pulls her close. "I have a better idea. You will not go back to your United States after all." His snake-like eyes are beady and cold. "Yes you little whore, I have plans for you. I am staging a little drama. And it needs a heroine."

Hernandez releases his grip. Bailey falls to the floor, covering her face with her hands. Soldiers take her to a waiting jeep. She passes the truck where Ernesto sits. For a moment their eyes meet—she reads his despair. But there is nothing she can do. She looks away.

Bailey is in the back of a jeep still wrapped only in a sheet. The truck bearing Ernesto pulls away.

"No! No! Don't! Please don't. . . !

"Bailey, wake up. Wake up. What is wrong?"

She opened her eyes to find Marcos staring at her. The sun was shining through the window above her head. Her hair was wet with perspiration and the side of her face hurt. She was back in the small house in Chihuahua. Acteal had been a dream.

"Are you all right? You were shouting in your sleep."

"It's nothing. Nothing at all. Just a bad dream. I'll make coffee." Bailey rose and brushed by him into the kitchen. As she waited for the water to boil, she touched her hand to her cheek, feeling for the phantom bruise. But it was not there. Of course not.

CHAPTER 12

THE DULL ACHE BEHIND TED'S EYES forced him awake. Damned tequila. He should have kept his vow never to drink that poison again.

It was daylight and he could hear movement in the adjoining room. He did not want to get out of bed. He had made a complete fool of himself. Different country, different woman—but the same old pain, that familiar empty feeling in the pit of his stomach. He should never have let himself dream.

Bailey was making coffee in the kitchen. There was no sign of Marcos. "Good morning," he muttered. He could not bring himself to make eye contact.

Bailey pulled out two wooden chairs and set coffee on the table. "Sit down, Ted, we should talk."

Ted wrapped his hands around his mug and stared into it. Bailey took the other chair. She did not look at him.

"So you are probably wondering what that was all about," she said.

"Like you told me, it's none of my business. If I recall your words," he said, "you do whatever you want, with whomever you want."

"Yes, I said that." She still was not looking at him.

Ted shrugged. "Look you can sleep with whomever you want. But what's this business about killing some army officer?"

"Remember something else I told you?" she asked, finally looking at him. "I'm trouble. You don't want any part of it. There are lots of things I haven't told you." She paused. "If the time were right, you and I might be good for each other." She placed one of her hands over his. "But it would be no good. Don't you see? I can't be with anyone until I finish this."

Ted did not respond.

"You don't understand anything, do you?"

"How could I? Anytime I ask you anything, you almost bite me," he said.

"Okay, here's what you have to know. Marcos means nothing to me. Last night was more about hero worship than anything else. But if I were to get involved with you, it would mean a lot more. This just isn't the time. I can't be tied to anyone."

Involved with him? This was surely black humour. This woman who has just rejected him for another man was telling him that she can't be involved with him because the timing wasn't right. Was he supposed to feel good about this?

"Who is Hernandez?" he asked.

"Someone I met a long time ago. He killed a friend of mine."

"A friend?"

"No, my lover, actually. A man I knew in Chiapas. Hernandez was in charge of the army detail that murdered him."

"Is that why you slept with Marcos, so he would kill Hernandez for you?"

"I won't sugar coat it. I'll sleep with all the men in Mexico if that's what it takes. Yes, I went into that room to make a deal. I knew exactly what I was doing." Her voice betrayed her. There was the slightest quaver in her words.

Ted had an impulse to put his arms around her, to tell her everything would be all right. But if he did, which woman would he touch? Would it be the Bailey who played with little Mexican girls and their dolls? Or would it be the terrorist who arranged jail breaks and shot pistoleros by the roadside? Or perhaps it would be the woman who hopped into bed with revolutionaries to make blood pacts for murder? She would probably slap his hand away, telling him never to touch her again.

While he hesitated, the door crashed open. Ricardo burst into the room, out of breath, his clothing dishevelled, blood running down his right arm.

"Federales!" he cried." The young man was wide-eyed with terror. They are right behind me. I've been hurt." He slammed the heavy door shut behind him.

Before they could react, there was an explosive banging. The doorframe collapsed and a tall soldier barged into the room, red in the face from exertion. He was carrying a submachine gun, held at the ready.

He pointed his weapon around the room. Bailey and Ted raised their hands in surrender. The soldier made an angry gesture towards Ricardo and swore an oath in Spanish. He motioned impatiently for them to stand against the wall. The soldier slammed home the bolt on his gun, and levelled it. The machine gun's muzzle loomed as a great black hole.

Marcos' room was behind the soldier. The door was standing open. The man's eyes suddenly bulged.

"Take it real easy, amigo. I don't want to see anyone get hurt, not even you." Marcos was pressing something into the soldier's back. "I will shoot you if I have to. Now lay that rifle down slowly. Yes, like that. Ricardo bind his arms and legs."

Marcos stood out from the shadows. He was masked, wearing his trademark balaclava. He was holding an empty tequila bottle. He stood in front of the soldier who was now trussed on the floor. "It is a good thing you didn't make me shoot you. This bottle was empty."

The soldier glared and struggled with his bindings. His lips were moving, but the gag in his mouth muffled his words.

"Don't worry. I won't tell your commander that you surrendered to a man with an empty bottle. Give the colonel my regards."

"Come, we have to get out of here," Ricardo said.

"Just a minute, my friend," said Marcos. Do you not realize that there is a lesson in this? In this rebellion it seems we are always fighting men with guns while we are armed only with empty bottles. But sometimes, an empty bottle is enough."

"Yes, yes, Marcos, this will make a fine story for a campfire someday," Ricardo said, "but the police are searching house to house. They almost caught me, and they will be here any second. We must get away."

"Ricardo, when will you learn? If you are ever to lead men, you must have a sense of the moment. Conflict is mainly theatre. If the campesinos believe that their commander can defeat a foe with an empty bottle, what is to stop them from doing the same? But yes, there is also a moment when we should run away. It is now."

They left by the back door, which opened into a narrow lane. Sirens and the sounds of men shouting came from the front of the building. They ran down one lane and then another until they entered a maze of streets and alleys in the oldest section of the city.

Marcos waived his arms for them to stop. "Slow down. There is no need to run. The police will not be able to follow us here. There are many places to hide and we are among friends."

Marcos rapped on the door of a small cantina. The shutters were closed, the chairs stacked on tables. The door opened a crack, and a man ushered them in. The man bolted the door behind them.

———

They sat around a tiny table sipping strong coffee.

"This city is no longer safe for any of us," said Marcos. "The police must know that I am here and Hernandez will do anything to get his hands on me. We must . . . "

"Wait!" Bailey said. "Did you say Hernandez? Captain Hernandez?"

"Yes," said Marcos, "the one and the same. Except now he has been promoted to colonel and is in charge of the intelligence forces for all of Mexico. He is responsible for the deaths of hundreds of our people. He leads a death squad known as the Red Mask."

"So he has been here all the time." Bailey's heart was pounding. "That nonsense about me returning to Chiapas was just a ploy. Why didn't you tell me before? You weren't serious about helping me with this . . . "

"Slow down." Marcos held up his hands. "I told you that I would help you, and I shall. One day I will surely kill him. Not only for you but for the sake of all of his victims. But you must be patient. The peace process is very delicate, and now he is too strong."

"He is the only reason I returned to Mexico. If he is in Chihuahua, tell me where, so I can find him."

"No, Bailey, you must not do that," said Marcos, leaning towards her. "I don't blame you for wanting to kill him. But to attack him here, with his garrison around him would be suicide. We should leave here and return to Chiapas and carry on with our struggle. Hernandez comes later."

Ted placed a hand on her shoulder. "He's right, Bailey. You won't be helping things by getting yourself killed. We should do as Marcos says."

Bailey glared at him, fire in her eyes. She slapped Ted's hand away. "I told you never to touch me!" She sprang to her feet, kicking over her wooden chair.

"Cowards! He slaughtered the men, women, and children of Acteal, but you say we should run away because he is too strong. Too strong? If you will not help me, I will kill him myself. You make me sick!"

Bailey's face was scarlet. She stormed from the room, out the door of the cantina and into the street. It happened so quickly that no one had the presence to stop her. By the time they got to the doorway, the alley was empty. They searched for her, but she was nowhere to be found.

CHAPTER 13

WHEN HER PULSE SLOWED, Bailey found herself alone. What now? She was lost in the back streets of Chihuahua. The adobe buildings and tiny churches all looked alike. She wandered in circles down lanes without names, passing the same landmarks again and again. The local people eyed her suspiciously. Their faces were closed and unfriendly. A lost white woman was what they thought of her, just another stupid white woman.

A stupid white woman—that's exactly how she felt. She was a stranger here. She didn't know a soul, not even a name. Her Spanish was passable, and she had money, but the police were looking for Marcos and his companions. She saw police cars in the distance, their sirens blaring. There was no way of knowing whether they had her description.

She found a main avenue that brought her to an expensive hotel. She checked in under her own name. It was risky, but it was her only choice—she needed the credit card to pay for the room. She doubted the Hilton reported the names of its American guests to the police.

The desk clerk noticed her lack of luggage. Bailey saw his suspicious look and reacted quickly.

"Air Mexico—those fools have lost my luggage again. When it arrives, send it up to my room."

"*Si*, señorita. It happens all the time. You can find what you need for tonight in the gift shop. It is open until nine."

Once in her room, Bailey headed to the bathroom to splash cold water on her face. She needed to think. Where to begin?

What a mess she had made of things. Two days ago she was travelling across northern Mexico. She was just starting to enjoy the man's company and almost forgot her reason for being here. She had even thought of going home when it was time for Ted to leave. Now two men were dead and the police were on a manhunt. And here she was hiding in a tourist hotel without the slightest idea of what to do next.

She had planned all along to come to Chihuahua—Hernandez' headquarters were somewhere in the city. She'd bought that damned gun and travelled all the way here to kill him—that was as far as her plans had got. But when she met up with Marcos, she was sure he would help her. Now she was on her own and didn't even have her gun. It had been left behind when they fled from the police. She thought about hiring a professional killer, but she didn't think she had near enough money for that. Here she was armed with only the small camping knife given to her by Antonio's daughter. The blade was sharp, but as a weapon it was useless. *A lot of good this will do.* She tossed it into her handbag.

She thought briefly of Ted. She had lied to him, let him go on thinking she had slept with Marcos. There had been a hurt-puppy look in his eyes. Did she want him to go on thinking the worst of her? Yes, probably. Ted was a complication. They had become too close. And she had no time. No time for anyone who might care about her.

But then this was hardly new. Bailey had been running all her life, committing reckless acts to drive others away.

The next morning the daily paper was delivered to her door. It contained no account of the deaths of the pistoleros and nothing of a manhunt for Marcos. The streets outside her window were quiet. She began to think of a plan to find Hernandez.

After another day without incident, Bailey ventured out. It was evening—the streetlights were on. She had washed her clothes in the sink in her room. She brushed her hair, and once again applied makeup.

The same desk clerk was on duty.

"Can you help me?" she asked. "I need some directions."

"Certainly, señorita, anything."

"I'm supposed to meet my brother for dinner tonight, but my luggage hasn't turned up and my appointment book was in it. We agreed on a restaurant in the downtown, but I don't know which one." She gave the clerk a hopeful smile.

"There are many restaurants in the area. Do you remember the name?"

"No, but he is doing some consulting with the Mexican army—he said the officers meet there all of the time. Does that help?"

"It was probably El Condor. It is favourite eating place of the military. Here, I will draw you a map . . . "

Bailey stopped at a shop in the hotel. She picked through a rack of sundresses and selected a bright red one and then browsed through some of the other displays. She noticed a pile of wigs on a stand nearby, grabbed a blond one, and ducked into the change room. She emerged in a new outfit, complete with sandals and costume jewellery.

Inspecting herself in the mirror, Bailey was satisfied. The dress was just the thing, tight fitting and cut low in front. She signed her purchases to her room and packed her old clothes in her handbag.

El Condor was a large restaurant consisting of a centrally located bar surrounded by booths set against the wall. The room was softly lit, the tables covered with red and white chequered cloths. Cigarette smoke hung in clouds. Conversation hummed above the clink of glassware.

Bailey found herself a place at the bar and ordered a drink. She toyed with her glass and let her eyes roam about the room. The clientele consisted of assorted fat Americans in loud clothes, Mexican businessmen, and local lounge lizards. Groups of soldiers were having drinks. She identified a group of army officers, distinguishable by the cut of their uniforms and the insignia on their caps.

Soldiers flocked to her like bees to honey, her blond hair and the tight red dress as effective as a written invitation. Bailey accepted the drinks but rejected the propositions. An hour later she had the information she needed.

"*Intelligencia?*" asked the fresh-faced soldier. He lowered his voice. "Why would you want anything to do with them?"

"I have a friend I need to meet," she said. Bailey touched the soldier's hand across the table.

"Behind us, that group of officers. They are *Intelligencia*. But don't tell them I told you. Be careful, señorita." The boy emptied his glass and left.

"So would one of you gentlemen like to buy me a drink?" Bailey struck a pose, one hand on her hip.

"Certainly, señorita." The officers stood as one, and a chair was proffered.

"Thank you," she sat down. "I'm just waiting for my brother, but I couldn't help but admire your uniforms. Men look so dashing in uniform."

The officers smilingly acknowledged the remark.

Introductions were made.

"My name is May-Belle, but you can call me May," she said. "I'm here on holiday from Atlanta. Your country is so beautiful. And the people have been so friendly."

The soldiers exchanged knowing smiles. Bailey did not have to read minds to know what they were thinking. Glasses were raised in a toast.

"To beautiful women and the Mexican Army. May they always go hand in hand."

Smiles and laughter.

"And what part of the army are you in?" she asked . . . "Oh, intelligence . . . isn't that fascinating?"

As the conversation progressed, Bailey told more easy lies. She asked the time as if waiting impatiently for her brother. *This was too easy.* She could almost smell the testosterone in the air.

"I've read something about your army intelligence," she said, "in *Time Magazine*, I think. It was about an officer by the name of Hernandez—Colonel Hernandez, I think. Is he your commander?"

"*Si.*"

"He looks so handsome in his photograph, I'd love to meet him. Does he ever come in here?"

"Often, but not tonight. Two, three times a week. We will introduce you."

"Thank you, I would like that," she said. For once her smile was genuine.

After one more drink and more ritual pleasantries, Bailey excused herself. "I must be on my way, but I'm in town for another week. Perhaps I will see you again."

She received an enthusiastic invitation for drinks the following evening.

After two nights, Bailey was a fixture at the officers' table. The men vied for her attention, behaving like stallions after a mare in heat. The conversation was charged with sexual overtones. Bailey flirted casually, but she always left early, and alone.

———

She saw him walk in the door. He was not in uniform, but rather wore a soft grey suit. Only the bulge made by his sidearm distinguished him from a successful businessman. The officers stood to attention.

Bailey recognized him instantly. Her breath caught in her throat. Hernandez was smiling as he approached the table; he seemed to be looking only at her. Had he recognized her?

"Colonel, may we introduce you to our new friend. May-Belle, this is our commander, Colonel Hernandez."

"Señorita," he said with a nod.

Smile, keep your voice level. Make eye contact.

"Colonel, I've heard so much about you. Please join us," she said. She made herself look up into his face, forcing her features into a winsome smile.

Bailey was terrified. Had her expression betrayed her emotions? This was so difficult. But it must have been going all right. Hernandez' eyes showed nothing.

"May I buy you a drink? Emiliano Hernandez, at your service." He still wore a moustache, and his face had the same gaunt and sallow lines, even when he smiled.

It was Hernandez' eyes she remembered most clearly. They were dead, like pieces of stone set in deep orbits. He stared frankly at the neckline of her dress. It was all Bailey could do to stop her hands from clawing at his face.

This is it, Bailey. Put your feelings away. Do whatever needs to be done. Just get him alone.

Hernandez was no sooner seated than the other officers began to make their excuses and to get up to leave. Bailey intercepted the subtle signals. With a flicker of his eye and a slight wave of his hand, Hernandez dismissed the other men. Within minutes they were alone.

"You Mexican gentlemen have the best manners," she said. "Here's little old me, all alone in your country, and your officers have been showing me the pleasure of their company." She tittered at the end of each sentence and gave Hernandez her best attempt at a come-hither smile. She touched him lightly on the arm.

Hernandez did not remove her hand and appeared to enjoy her attentions. "Please stay. You must have dinner with me," he said.

"Well certainly. It would be my pleasure," she said. "My friends are out, and I'm all alone tonight."

His eyes narrowed.

They ordered from the table. The waitress brought them more drinks—shot glasses of tequila followed by thin Mexican beer. Bailey made a show of coughing and sputtering as she drank the harsh spirits. He suggested another. She giggled and agreed. She feigned being overheated, fanning the air and then undoing a button at the top of her dress. Hernandez' eyes followed every movement.

Bailey made her mind go into neutral. This was a drama, a high school play. Her part was the seductress. Don't think about what comes next—just say your lines.

After three tequilas, Bailey was laughing at Hernandez' every word. Her hands were in constant motion, casually brushing against his arms and shoulders. She whispered nonsense in his ear.

They had barely touched their meals when Hernandez rose to his feet, taking Bailey's hand. She accompanied him from the restaurant, leaning drunkenly on his arm.

"Where're we going, sweetie? Aren't we going dancing?"

"Later," he said. "First we should get to know each other better." He placed his arm around her waist.

Bailey leaned into him. "I'd like that."

He led her to the elevator and up to the third floor of the attached hotel. He guided her through the doorway of his room with his hand. Hernandez removed his jacket, and hung his holstered pistol on the back of a chair.

Bailey stroked his shoulders, standing very close. "Now I'd like you to do something for me."

"What's that?" He pulled her closer, running his hands down her sides. He pressed his lips into her neck. Bailey turned her face away.

"No, not yet."

Hernandez continued to pull her to him, his hands stroking her buttocks. Bailey placed her lips against his ear.

"I want us to take our time. I've got something special in mind."

"What do you mean?"

"I'd like you to have a shower," she breathed in his ear.

"A shower? What, alone?"

"Yes, alone. I want you to be very clean." She kissed him lightly on the cheek and pulled away. She stood with her back to him, unbuttoning the front of her dress.

"Get going now. And I want you very clean. Especially you know where," she said.

When she turned around he was gone. The water in the shower was running.

Bailey closed her dress and crossed the room. She picked up Hernandez' holster, released the clasp, and wrapped her hand around the handle of the pistol. The oversize automatic dwarfed her hand. She clicked off the safety and sat down to wait, facing the washroom door.

Hernandez emerged wet-haired from the shower, wrapped in a terry robe.

Bailey held the automatic outstretched in both hands, the barrel aimed at his chest.

"Hold it right there," she said.

"Well, well." Hernandez curled his lips in the slightest of smiles.

"Keep your hands where I can see them."

"So what is this? And holding my own gun in your hand? What game are we playing, Bailey?"

Bailey? How did he know her name?

"You are surprised I know your name? But of course I do. You forget I am in intelligence."

"How. . . ?" she asked. She kept the automatic pointed at his chest, but her hand was quivering.

"I have known you were here since you crossed the border. I have been waiting for you."

"What?"

"How stupid for you to travel under your own name? And to check into a hotel using a credit card. Bailey you disappoint me. But then again, I thought you were dead. However did you survive?"

"It doesn't matter, this gun is all that matters. This is the end. I'm here to kill you."

"Give me the gun, Bailey. You are not going to shoot me. Give it to me before someone gets hurt." He extended his hand.

"No, stay back."

"So, shoot me then. If you think I deserve to die, go ahead. Shoot me." His lifeless eyes were locked on hers. He advanced across the room.

"Shoot me. Come on. Shoot me." He was closer, almost touching the gun.

She fired.

"Bang!" Hernandez mouthed the word as the hammer dropped on an empty chamber.

"Click! Click! Click!" She kept pulling at the trigger.

She threw the pistol at him; he ducked under the throw. She grabbed her handbag from the table and flung it at him. Hernandez deflected it with his arm, the contents spilling across the floor.

Bailey started for the door, but he cut her off. Hernandez pinned her with his body against the wall.

She scratched at him with her hands. Her nails dug into flesh.

He slapped her across the face. "Bitch! Thought you would kill me with my own gun, eh? You should have checked for bullets."

With both hands he ripped open the front of her dress. The buttons tore from the thin fabric, bouncing across the floor.

"So how about some of that fun you promised?"

"No! Stop!" she cried.

"Scream. Go ahead. Scream your head off if you like. No one will come. In this room, screams are not unusual." A vein pulsed in Hernandez' forehead.

Bailey was pressed against the wall. Hernandez' hands were beneath her bra. His robe fell open. He was naked beneath it, and his penis pressed against her thigh.

She clawed at his hands, desperate to escape. She raised her knee to his groin. Hernandez pushed her back onto the bed. He crushed her with his weight. He tore at her panties, one hand clasped painfully on her left breast.

"Come on, you little bitch! Give it to me!"

"No! No! Please stop!"

Hernandez grabbed her hair and pulled off the wig and dragged her off the bed and onto the floor. He pushed her to her knees.

"Now for some special attention. Now, if you know what's good for you."

He pulled her face into his groin. His penis pushed against her lips. She averted her mouth.

Bailey's knee struck something hard. She recognized the camping knife from her bag. She found the handle and gripped it tightly.

"Okay, okay, stop pulling my hair. Give me some room."

Hernandez pulled away ever so slightly, arching his back. His hands were entwined in her hair, pulling her into him.

"Kiss it, bitch."

Bailey yanked the knife from its sheath.

"Kiss it bi—"

She thrust upwards. She buried the knife into the flesh between his legs.

Hernandez howled—the bellow shook the walls. Bailey was sprayed with hot blood. Hernandez clamped his hands to his groin and fell heavily to the floor.

She pulled the knife from his groin and held it like a crucifix in both hands. She took a deep breath, fighting the urge to run.

Finish it! Kill him now!

Hernandez was emitting guttural moans through clenched teeth. She knelt over him, setting the tip of the blade in the hollow of his throat.

"Shut up, you bastard." She applied pressure to the knife, and he choked into silence. A thin trickle of blood ran down his throat where the point punctured the skin.

"I'm here to kill you. The 'American whore' from Acteal has come back for you. This is for all the good people you killed."

Hernandez' eyes were glazed with pain. He was barely able to mouth the words, "Acteal . . . not my doing . . . only following . . . " His eyes closed and his body went limp.

There was no sympathy in her—Hernandez deserved to die. Her goal was within her grasp. Just a little more pressure on the knife and it would all be over. Just a little push . . . She hesitated. The seconds seemed to extend endlessly. She was holding her breath.

It was no good. This was not the scene she replayed endlessly in her mind, standing over Hernandez while he begged for his life. There could be no climax to this drama. She paused, hoping the anger would come back and drive her to finish it.

Finally, she sighed and removed the knife.

She dressed and wiped the worst of the blood from her face. At the doorway, she looked back. Hernandez lay on the floor, oozing blood. Beside the body lay her black lace panties. She felt hollow inside.

Got to get out of here. She ran, clutching the front of her dress. Outside the hotel, through the streets. Her mind operating at the most primal level, *"Run! Escape! Hide! Find Ted!"* People stared in amazement as she ran past them, headlong into the dark ghettos of Chihuahua.

Bailey was oblivious to her surroundings and ran without thinking. Instinct was her only guide. Down one street, through back lanes, into the darkest corners of the city. One thought filled her mind—she must find Ted. He was her beacon—she had to find him.

She finally stopped, out of breath. She was in a maze of alleys, miles from the hotel. Behind her the night was alive with the clamour of sirens. She was not afraid—let them take her.

A Mexican boy appeared out of the night. He took her hand, tugged and motioned that she was to follow him. Bailey obeyed without question. He was taking her to Ted.

The boy showed her to a small adobe building. It was dark and empty. Bailey was disappointed. Where was Ted? Why wasn't he here?

The boy spoke in broken English, "Señorita, stay here. Miguel, come back soon with friend Ted."

"Yes. Find him. Please, Miguel."

The boy smiled. "Si, señorita, Ted is big friend of Marcos. I bring. You wait." He was gone into the night.

Bailey sat huddled in a chair in the dark. She could feel the hot blood splashing against her face. She rubbed at her skin trying to remove the stains. Her shoulders shook and her lips trembled. She shivered as if from cold.

Time stopped. She sat alone for minutes or perhaps hours. She smelled him before he spoke—his presence was like a warm wind. Finally his arms were around her and she was safe. The last of her self-control was gone as convulsions wracked her body. Her tears came hard and fast. She huddled in Ted's embrace.

CHAPTER 14

BAILEY TOOK THEM BY SURPRISE when she ran from the cantina. Ted followed her into the streets, only to find she had vanished. He spent the rest of the day searching. With help from Ricardo he scoured the nearby streets, up one block and back the other. Meanwhile, Marcos directed a small army of supporters from his table at the back of the cantina. By nightfall the searchers reported they had found nothing.

"She has vanished, Subcomandante. We have looked everywhere."

"Thank you my friends. I know you have tried," said Marcos.

"We can't give up. The police are everywhere. She's in danger," Ted demanded. "We have to go on looking."

"We will not give up, compadre," said Marcos. "We have contacts in many places. If she is not found tonight, we will look again tomorrow. And the day after if necessary. Our people will help you, but sadly I cannot stay myself. There are pressing matters in Chiapas. I must return."

Day after day, Ted refused to give up hope—a legion of Zapatistas helped him comb the city. He received regular reports through a young boy, who passed along the disappointing lack of news.

He spent his time visiting the local restaurants and bars. "Have you seen an American woman? She has dark hair and . . . " He had repeated the question too often to count, enduring the resulting shrugs and shakes of the head. From time to time he would start at a woman's hair or a face in a crowd, only to be disappointed. He ate little and slept hardly at all. His eyes stung from lack of sleep.

The questions would not stop. What was she doing right now? Was she hurt? Was she in trouble? The worst was knowing there was no way to stop her—nothing he could do to prevent some act of self-destruction. How did he ever let it get this far? How did he let her get away?

What a shit I've been.

Ted was waiting for his messenger in a darkened cantina when he heard the wail of sirens and the roar of rushing vehicles. The word of mouth telegraph brought the news. Two young men were talking excitedly in Spanish, and Ted was able to overhear.

"An army officer. He was attacked."

"*Qué?*"

"*Sí*, an officer. He was stabbed by some gringo woman."

"This is good. May he die a painful death."

"He may. He was stabbed in the *cojones*."

"Hah! That will serve him right!"

"We must be careful, Manuel. The city is crazy with soldiers. They are looking everywhere for this woman."

"A gringo woman who cuts a federale in the *cojones*! I hope she gets away."

"Eh, Paulo, but I would not want to meet such a woman."

It had to be Bailey. He must find her. Ted slapped a few pesos on the counter and was turning to leave when his messenger ran up to him. The boy grabbed his sleeve.

"Señor Ted, Señor Ted, come quick. The señorita, she asks for you. I think she is hurt." The boy pointed to his face. "She has blood."

Bailey was sitting in a chair with her back to the doorway, staring at a wall. Her hands were to her face, rubbing at her cheeks. Ted rushed to her, kneeling by her side and taking her hands in his.

"Bailey! Thank God. Are you okay?"

Bailey was mumbling something. Ted inclined his head closer to hear.

"*El diablo . . . está muerto . . . está . . .* " The rest was inaudible.

"It's me. It's Ted. I'm here."

Her head turned to face him. "Where were you? I needed you." Her lips trembled, she began to shake. Tears welled up and streamed down her cheeks. Ted took her in his arms, stroking her hair and whispering in her ear.

"Easy, no one's going to hurt you. Take deep breaths. Easy now."

Her response was in Spanish. The word "*muerte,*" Spanish for death, was all he could make out.

Somewhere behind them, Miguel lit a kerosene lamp, filling the room with soft orange light. Bailey's features were revealed from the shadows. She looked like a creature from the crypt. Her face was covered with dried blood through which tears had carved deep channels. Her eyes bulged in their sockets.

"Miguel, a rag, and some water," Ted said.

"*Si*, right away."

Ted dabbed at Bailey's face with a wet cloth, and her skin slowly emerged from the gore. Except for a darkening bruise across her cheek, he saw no injuries. He pushed her hair back from her face.

"There, that's better. You'll be all right. Here, drink this." He raised a glass of water to her lips.

Ted motioned to the boy that he should leave. Miguel gave a small bow and was gone.

"Ted, I've done something bad. You can't imagine what I've done."

"Ssshh, you don't need to talk about it. I know everything. It's okay."

"No! It's not okay! I stabbed him—it was bad." She swallowed hard, and for a minute was unable to speak. She put her face in her hands and rocked backwards and forwards.

She was a wreck. The self-assured woman was gone, replaced by a frightened little girl. Her defences were gone—she was vulnerable. She needed him.

I love her.

The thought surprised him. It bubbled up from somewhere deep in his subconscious, like a flash of sunlight in his brain. *He loved her.*

Regaining some control, Bailey began to talk. She told him about Hernandez, about the attack, and how at the last moment she was unable to kill him. She rambled. Much of it made no sense. Caves and jungles. Soldiers and guns.

Tears continued to roll down her cheeks, but she was no longer crying hard.

She spoke in a monotone punctuated with occasional smiles and inappropriate laughter.

"And back to Acteal . . . the birds, the flowers . . . see the black earth come up to meet me . . . the men with the guns will never be again . . . the blood on my hands, on my face . . . the night . . . the night will never end. The dead know what I've done. They are laughing at me now, they are all laughing . . . hear them . . . "

The words would not stop—she could not stop. Whatever was inside had to come out. She seemed to have some desperate need to confess, to unburden her soul. The words poured from her.

Ted was her silent supporter. He listened though he understood little of what she said. Most of it was gibberish, but he recognized snatches of stories from her past.

There had been many men but little love. She talked of alcohol; she once had a problem. And drugs, prescription drugs it sounded like. One name was repeated many times.

"Ernesto, my love . . . my love." The tears started again. "I killed him, I killed them all."

"No, you didn't. Don't talk like that."

"You don't think I'm a killer? I'm a murderer. I killed them all."

"No, don't . . . "

She sat straight up, her eyes clear and staring.

"I'll tell you. The story behind my name, you asked me, you wanted to know. So I'll tell you. I killed both of my parents. What do you think of that? Do you want to know the whole story?"

"Yes, tell me."

"That's where it started."

She spoke in phrases, gaps of seconds between each.

"The story I told . . . they couldn't agree on a name . . . that was true . . . but that was before I was born . . . It was a breech delivery . . . There were problems . . . My mother . . . in labour . . . for twenty hours . . . She died." Bailey lapsed into brief silence.

"Go on," Ted said.

"When I was a little girl . . . I used to look at pictures of her in scrapbooks . . .

She was beautiful . . . She would have loved me."

"My father never forgave me . . . Her death was my fault . . . He never got over it . . . a haunted man . . . for the rest of his life . . . Wouldn't look at me, wouldn't give me a name . . . his way to punish me . . . to remind me every day that I killed . . . I killed . . . I killed the woman he loved.

"Bailey, the girl with no name, the girl who killed her mother. So what do you think about that?"

Ted wiped at her tears and stroked her hair. "It's all right. Let it go."

"I was raised by nannies . . . He drank. I could hear him up in his room smashing bottles and screaming at God for taking her . . . I was thirteen the year he killed himself . . . In his note, he wrote he couldn't live without her. Not a word to me, but I knew . . . He hated me . . . I killed him, too."

Ted tried to take her hand, but she brushed it away.

"Don't you understand? Don't touch me—nobody touches me. That's what my father taught me. The only thing he left me was money. When I came of age, I started to spend it as fast as I could. Cars, trips, drugs, men—I had them all. But nobody touched me. No ties. No commitment, no pain."

"Then Mexico—things changed. I had no history here, no past. People needed me. I needed them.

"They even gave me a name, a pet name, my first name ever. For the first time in my life I was somebody—I existed. But that's the past. It's all gone now."

"What was the name? I'd like to know."

She shook her head. She was becoming agitated, eyes darting, hands restless.

"No, I don't have the right to a real name. I'm an animal, just like him. Who can ever forgive me?" Again, Bailey's hands began stroking her face.

"I can forgive you," Ted said.

"But God doesn't forgive me. He doesn't, does He? There are things no one can forgive. The blood is on my hands! Look!" She held them out for inspection. Her jaw trembled.

She put her face into her hands. "Leave me. Let me be alone now." She said nothing more but made no move to escape Ted's embrace. After a long time, her breathing became deep and regular and her eyes closed.

Ted lay awake holding her. Her body was hot, as if the pain inside was radiating through her skin. The night sounds turned to the morning birdsong before he slept.

When he awoke, she was gone. The door was standing open. Leaping out of bed, Ted feared the worst—that she had kept on running.

CHAPTER 15

SHE HAD NOT RUN FAR. He found her sitting in the street just outside the door. Her feet were bare, her eyes vacant. She was sifting handfuls of dirt through her fingers, and rubbing her palms against her cheeks.

"Bailey! Bailey, what are you doing? Come back in." She did not look up or turn her head.

Ted brought her to her feet and led her inside the house. She gave no resistance, her body limp like a rag doll. She sat on the bed with her hands in her lap, listless, staring vacantly at nothing.

"Bailey, what were you doing? What's wrong? Talk to me."

She would not make eye contact and instead stared over his head at a point on the wall.

"Bailey, say something. Bailey . . . "

She was whispering to herself, repeating the same words over and over. Her words were a mantra in Spanish. "*Muerta, es muerta, es muerta, es muerta, es muerta, es mu . . . *"

After half an hour and no change in her condition, Ted was beside himself. Bailey was stroking her face with her hands, continuing to chant. Was this her mind's reaction to the assault, shutting down in response to what she had done? He needed to find her a doctor. But how? In the distance he could hear sirens. Through a crack in the shutters, he saw army trucks rolling by. And he did not dare leave Bailey alone.

There was nothing to do but wait, and hope that Miguel would return. Without help they were doomed—there was no way he and Bailey could avoid capture on their own. Ted sat staring into the vacant alley, willing the boy to appear.

"Come on, kid, don't desert us. You said you would be back. Come on now."

Within the hour he spotted Miguel racing up the street towards him. Ted's heart leapt at the sight. Here was his saviour—a runt of a Mexican street boy. The boy flew across the cobblestones, his bare feet barely touching the ground. Ted had never been more relieved to see anyone in his life.

"I have brought some food," Miguel said, out of breath. "They almost caught me." He placed a parcel tied with twine on the table.

"The soldiers are everywhere. They are showing her picture. They ask me where I go. I say, my sister is virgin and I would bring her to them. *Bastardos!*" He spit on the floor.

An involuntary smile came to Ted's lips. "Your sister?"

Miguel's face cracked in a grin. "I have no sister, but federales think only with their *pistolas.*"

"What have you heard of Hernandez?" Ted asked.

Miguel had little news. Hernandez' identity had been confirmed but nothing more. There were competing rumours—some that he was dead or that he was in hospital. Other versions had him leading the search for Bailey. There had been no official statements and the newspapers carried no accounts.

Bailey remained on the bed with her back to the room. "What is wrong with lady? Did soldiers hurt her?" Miguel asked.

"I need to get her to a doctor and out of Chihuahua. I have money. Can you help?" Ted pulled a wad of pesos from his pocket.

"No, I not do this for money. Miguel is Zapatista. I do this for sake of Revolution."

"Thank you. I will tell Marcos you have been a big help."

The boy stood to attention, feet together, head up, shoulders straight. "Marcos is a great leader. Someday I be like him."

"Okay, but enough about the Revolution. Right now we need a vehicle."

"Car is no problem. Miguel is great driver. I drive us." The boy puffed up his chest.

"No, I don't need you to come with us. Just tell me where I can find a car."

The boy shook his head, crossing his arms over his chest. "Is no problem—Miguel is good driver."

"You can't come with us. How old are you, ten, eleven? What would your parents say?"

There was a short pause—Miguel looked away as he spoke. He had been speaking English, but now he slipped into Spanish. "*Mamá y papá están muertos. Miguel es solo muchacho. Miguel esta solo.*"

"I'm sorry, I didn't know."

Miguel appointed himself Ted's amigo and chauffeur. He promised to cook, to clean, to fetch tequila and to be no trouble.

"All right, Miguel. You have a deal. We are compadres. But one thing—I do the driving." A sly smile lit up Miguel's face as he dashed away.

Bailey had said nothing during the exchange. Her eyes were open, but Ted did not know whether she had understood.

"You heard that, Bailey? Miguel's getting us a car. We're leaving here. That's good news."

He might as well have been talking to himself.

As the day wore on, Bailey continued to stare at the wall. Ted fed her a little bread and some water, but she did not respond other than eating what was offered. She said nothing; even her chanting had stopped. He tried holding her hand in the hope that his touch might reach her. It did not help.

It was early evening and a single lamp lit the room. Ted could not sit still. He had been pacing the floor for hours. There was the sound of a vehicle—a motor stopped, doors slammed. Miguel entered with two Mexicans.

"This is Jose and his mother, Consuela," Miguel said. "They do not speak English. We can trust them."

Ted nodded and ventured the few words in Spanish he knew to be a greeting.

"I have found us a vehicle," Miguel said. "It is a very fine one. Come see."

Outside in the lane stood a battered Buick. It was faded black in colour and looked to be about forty years old. Its bulbous fenders almost touched the houses on either side of the alley.

"We're going in this?" Ted asked. "Are you sure this thing will hold together long enough to get us out of here?"

"Of course. It belongs to the undertaker. He uses it almost every day."

"And he let you borrow it?"

"Not exactly." Miguel's eyes became hard. "He finds it better not to support the Revolution. Instead he gets rich burying people the army kills. Now he can do so without his car."

The old woman shooed the men from the room and helped Bailey dress in fresh clothes, pants and a plain blouse. Ted wrapped her bloodstained red dress in paper and fed it into the fire. The synthetic material burned with iridescent green flames.

They made plans for their escape. Ted and Bailey would hide in the Buick's cavernous trunk while the Mexicans rode in front. Ted hoped that to a passerby they would look like a normal family out in their car for a drive.

"If we're stopped, tell them you are visiting a sick relative," Ted said. "Remember, Jose is your father and you're going to visit your grandfather."

"*Si*, I will do as you say," Miguel said.

Miguel ventured out first and whistled to report there was no one about. One by one they left the house and walked the short distance to the car. The houses around them were dark—the entire neighbourhood seemed deserted.

Ted opened the car's trunk, climbed in, and settled onto a pile of blankets. Bailey was helped in to lie beside him. Her eyes were open and staring. Ted held her by the hand.

"There's nothing to worry about. The trunk is going to close now, but I'll be here with you. We must be very quiet."

The lid closed over their heads—it was like being sealed into a coffin. There was no light and little air. Bailey stirred beside him, her fingers digging into his flesh. *This was madness!* The protest died in his throat as the motor roared into life. The Mexicans slammed the doors and the vehicle set off through the darkened streets.

In the trunk Ted and Bailey experienced the trip through sound and movement. Their compartment was dark and airless, and the exhaust pipe thundered and rattled. The crunch of gravel and the bouncing of the suspension marked the car's progress.

The vehicle stopped so suddenly Ted was thrown against the front of the compartment. Outside there were shouted commands. *"Alto, Alto!* Out and show your papers!"

There was the crunch of tires from another vehicle and the pounding of metal-shod boots. Men's voices came muffled through the steel. The doors opened and the vehicle lurched as its occupants were pulled from the car. Sounds of a scuffle and shouts. "All of you, hands on the car!"

Bailey became restless. "The soldiers, they've come back. Ernesto, they've come back to kill us."

"Shhh, we must be quiet. It will be all right." Ted tightened his grip on her hand.

"No, No . . . NO!"

Ted clasped his hand across her mouth. She struggled in his grasp. *Had they been heard?*

The interrogation continued—the sounds from the trunk apparently unnoticed. Ted heard a body brushing against the lid over his head and the vehicle sagged on its springs. A soldier was sitting on the fender above his head. The man was so close he could almost smell him.

Ted was covered in perspiration. Bailey was thrashing and clawing at his hands. He held her down with all his strength, with his hand across her mouth. But she was strong. How much longer could he hold her?

"Where are you going, old man? What is your business so late at night?"

"My father he is . . . "

There was a thud as something soft and heavy slammed into the side of the car.

"The truth! Don't lie to me! Where are you going?"

"My father he . . . "

Bailey was kicking her feet, the sound of her shoes banging against metal rang loud in Ted's ears. *The soldiers must have heard. They were going to open the trunk. It was all over.*

A crunch of bone hitting flesh. "I warned you. Hold him up!"

Ted couldn't hold Bailey much longer. She was writhing in his grasp. She bit his hand, freeing her mouth. "Help—"

Miguel's voice rose shrill and loud. His small fists pounded on the trunk lid, drowning out Bailey's cries. "Stop! Stop! Don't hit him! My father did not understand. He tells the truth."

"Stop the noise and explain. Quick, *chico*, before we shoot your papa."

"His father is dead! We go to honour him on *el Dia de los Muertos!* The grave is in the south. It is many weeks to travel there and make preparations. It is the truth!"

There was no immediate reply. Inside the trunk, Bailey ceased her struggles. She seemed to be listening. The soldiers muttered in conference. Seconds dragged by with Ted holding his breath. Would the next sound be a gunshot?

"Boy, help your father up. You should have told us before. We mistook you for rebels. Your journey is sacred, and we did not mean to interfere. Carry on. Go with our blessings for your departed ancestor."

Hands slapped the fender as the car pulled away. "Go with God. Remember us to your father!"

Ted released his hold on Bailey and sighed in relief. El Dia de los Muertos—*the Day of the Dead. Go with God. All for the sake of a dead relative. What a bloody country. No respect for the living but in love with the dead.*

———

An hour later the car stopped on the side of a dirt road and the trunk opened. In the distance, the lights of Chihuahua sparkled. In the foreground, a line of headlights marked the main highway.

Ted clambered from their hiding place, helping Bailey out after him. "Help me with her, Miguel. Let's get her into the back."

"I'm all right. I'll get there myself." Bailey opened the rear door and settled into the seat. She closed the door, sitting alone in the car.

Ted and Miguel exchanged puzzled looks. Something had shaken Bailey out of her stupor. "I thought we were done for," Ted said. "How did you ever come up with *el Dia de los Muertos?*"

"In Mexico it is the most important day in the year," Miguel said. "Not even federales dare interfere—it could cost them their souls."

Miguel conferred with the man and his mother. "They leave us and walk to city. We should be safe. The highway is not far."

Ted pressed some money into the Mexicans' hands and thanked them for their help. The old woman made the sign of the cross and murmured a benediction. Then they turned and melted into the night.

They were alone. The air was cool and the stars shone brightly. It reminded Ted of the night he had escaped from jail. A beautiful night in the desert with not another soul for miles around. It was enough to let him pretend he was safe and the men with guns were not real. Ted started the car—the dash lights bathed the interior in pale light.

Bailey was awake and seemed aware of her surroundings. "You almost got us killed you know," Ted said.

"Are you listening? If it hadn't been for Miguel's fast thinking, we would have been arrested, probably shot."

"I don't care," she said in a monotone.

"Whether you care or not, you're going to behave. One more trick like that and I'm going to tie you up and you can ride the rest of the way in the trunk. Do you understand?"

"Yes." Bailey turned away into the back seat.

"We take that highway to the American border," Miguel said, pointing to the lights in the distance.

"No, they'll be expecting us to go there. Instead we'll go south."

"South, compadre? To where?"

"We will go to Chiapas," Ted said. "It's our only chance. Marcos can protect us."

"Yay!" Miguel cheered. "We go to Marcos. We will join the army. We will kill federales and . . . "

"Calm down, calm down," Ted said. "Let's just get there first. It's a long way."

Bailey sat up straight and leaned her head into the front seat. "No, I can't. I can't go there."

"We have no choice," Ted said. "It'll be all right."

"You don't understand. I can't go there. I can never go back."

"You heard me. We have no choice. Get some rest. We'll talk in the morning."

"You should have let the soldiers have me," she said. She lay down on the back seat with her face turned away.

"Now I will drive us," Miguel said. "I am a very good driver."

"You're too young. What if someone sees?"

"Was I too young when you needed the car? I borrowed it. I should drive."

"All right," Ted said, "but only to the highway. I'll take over there."

Miguel slid into the driver's seat, and sat on a pile of blankets. He could barely reach the pedals and at the same time see over the steering wheel. He started the car, let out the clutch, and pulled away smoothly.

"Why do I think this isn't the first car you've borrowed?" Ted asked.

"*Qué?*" Miguel was concentrating solely on the road ahead. The reflected glow of oncoming traffic revealed his sparkling eyes.

Nearing the main roadway they switched places—Miguel in the back and Bailey in the front with Ted. Moments later when Ted checked on him, the boy's eyes were closed. In sleep, Miguel looked like a little angel.

The traffic was light and they spent the night driving, to put as much distance as possible between themselves and Chihuahua. Bailey sat in the front seat, awake but silent. She made no further references to their destination, and he knew better than to try to engage her in conversation. He had been hard on her, and in a way he felt bad about it, but she had almost got them all killed. Why was she so reluctant to go to Chiapas? He left it alone. He was in no mood for unravelling more mysteries.

They stopped briefly just before dawn and set off again with the sunrise, heading due south on the main highway towards Chiapas. Ted was operating on a mixture of adrenaline and caffeine—too tired to sleep, and too scared to stop.

Bailey seemed to have recovered from whatever had afflicted her. She had regained her power of speech but for the most part simply stared out the window. She rode in the back, leaving Miguel in the front seat with Ted.

It was years since Ted spent time with children, and he had forgotten what they were like. Miguel was full of questions. Questions, questions, and more questions. His curiosity was insatiable. He seemed to never stop talking.

"What is it like in Canada? . . . Is it cold? . . . What is snow? . . . Frozen water? How does water freeze? . . . Do you live in ice houses?" He wanted to know about being a lawyer and why Ted was in Mexico.

Ted sanitized his answers, but even so, his explanations seemed to confuse Miguel. "I came on a holiday. My boss told me to go to Mexico."

"Why you come to Chihuahua? Are you and lady here to help Revolution?"

"No Miguel. I just want to get back home."

"But your home is north. We are going the wrong way."

"Yes, I know."

"How you get home?"

"You've got me on that one," Ted said.

Miguel tried involving Bailey in his "question game" but soon tired of her one-word answers. Ted became the focus of his energy. The experience was exhausting.

Through his non-stop chatter, Miguel revealed a good deal about himself. He did not know his own age. He guessed it was either twelve or thirteen, but his birthday had never been celebrated.

They passed many small land holdings, each a few acres, the houses little more than shacks.

"We had farm like that. Papa was campesino. It is gone now," Miguel said.

"What happened?" Ted asked.

"They dead now."

"How?" Ted checked the rear-view mirror for the thousandth time.

"Pistoleros—they killed them."

Ted turned off the radio. "Tell me about it. Who was killed?"

"All of them. Mama, papa, sisters."

"Why?"

"For the land. Hacendados wanted Papa's land. He say, 'No, we stay.' One day pistoleros come. They burn house. Mama and sisters they burn all up. Papa they shoot. I run away, become Zapatista."

Ted took his eyes from the road. Miguel's steady gaze met his. "Someday there be many Zapatistas. We kill pistoleros, take back land, be happy."

"I hope that you're right." Ted felt a tear in his eye.

In the next moment, Miguel changed the topic. He was a boy again, full of a sense of wonder. "Look a golden eagle! And many hawks! I knew a man who hunted with hawks. How do they know to come back after they kill?" Birds were one of his special interests, from eagles to carrier pigeons. "How they know which way is home? Do they fly by the sun? Tell me, Ted." So the hours went, from geology, biology, history to science. Ted gave answers and explanations he forgot he even knew.

Some of what he didn't know, he made up. "The sky is blue because it reflects the colour of the oceans."

Once Ted tried changing the game by asking Miguel questions, but the boy made it clear that this was not the natural order of things. It was his role to ask and Ted's to answer. The miles rolled quickly by.

―――――

On one monotonous stretch of highway, Miguel proposed a game of counting the dead animals. "Two points for a dog, one point for a bird, and three points for a donkey or a cow."

"A donkey or a cow?" Ted asked. "Live ones or dead?"

"Dead, of course. Yes, and ten points for a dead federale."

In the span of a hundred miles, they counted six dead dogs, ten animals too mangled to identify, numerous flattened birds, and one donkey—its four legs pointed straight up at the sky. The game was called to a halt when they passed a body covered in rags.

"What was that?" Ted asked.

"Probably a federale killed by the Zapatistas. That means I win." But Miguel's expression had turned grim. "I don't want to play anymore."

South of Mexico City, traffic ground to a halt for over an hour, the roadway blocked by a herd of cattle grazing on the roadside grass. While truckers honked their horns and motorists cursed, a group of vaqueros sat astride their horses, puffing cigarettes. There was a standoff, the vaqueros refusing to move their herd until a collection was taken from the stopped vehicles. A young boy moved from vehicle to vehicle with a straw hat. Ted deposited his pesos to a smiling response, "*Gracias*, señor." The vaqueros collected their booty and herded the cattle from the highway.

Ted shifted the car into gear. "What was that? The Mexican version of a toll booth?"

"What's a toll booth?" Miguel said. "Tell me."

"Never mind."

Bailey remained a brooding entity occupying the back seat. She would reply when spoken to, but her responses consisted primarily of monosyllables.

"How are you doing?" Ted asked.

"Fine. I'm fine."

He risked a glance away from the highway. "Is there anything I can do? Anything at all?"

"Just let me out of the car."

"I can't do that. Tell me what is going on."

"Watch the road," she said.

Her mouth was pulled down at the edges. As to what dark thoughts filled her mind, she gave no clues.

As they travelled ever southward, the countryside gradually changed. They emerged from the monotonous dry badlands into an area of gently rolling hills. After weeks in the deserts of northern Mexico, it was a relief to see some green again—as if they had come through a winter where everything was brown and dead and now were emerging into spring.

On their third day, they climbed into rugged hills as they wound their way into the highlands. Passing through the city of Tuxtla, they left the main high-way. The old car strained to climb hills on secondary roads that were only half paved. The way became narrower, and finally the pavement ended. The countryside was wild and sparsely inhabited.

"So this is Chiapas," Ted said. "How do we go about finding Marcos?"

"We go to the town of San Cristobal. There we will get directions. I know the passwords," Miguel said.

Later that day they arrived at a town perched on the edge of a forest. Clapboard buildings surrounded a square filled with vendors. The people were dark-skinned and dressed in peasant attire. There were no other vehicles in evidence, and their car was the focus of much attention. Small boys ran up to touch the paintwork.

"I will be back," Miguel said. He left the car and entered into a conversation with an old woman with skin like tree bark. There was gesturing and animation. Apparently satisfied with Miguel's explanations, the woman pointed to a cut between the trees on the outskirts of the town.

Miguel returned to the car. "We are to travel that road until it ends. There the Zapatistas will find us."

"How will they know we are coming?" Ted asked.

"See there," Miguel said, pointing to the sky. The old woman had released a pigeon from a cage. The bird took flight and winged south towards the forest.

———

They were travelling on a rutted trail, the bush enclosing them on all sides. It was midday, yet little sunlight reached the forest floor. The way was barely navigable—no vehicles had passed this way in recent times. As they crested a hill overlooking a gorge, the road ended. Ahead lay only a donkey track. Mist rose from a river snaking along the valley bottom, half a mile below. The horizon was dimly visible through the haze—the air hung heavy with humidity and smelled of vegetation.

It was like a fairyland. The steamy feel, the lush foliage, and the vastness of the valley cast a spell. Leaving the vehicle, they instinctively hushed their voices. Their footfalls made no sound, cushioned by the spongy ground. Ted was aware that he was holding his breath, as if straining to hear the beating of his heart.

They walked in single file up the narrow path.

A form materialized from the underbrush. It was a man dressed all in black, his face covered by a balaclava of the same colour. He carried an assault rifle in his arms. Ted had a bad moment. Then he saw the bright yellow-green of the man's eyes—a cat's eyes.

"*Buenos dias*," the masked man said.

"Marcos. It's good to see you."

Marcos embraced him. "Welcome to Chiapas. You have come a long way."

Marcos opened his arms to Bailey, but she pulled sharply away. "Don't!" she said. Marcos' eyes narrowed at the set of her face.

"I'll explain to you later," Ted said. "There has been trouble. Have you heard the news from Chihuahua?"

"Yes, I know," said Marcos. "We will talk of it later. But first to camp. And you, too, my young friend." Miguel had been standing awkwardly to one side waiting to be noticed. "You have done very well, Miguel. I am proud of you."

Miguel was standing to attention. "Thank you, Subcomandante."

"Come." Marcos put his hand on Miguel's shoulder. "We have food waiting and comfortable beds."

After the unending tension of the past few days, Marcos' greeting was like a tonic. For the first time in days, Ted dared to hope—maybe everything would be okay. They hiked up the trail and into the jungle.

CHAPTER 16

THE SMALL SETTLEMENT WAS CARVED out of the deepest jungle. The forest canopy blocked out the mid-afternoon sun, casting the scene into permanent twilight. The tendrils of the rain forest trailed to the outermost buildings, creeping up the walls as if trying to envelop them. The air hung with the odours of damp and fresh vegetation. The ground was so moist it appeared to steam.

There were about fifty buildings, small and windowless, but freshly painted. The camp hummed with a sense of order. Black-shirted soldiers were moving about, some masked like Marcos. Men and women were represented in about equal numbers, but there were no children. Some carried machine guns, but most were armed with old rifles or machetes. The troops were drilling and training with their weapons, and the occasional salute was thrown. The wildness of the environment stood in sharp contrast to the organization of the camp.

"This is our main encampment," said Marcos. "This is where we invite the press of the world to see our army. And so we march around a bit. And give interviews of course." Marcos was wearing his typical wry expression, recognizable even behind his mask.

He gestured towards some huts that were larger than the rest. "Over there, that is where we keep the reporters. They come from all over the world—France, Spain, even Russia—to interview the famous Marcos and his band of Zapatista rebels. We are careful to give them what they want. Lots of stories and photographs of poor starving people and the nobility of our cause."

Miguel had wandered off a few paces and was engrossed in the sight of soldiers drilling with their weapons.

"Miguel, would you like to join our army?" asked Marcos.

Miguel nodded vigorously. "Oh, yes, Subcomandante. Very much."

"So then you must have a mask," said Marcos. "It would not do to have the press of the world recognize you as the famed terrorist from Chihuahua." He winked at Ted and presented Miguel with a black balaclava and helped the boy fasten it around his head. Miguel straightened his shoulders and saluted. Ted doubted that he would take off the mask to sleep.

Marcos led them through the camp and back up into the jungle. Again they climbed through heavy vegetation along an overgrown trail. Tall ferns shaded the path, dripping moisture on their heads. After about a mile the trail broke out of the forest at the base of a tall limestone cliff. The rock face sprang abruptly from the ground before them and towered over their heads.

"This is my headquarters. Follow me," said Marcos. He ducked into a hole between the rocks.

Inside the opening they entered a long passageway that led to a broad, high chamber. The way was lit with overhead electric lights; the ground was smooth beneath their feet.

"Welcome to the world of the Mayans," said Marcos. "This is known as a cueva, a Mayan cave. Our ancestors have inhabited this one for over five thousand years. It provides us with fresh water, shelter, and safety from our enemies. It has all the modern conveniences—electric power, mobile telephones, even our own website. I can be contacted both on the internet and by carrier pigeon."

Miguel was drawn to the caged birds, and stood with his fingers looped through the wire. Ted wondered if he was looking for their navigational equipment.

The cave contained evidence of many old fires. Black smudges covered the roof and ancient rock drawings adorned the walls. The floor of the cave had been worn smooth by thousands of Mayan feet. It had the consistency of polished tile.

"These caves are common everywhere in the Yucatan. Come now, sit, eat," said Marcos.

They sat at a table in the middle of the cave and were served the traditional meal of beans and tortillas along with unidentifiable roasted meat. Bailey had not spoken since their arrival. Her eyes darted back and forth, taking in the cave. She did not touch her food, and Ted ate little of his for watching her.

Ted began to tell Marcos of the events in Chihuahua, but Marcos was already well informed.

"Yes, I have been told," said Marcos. "It is very bad there now. You were lucky to have escaped." He directed his attention to across the table. "Bailey, you are in great danger. What you did was very foolish. But don't worry, we will take you somewhere safe." Marcos reached for her hand.

Bailey pulled back her hand and held it behind her back. Her eyes were frantic. "Keep away! You can't keep me here. Ernesto will not let you. Keep away from me!" She stood up, overturning her chair. She backed away.

Marcos caught her arm. "Now, now. There is nothing to be afraid of. No one here is going to hurt you."

She struggled in his grasp and Marcos released her. She retreated to a far corner of the cave.

"Come, I will not hurt you," said Marcos. "You remember me. I am your friend." He held out his hand until finally she took it.

"It is like this then. I am not surprised," said Marcos. "First Acteal, and now this. You must have time to rest. We will take you to the nuns of San Cristobal. There you will be safe, and they will care for your soul." He motioned to a woman who had been standing in the shadows.

"Maria, see to her. And be certain she is not left alone." The woman took Bailey by the arm and led her from the chamber. She left with her head down, shuffling her feet.

Ted had jumped to his feet during the outburst and remained standing by the table.

"Sit down, sit down," said Marcos. "She will be fine now. Maria will care for her. Now let me tell you what I know. I have had reports from the north. Hernandez did not die, but he is in hospital. I fear what he will do when he is released. We have had much trouble with him before, but now this . . . He may be more a monster than ever."

"Marcos, I've been thinking about what I should do," Ted said. "I want to go to Acteal. Bailey was there at the time of the massacre and has never recovered. It's probably futile, but I might find something there. If I could only understand what is wrong, then maybe I can . . . "

"Acteal was very bad," said Marcos. "Many people were killed and more are missing, probably dead, but their bodies never found. It is deserted now. Few people dare even go there. It is said that the dead still walk the village and the souls of those who are missing cry out for their rest. I do not think that you will find any answers there."

"You are probably right, but I can't think where else to turn," Ted said. "Can you find someone to take me?"

Marcos thought for a few seconds and finally nodded. "It is probably for nothing, but there is no harm in it. You can go soon. It is about two days by donkey. I have a man who will take you. Maria will take Bailey to the convent tomorrow. She will be safe there until you return. Miguel can stay here with me."

Miguel spoke up without hesitation, "*Gracias*, Subcomandante, but Señor Ted is my compadre. I go with him."

"Miguel, this is a trip I should take alone," Ted said. "You should stay here with Marcos and learn to be a soldier."

"I be soldier later, now take care of Ted."

CHAPTER 17

HERNANDEZ FLUNG HIS WATER GLASS at the cowering nurse. "Out, bitch, before I have you shot! Find me the doctor! Now!"

The nurse retreated, stumbling over the chair beside the bed. "Yes, Colonel. Right away, Colonel." She disappeared down the hallway.

Damned stupid nurse. Indian by the look of her. That was the problem with this country. Indians. Damned dirt-scratching campesinos who think they are as good as white men. He had seen the expression on her face when changing his dressing. *She was laughing at me—she thought it was funny. They were all laughing at me. "Did you hear about Colonel Hernandez? Stabbed in the* cojones *by a woman. Almost died."* He could all but hear the giggling from the nurses' station.

Hernandez lay in a comfortable hospital room, and at last the pain was under control. But it was his mind that was in agony, a burning pain that would be with him the rest of his life. Every time he urinated and had to hold that mangled organ, he wanted to scream. He wanted to kill. Kill her, kill those damned nurses, kill them all.

He was going to find that bitch if it was the last thing he did.

The planning had been so delicious. That woman and her inept plans to assassinate him. It was pitiful. He had been tracking her since she entered Mexico; her hotel room had been under surveillance for days. Admittedly, it was a nice bit of work for her to find the bar his officers frequented. But still, if she had not found him, he would have found her. The look on her face when she realized the gun was empty and that she was trapped—it was worth all the effort. And then. And then . . . damn it to hell!

94

How could he have been so stupid? One tiny slip. A knife scarcely big enough to peel a potato. And she almost killed him . . . could have killed him. The last image before he passed out was her pressing the blade into his throat. Why hadn't she finished it? She should have. It was a decision she would regret.

The "American whore from Acteal"—that was what she called herself. She was out there somewhere, and he was going to find her. Images boiled in his brain. This time no mistakes, no escape.

For the moment his doctors were the targets of his wrath. He did not want their damned explanations—he wanted it fixed. He could not even piss straight. They just shook their heads.

"Some things cannot be done, Colonel. The nerves are severed. The damage is severe."

"Don't give me that bullshit! I want it fixed. Do whatever you must, but get it done."

"Perhaps in time, after the swelling goes down, perhaps plastic surgery. We can make you look almost normal."

Hernandez hated the way they talked. As if they were better than him. "And how about sex? Will it work again?"

"Well, sex, that may be a problem. You see . . . "

"Get out! All of you! Out!"

Hernandez was lathered with perspiration. No more sex? They could not be serious. No more taking the village girls? He had liked it best when they fought back, even better when they screamed. No more.

"Corporal! Corporal! Come here! At once!"

"Yes, Colonel."

"What news? Have you found her yet."

"Nothing sir. I have heard nothing."

"Imbecile! Get out of my sight!"

Forty-five years of age, Hernandez had been a soldier for twenty years, the last ten in military intelligence. He was of the officer class and thought himself Castilian rather than Mexican.

Even in hospital he remained in command. He had given orders that Bailey be found at any cost and demanded reports on the hour. At first there was nothing, as if she had vanished into the air. Hernandez railed at his officers' incompetence. He suspected his men drew lots to determine who would deliver the lack of news.

After a day of road blocks and house-to-house searches, there had been a break. A peasant woman and her son were caught walking back to the city in the middle of the night. They were reported as nervous on arrest. Hernandez ordered them questioned, tortured if necessary.

The next morning a lieutenant reported to the hospital room. Hernandez put down his book. "Well?"

"They will not talk. They tell us nothing."

"Do you understand nothing of interrogation? What are you some weakling *mujer*, afraid of a little blood? Cut off the woman's hands. Make the man watch you do it. Then he will talk. You will see." Hernandez picked up his book and resumed reading.

———

The lieutenant returned within the hour. "Colonel, we have information. It was difficult . . . The woman, she died."

"Don't bother with details. What did you find out? Quick now!"

"The man, he finally told us. He took the woman, a tall gringo, and a street boy in a car and left them outside the city. He and his mother were walking back to the city when we caught them."

"What else did you learn?"

"The man knew little more. Even under torture he could not tell us. Only that the boy was a Zapatista and the car was headed south."

Hernandez smiled for the first time during the briefing. "So there are three of them. And they can only be going to one place—they are running back to Marcos. Good, we will catch them all together. I will be ready to travel in a few days. Prepare my personal guard to travel to Chiapas. We will finish this once and for all."

"The other prisoner, what should we do with him?" the soldier asked.

"Kill him. Pin a note on the body and dump it in the street. I want her to know I am coming."

CHAPTER 18

THE CONVENT WAS A LIMESTONE EDIFICE perched on a steep hillside. It overlooked a broad valley, and from the upper windows a watcher could see for miles. Behind the buildings the rain forest engulfed the land. A refuge from the world, the place exuded peace and tranquility. The air was filled with birdcalls and the hushed voices of nuns at prayer. Merchants and artisans came and went, and the occasional worshipper visited the chapel.

Bailey was confined to a small cell. Her presence in the convent was a matter of the utmost secrecy—she was one of the most wanted fugitives in all of Mexico. Even walking in the yard was an unacceptable risk.

But there was another reason for her restriction, and Bailey knew it. She was being kept as a patient. The nuns feared she would harm herself if released. The way they crossed themselves at her doorway and their grave expressions revealed what they thought of her. They believed she was mad, and perhaps she was.

She rarely spoke and responded only to direct questions. She could speak when she wanted to, but there was just nothing she cared to say. She spent her time examining the pattern the sunlight made on her wall. It made her sad.

She felt detached, floating in nothingness. She vaguely recalled what she had done to Hernandez, and that men were searching for her, that they would kill her if they found her. Bailey did not care. She had no interest in anything, and ate barely enough to stay alive. She rebuffed anyone who pried into her affairs or tried to be of comfort. She wanted to be left alone.

The nuns believed her to be possessed. Some would not enter her room, and those who did would first make the sign of the cross and clutch their crucifixes. They talked endlessly to her of God's love. She did not believe them—God had no love for her. Finally she screamed at them, threw things, drove them away.

There was one nun who was not afraid. She was older than the rest. Her name was Magdalena, and she was the Mother Superior. She was small and plump, not much more than five feet tall, with a round brown face that was smooth and wrinkle free, as if the world had left her untouched. The nun's strength shone out through her eyes, which were steely grey and seemed to see inside Bailey's head.

"Child, what is this vision in your mind?" Magdalena demanded answers and Bailey found herself bending to her will.

"Open your heart. Tell me your problems—the Lord will help you."

Bailey probably revealed more than she should. She told Magdalena things that she thought she had forgotten. The old nun would listen quietly, and then asked her to pray. Bailey just went through the motions. It would not matter in the end. Mostly she just sat and waited.

Other than the nuns, she had only one companion. Emilidia was a Mayan; she was tall and angular with silver hair that hung down to the small of her back. She was probably sixty, but retained the smooth skin and limber body of a younger woman. Like Bailey, Emilidia was a patient here, and like Bailey she too was suspected of being possessed by the devil. She had been found unconscious in the jungle under the influence of a powerful drug. The nuns suspected she had been practising Mayan witchcraft and had brought her to the convent. They had conducted rites of exorcism but it had not succeeded. Now they were trying to reform the woman through the power of prayer. She spent hours each day with Bailey, just sitting.

There was little conversation, but the women had reached an understanding. Both were waiting for a sign, something to guide them. Their destinies were to be intertwined.

Bailey felt the blood on her face. She could not remember where it came from, but it would not come off. She rubbed at it but still it remained. She washed her face constantly, but the stains came back. The nuns tried to stop her. They told her there was no blood, but she knew they were lying—she could feel it. She could see the blood, even reflected in the pool of sunlight on her wall. The nuns warned her she would hurt herself, and they even tied her hands. She screamed until the bonds were removed.

She was taken to prayers in the morning and the evening, but she did not say the words. Her prayers were not to God. There was no one there to hear her. The prayers she did say were to the souls of the dead. She begged her lover Ernesto to intervene on her behalf, to make the others understand that she had no choice. It was no use. Forgiveness was refused.

There was a trail before her. She could not see it clearly, but it was out there, and in time it would be revealed. The dead whispered of it in the night. They spoke to her, calling her by name, a name she had not heard for many years. She said nothing of these voices to the nuns. They would not understand, not even the old one. She maintained her silence and waited for the sign. It would come.

CHAPTER 19

THE JUNGLE ASSAULTED HIS SENSES. The air weighed upon his skin, humid and sticky. Perspiration ran down his skin, puddling in his shoes. Clouds of steam obscured the trail ahead, acrid mist settling on the tip of his nose. Ted could taste each breath, mouldy and earthy, as if the decaying undergrowth were flavouring the air.

They trekked along a path too narrow to ride their donkeys. The mud beneath their feet made sucking sounds with every step. *What was he doing here? Why had he insisted on going to Acteal?*

Their progress was accompanied by the sound of water gurgling in unseen streams. And the whine of the mosquitoes. Slapping, twitching. Rivulets of sweat indistinguishable from the lighting of insects. Trying to ignore them, willing his feet to keep on moving.

The undergrowth was like a vast green sea, parting with their passing and filling in behind. Leaving no wake. They travelled slowly, hacking their way through dead falls and woven vines, the silver blades of their machetes rising and falling.

The jungle contained a million eyes. Ted felt them watching him. The air hung thick with sounds and smells. The undergrowth rustled, trees bent with unfelt breezes. In the near distance something screamed. Further off, howler monkeys created a din of discordant shrieks.

Their guide, Ramone, was a middle-aged Mayan. He was heavily dressed in thick denim and a felt hat, but seemed unaffected by the heat or the insects. He did not sweat. He swung his machete in an effortless flowing stroke, the brush melting away before him. Unseen creatures started in his path, but he never stopped. Ramone was contemptuous of his companions' unease. His body language spoke for him, "This is the jungle. Get used to it."

To bide the time, Miguel and Ted kept up a running conversation. The sound of their voices helped keep the weight of the jungle at bay. They spoke louder than was necessary.

"Why we go to Acteal?" asked Miguel.

"I don't really know," Ted said. "Bailey was working there when the attack took place. It's probably a good place to start."

"What will happen to the señorita?"

"I wish I knew. She's not well." Ted told Miguel some of what Bailey had told him about her past. This was no time for keeping secrets—Miguel was part of this.

"She only has one name, and there's a bad story behind it," Ted said.

"Why she unhappy about name? Miguel my only name. Is okay."

"Where do we stay in Acteal?" Miguel asked.

"I don't know. I haven't given the matter much thought."

"No problem, I find us place. We stay together."

Something in Miguel's voice made Ted turn to look at him. The boy's big brown eyes were twinkling.

"This be big adventure. We find answers," Miguel said.

Why was he really going to Acteal? Ted had trouble explaining it even to himself. It was not just Bailey, although certainly she was part of the reason. Ted felt drawn to Acteal, drawn to what had happened there. It had been a senseless slaughter in the remote jungle—nothing that involved him at all. But somehow he felt he was involved. Something waited for him there. He had a premonition that the village held answers. Whether they were about Bailey or himself he did not know.

The first night they slept in the jungle. They made their camp in a small clearing by the side of a river. The ground was covered with a dense and interwoven mass of wet leaves and vegetation. They cleared a spot for their tent, hacking and slashing with their machetes. All around Ted could imagine small creatures scampering and slithering away. About ten feet from their tent, Ramone swung his machete at something on the ground. He stood up, holding a writhing snake. It was at least eight feet long, and as thick around as his arm.

"Bushmaster," he said, pointing at his prize, "good to eat."

Ramone made a motion of drawing his free hand across his throat. "Also good to kill you. Very dangerous."

Ramone skinned the snake while Miguel scavenged for dry wood. Night fell quickly and there was no moon. There had been only enough dry wood to cook their meal and they were soon in total darkness. Ted sat with Miguel in their tent chewing pieces of sinewy meat. Ramone set up his hammock between two trees.

The sky opened and the nightly rain began. As if the air had turned to water, the torrent seemed to come from all directions. The soil was already saturated and unable to absorb the deluge. Water pooled and flowed around their feet. The canvas of the tent provided no protection. Rain poured through every seam, and within seconds they were drenched. The storm passed as suddenly as it began.

A mere shred of canvas protected them from the jungle. Boughs creaked as wind whipped the long wet grass. Ted was aware of every sound. His imagination created monsters in the night. He had a prescience of something nearby, something large and very dangerous. The pack animals moved about, stamping their feet and shaking their ears. Finally he slept, but his mind tumbled in and out of nightmares. In his dreams, he was attacked by jungle cats, huge mottled beasts that chased him through the night.

A scream jolted Ted awake—a shrill banshee cry, so loud and close it seemed to come from within his head. He heard it only once. He sat up, covered in sweat, the hairs on his neck tingling. The night had gone silent. Neither Ramone nor Miguel had stirred in their sleep. Had he imagined it? Was it just another nightmare?

He closed his eyes, but sleep would not come.

Ted was up at first light, half expecting to find their animals killed while they slept. Instead the donkeys remained tethered outside the tent, peacefully munching grass.

Ted asked Ramone about the scream he had heard. "It sounded like a cougar. It was very close."

"You are mistaken, gringo. The jaguar is the only cat who ever lived here, and he has been gone for many years. It was just a bad dream."

Morning in the high jungle was magical. The sun cut through the mists and lit up every leaf. The plants dripped and sparkled. In the interlude between dawn and the heat of midday, they set out to travel as far as they could. Again, they beat and thrashed their way down the disused trail, making slow but steady progress.

Shortly after noon they neared their destination. The forest had thinned and open spaces appeared where the jungle had been cut back. They rode their donkeys across neglected fields, through pastures high in weeds. Scrub trees grew in the midst of what had once been farmland. Orchards stood barren; the trees were unpruned. All around, the jungle was advancing upon the land. Before long, all evidence of cultivation would be gone.

Over a small rise, they saw houses in the distance. Ramone dismounted. He made the sign of the cross and motioned he would go no closer.

"Acteal. You go now. *Es lugar de la muerte.* The dead who know no peace live there." For once, Ramone had broken a sweat.

Ramone threw his leg over his donkey and rode away without looking back. Ted shook his head. How could this man kill venomous snakes without a qualm, yet be afraid of a little superstitious nonsense.

"Come on, Miguel. You're not afraid of ghosts are you?" They set out for the village, trailing their donkeys.

The village consisted of ramshackle houses set in roughly aligned streets. The buildings were built of plywood with thatched roofs. They all looked to have been deserted for some time. The roofs were in tatters, the plywood siding was weathered and broken. Doors hung open on their frames, some swinging in the breeze. Some houses showed evidence of fire—scorched timbers lay where other buildings had once stood.

They examined the first few houses for signs of life. They were all deserted.

Small shrines built of sticks, bottles, and photographs stood in front of every house.

Ted thought about what had happened here. If the buildings could talk, they could tell him. Even now they bore silent testament. They were laced with holes, each about an inch across. Ted fingered a pock-marked wall. Bullet holes?

The village was deathly silent. In Acteal, it seemed the birds did not sing. Ted had made light of Ramone's fear, but now this place gave him the creeps. He felt that someone was watching him. Perhaps Ramone had been right to run away.

"*Buenos dias!*"

"Wha—?" Ted ducked his head behind his donkey.

A middle-aged woman stood in the yard of a nearby house. She was dressed simply, but all in black. Her left arm was missing below the elbow.

"*Buenos dias*, señora," Miguel said.

The woman started to respond in the staccato of her local dialect but switched to Spanish.

Miguel translated. "She says welcome to her village. Her name is Rosa. But she wants to know what we are doing here. I told her we are friends, and we come from Marcos' camp."

There was more rapid chatter between Miguel and the woman. "She wants to know how long we stay?" He looked inquiringly at Ted.

"Tell her a few days at least."

Miguel answered for him.

"She says no one comes to Acteal. They fear the unburied dead. She also wants to know if we are hungry, and she says she would share her meal."

Miguel did not consult Ted before answering. "I told her yes, we would like to eat with her."

There were three monuments in Rosa's yard. Fresh flowers stood in vases beneath painted white crosses. The photographs, of two children and a man who must have been their father, showed signs of weather.

The woman had turned her home into a shrine. As he entered, Ted instinctively hushed his voice. The walls were adorned with artifacts. Photographs were draped with black silk. They were of the same man and two children. The boy and a girl looked to be about ten years of age. Ted did not dare to ask.

Ted guessed Rosa's age at about forty, but she looked much older. She had the flat-faced characteristic of the Mayan people, her skin weathered to the texture of canvas. Her eyes were sunken in her head and her mouth drooped at the edges. She wore her sorrow like a cloak.

She fed them on simple fare and barely acknowledged their thanks. The weight of the tragedy weighed on Ted. He ate in silence. But Miguel was naturally curious and chattered away, asking about the photographs and the names of her children. Within minutes he breached Rosa's silence. Miguel kept up a running translation for Ted.

"She is the only one here . . . She had a husband and two children—a boy about my age, and a girl . . . See, those are their pictures. One day the soldiers came. They took all the men away in trucks . . . Only the women were left behind, with the children and the old men . . . They were praying, in the chapel, but it is burnt now . . . The pistoleros came . . . The ones they call the Red Mask . . . They shot them even in the church. They killed the children . . . And even the women who were big with child. With machetes they cut the babies from their bellies . . . They ran for the jungle. Many fell. Rosa was wounded—her arm . . . A man fell on her, dead, and she knew nothing more . . . When the police finally came, the pistoleros were gone, and the people were dead. Now there is only Rosa."

The history was told without emotion, much like Miguel's account of the murder of his family. Rosa was not looking for sympathy.

"Miguel, ask her if there was a woman here, an American woman."

Halfway into the question, Rosa smacked the table with her hand. "Bah! Bah!" She turned away and began poking twigs into her fire. Miguel did not attempt to translate further. He looked at Ted and shrugged.

Rosa let them stay the night in the main room of her house. They were glad of the shelter. As the nightly rainstorm lashed the roof, they sat dry before her fire. She sang softly as she wove reeds into baskets.

"I know this song," Miguel said. "My mama sing this song. Is a lullaby to her children. She sings for them to rest in their graves."

Rain splattered on the roof. The fire flickered and shadows danced around the room.

CHAPTER 20

RAMONE WAS HALF ASLEEP IN THE SADDLE, riding along a trail at the edge of the rain forest. He was not keeping a look out—his donkey knew the way. Another few miles would take him to Marcos' camp.

This was as close as Hernandez dared to come to Marcos' army without a large force. He was accompanied by a small squad of his personal guards. A frontal attack was out of the question. His best hope of obtaining the information he needed was to ambush an unwary Zapatista.

He seethed at his lack of resources. Those spineless pricks in Mexico City! They talked of making peace with the Zapatistas, of giving in to some of their demands. To negotiations! That was no way to deal with bandits and criminals. The lash, the noose, and the gun—that was the way to deal with them.

If Hernandez had more men, he would have gone in and cleaned out that whole rat's nest, but his request to mobilize a division had been denied without explanation. With this damned talk of peace, all he commanded were his loyal guards. But it would be enough; these were good, hard men. They had been with him from the beginning, since before that business at Acteal.

Ramone was taken off his donkey with a single shot. The animal crumpled beneath him, shot in the heart, the man sprawling onto the ground. Before he could regain his feet, the soldiers were upon him seizing his arms. He was big and well-muscled, and it had taken four of them to wrestle him to the ground and tie his hands. They trussed him in a standing position, his arms spread between two trees. There was no question he was a Zapatista. Who else would travel these woods alone?

"So, my friend. It is your bad fortune to have travelled this trail. And even worse fortune to have fallen into my hands. So how goes our good friend Marcos? Is he still sleeping with all of your wives?" Hernandez got no answer. He gestured with his hand and one of the soldiers smashed the man across the face with his rifle butt. Blood streamed from a broken nose.

"It is impolite not to return my greetings. Do you Zapatistas have no manners?" The man received a rifle stock to the midriff, doubling him up in pain. He did not reply.

"There is an easy way and a hard way to do this. It does not matter to me, for in the end you will give us the information we seek. To resist will only cause you needless pain, and will of course entertain my troops. My name is Colonel Emiliano Hernandez. I am seeking two gringos—a man and a woman. What can you tell me about them?"

The man did not answer but merely spit a loose tooth onto the ground. He glared back at Hernandez. "And my name is Ramone. I want you to remember that name. Some day you will answer for my death."

Hernandez struck him across the face with the back of his hand. Ramone hung in his restraints, blood dribbling from his mouth.

"Such things do not bother me. If everyone I killed were to be avenged, I would die a thousand times. I do not think that is likely, do you? Sergeant, I leave him to you. Let me know when his manners improve."

This was a tough one—he would take some time. Hernandez found himself a comfortable spot to observe and perhaps to catch a nap. Screams never disturbed him.

His soldiers settled in for a long interrogation. Hernandez had taught them well. They were skilled in the varied tools of persuasion—threats, beatings, sharpened bamboo splints. Today they were using burning embers from the fire. Hernandez approved. Applied properly, they made for fine entertainment. A bottle was passed. A little tequila relaxed the men and made them more enthusiastic about their work.

The sweet smell of burning flesh filled his nostrils.

But there were no accompanying screams. Ramone stood mute. He refused to answer any questions, or even to cry out.

The soldiers became frustrated. There was little sport in inflicting pain on a victim who did not react. Knives were produced. They rained blows on Ramone's face and carved pieces from his flesh. But it was to no avail.

The sergeant returned to Hernandez. "Colonel, I am sorry but the interview does not go well. The Zapatista pig refuses to speak. He has not said a word. We have been careful to keep him alive, but he has lost much blood. He may die soon. Perhaps he knows nothing."

Hernandez raised himself to one elbow. "You idiots! Of course he knows something! Why else would he refuse to speak? Must I do everything myself? Out of my way!"

He saw that Ramone did not have long. He hung unconscious between two trees, held up only by the bindings on his wrists. His joints were swollen; parts of his skin had been burned away. Blood flowed freely from ragged wounds. He was missing several fingers and one of his ears.

"Revive him!" A pail of water brought Ramone back to sputtering consciousness.

"So, my friend, have my troops been keeping you amused? I hear that you are not one for conversation. That is too bad." Ramone shook his head, as if trying to clear his eyes. He did not respond.

"Let me explain your situation. You will die soon, you know that. I can see that is not a matter of great concern to you. You are a brave man. But have you considered what may happen after your death?" There was sudden interest in Ramone's eyes. Hernandez had guessed correctly. They had reached the moment during an interrogation he most enjoyed.

"After you die we can do one of two things. We could bury you in a decent manner. Perhaps even say a few words and put a marker up so that your family may find you." Ramone was blinking his eyes, straining to remain conscious.

Hernandez twisted his face into a scowl. "Or instead we may chop up your body into pieces and feed you to the animals. There will be no grave. You will never join your ancestors. You will be like the unburied dead of Acteal, forever seeking your rest!"

Ramone's mouth contorted.

Hernandez knew these people. Even the strongest of them were as superstitious as children. Their lives were as nothing, but their eternal souls were another matter. He had used this knowledge to advantage many times.

"Please, Colonel, I beg you, do not do that. I will tell you what you need to know," Ramone gasped, choking on his words.

"So, where is she? Tell me! Where is that bitch?"

"I will tell you, but it will do you no good. She is with the nuns, the ones at San Cristobal. But they have given her sanctuary—you cannot arrest her there." Ramone was exhausted by the exertion of speaking; his eyes began drooping closed. At Hernandez' signal, another bucket of water was splashed on the man's face.

"Thank you for that, Ramone, but there is one more thing I want you to know. There is no sanctuary for that one. Your suffering is trifling compared to what I have planned for her. And as for you, we will take our leave of you now. Perhaps you will live a little while longer, perhaps not, but there will be no burial. The animals can have you." Hernandez laughed at the mask of despair that spread across Ramone's face. This was his favourite moment, when his victims gave up all hope.

"Colonel. There is one more thing. Come closer." The words were croaked through shattered lips. Hernandez leaned towards him. The man muttered in his ear.

Hernandez yanked his pistol from its holster and fired. Gunsmoke and bits of flesh filled the air. He kept firing until the gun clicked empty. When he had finished, Ramone's shattered corpse hung from the restraints.

The soldiers sprang to their feet. They looked in shock at their commander. Hernandez stood with his gun in his hand, red-faced and shaken.

Had they heard? Hernandez' brain was on fire. *That pig!* Would the shame never leave him? As he had put his ears to Ramone's lips, the man had hissed, "I may never have my rest, but at least I will wander the underworld with my *cojones*. I am a man, not a *mujer* like you!"

If anyone had looked at him the wrong way in that instant, he would have killed him where he stood. Killed them all! If he knew, they all knew! Even the Zapatistas! They were all laughing at him! Death to them all!

"I'll see that bitch in San Cristobal!"

CHAPTER 21

THE NUNS WERE AT THEIR EVENING PRAYERS when the sound of heavy boots echoed in the chapel. Hernandez and his men entered the chamber. The music ended on a discordant note.

The Mother Superior challenged the soldiers from the altar. "Who dares to enter the House of God like this, to desecrate this place?"

The soldiers stopped where they stood. Several crossed themselves, one went down on a knee, the rest looked away. Hernandez pushed the kneeling soldier to the ground with his boot and brushed past his men.

He marched up to the Mother Superior. He brandished his riding crop in her face. "Where is she? The woman you hide here? The American whore?"

The nun was at least a foot shorter than Hernandez, but she bristled with defiance. "How dare you to speak to me like this! This is a place of worship. All who reside here are under the protection of the Church. Have you no fear for your soul?"

"Sister, my soul is none of your concern. What should be your concern is what will happen if you don't turn her over. If I give the order, this place will be burned to the ground. Along with all those who you claim are under your protection. What will it be?"

"Leave here at once! I will complain to the Bishop in Mexico City about this outrage."

"Out of my way, you old witch." He called to his men, "Search the place! Start in the nuns' cells upstairs." Hernandez roughly pushed the Mother Superior aside and with long strides started up the stairs towards the sleeping chambers.

The soldiers bowed apologetically to the nuns and backed out of the chapel. They followed Hernandez up the main staircase.

The soldiers kicked open the chamber doors. The wood splintered under their boots. Meanwhile the Mother Superior and her flock were at their backs, howling in indignation, like chickens in a henhouse, cackling after a fox.

They stormed from room to room but found nothing. The cells were deserted—the nuns had been at prayer. Each chamber was as the one before, neat and sterile, places of prayer and reflection.

At the entrance to the last cell, the nuns redoubled their efforts to prevent the soldiers' entry. One nun threw herself in front of the door. The soldiers hesitated. Hernandez seized the woman under both arms and lifted her out of the way. He dumped her on the floor.

This was it—he had her now.

The door opened easily. The soldiers rushed in but stopped short. The room was chaos. Clothes were strewn everywhere, dirty plates covered the table, and the bed was unmade.

The disorder of the room was the least of its wonders. It looked like the scene of a battle. From one end to the other, spread all around were great swatches of dark brown hair, laying in clumps. Some of the hair was wet and sticky. Splashes of blood stained the walls and floor. A small knife lay on the floor, stained red.

"What is this? Where has she gone? What have you done with her?"

The nuns' stunned expressions told him they were as surprised as he was. They expected the woman to be in her room—she had obviously fled. Or been taken? And why all the blood?

CHAPTER 22

SHE FINALLY SAW THE SIGN the voices had promised. In the reflection of sunlight on her wall, the shadow of a huge bird appeared. Bailey sprang to the window—it was a golden eagle perched on the ledge. She approached the bird, but it dove away towards the jungle floor, beyond the convent walls. It hit the ground at top speed, and then rose on its broad wings. It wheeled and returned close by Bailey's window to display its kill. From its talons hung a writhing snake with a white underbelly and a bright red head. The eagle let out a single scream, gained altitude, and flew north across the jungle.

Bailey knew what she must do. She must leave this place. She must go north after the great bird.

The nuns always brought her meals to the room. They were unaccustomed to guarding a prisoner, and it had been easy for Bailey to pocket a small serrated knife. Now she retrieved it from under her mattress and began to cut away her long brown hair. The knife was dull and she was forced to saw at the strands. The hair came off in clumps; she let them fall to the floor about her feet.

She cut herself. At first the knife had slipped and nicked her scalp. She felt the sticky liquid on her skin. She understood. The snake's red head was meant to be part of the vision—bald like the eagle, blood red like the snake. She began to slice thin lines across her scalp. She felt nothing. When she was finished, her head was roughly shaved, with tufts of hair still in place, and it gleamed with flesh wounds. She was without a mirror but ran her hands through the bristles to check her handiwork. They came back sticky with blood. This was not like the blood she had tried to scour from her face, this was her sign. The sign by which the dead would know her.

She wrapped herself in a shawl and fled. There was no one to challenge her—as she left the cloisters, the nuns were at their evening prayers. On her way she heard shouts of angry men coming from the chapel but did not stop. Matters here no longer concerned her.

She was not alone, Emilidia walked close behind. She must have seen the eagle. It was her sign as well. Good. Bailey had felt the connection before. Emilidia said nothing; she simply followed. They passed through the main gates, slipping unnoticed into the night.

Outside the convent they headed up into the surrounding jungle. Bailey had no fear—the eagle would show her the way. From far away she could hear the voices. They were closer now. The dead were calling her.

CHAPTER 23

TED AND MIGUEL MOVED INTO their own house the next day. Miguel selected one in better repair than most. Its roof was still solid, and the glass remained intact in the front window. The house sat on the edge of the settlement and looked over a gorge that ran towards the valley. They spent a day on cleaning and repairs. The door was rehung on its hinges, the window wiped clear of grime. Years of debris and animal droppings were swept from the floor.

On their second night in their new home, they invited Rosa to share their meal. She surprised them with a present of a chicken and a bag of beans. Miguel cooked tortillas, and Rosa cooked the chicken and hot chillies. She sang for them again, some of the same sad tunes, but happier songs as well. Miguel hummed some of the refrains. Ted listened but did not join in.

That night they slept on palettes of fresh straw. It was an experience Ted found strangely satisfying. After a month of sleeping in strange houses, storerooms, and haylofts, he was lying in a bed he could call his own.

Miguel was exuberant. He ran from room to room, revelling in the joy of ownership. This was the first home he had known since the pistoleros burnt out his parents. Ted was happy for him.

It was like living in a dream. It was hard to imagine that anything was real, that the massacre had happened here. Not a day went by that Ted did not wonder what he was doing here, and that he should not be here at all. He was trespassing in a graveyard.

The village was a shadowland. It was deserted and isolated in the high jungle. No roads passed nearby. Access from the valley below was by a dirt track mostly overgrown from disuse. Day by day the jungle grew closer, the fields more overgrown. In another season the path would be gone, the way forgotten. It was only a matter of time before the village became a memory.

Ted had come here with a purpose. He was seeking answers—answers that had so far eluded him. But the trip that had started with a thin hope was bearing some fruit. Although he had learned nothing of the secrets in Bailey's past, he was discovering something about himself.

Acteal was getting to him, but in a good way. The black thoughts that had plagued him seemed less important here. He seldom thought of home, and when he did, his thoughts were no longer despairing. He had experienced no more fits of rage. For the first time in years, he was at peace with himself. It struck him as strange—finding peace of mind in a village steeped in death.

They lived by the sun. They got up at sunrise, napped in the heat of the day, and ate their dinner when the sun went down. Time itself had no meaning. Ted stopped wearing his wristwatch and stuffed it into his knapsack.

In the first few days, Ted and Miguel were busy repairing their house. The roof was patched so it no longer leaked, and fresh sand was raked across the floor. Miguel had scrounged some whitewash and was painting the dwelling inside and out. It was primitive—there was no plumbing or electricity—but Ted did not mind. When he walked in the door, he felt the pride of ownership. This was his home.

In the evenings after dinner, he would sit with Miguel on the veranda. The warm breeze swept down from the jungle, bringing with it the scent of flowers and wet grass. Ted wished he smoked a pipe. The time and place were perfect for reflection.

Ted was almost ready to believe the village's reputation of being haunted. If anywhere in the world held ghosts, this would be the place. Rows of empty houses stood in every direction; open doorways yawned into darkened interiors. The wind made a hollow sound as it whistled through the rooms. To walk by the gaping windows was to feel eyes on his back. The days were eerie; the nights forbidding.

His senses played tricks on him. He was forever catching movement just out of his line of sight. Time and again he would turn quickly, thinking to catch something behind him, but there was never anything there. It became a distraction. He asked Miguel, "Do you ever feel here . . . something odd . . . like there's somebody else here."

"Si, Ted, it is nothing. It is just the spirits looking over our shoulder to see that we are okay. Don't worry, they will not hurt you."

"Thanks, Miguel, you're a lot of help." The boy made him smile. About some things he was so innocent. Of course there were ghosts; everyone knew that.

———

Ted and Miguel would talk for hours. Miguel had given up his question and answer sessions. That had been his way to break the ice. Now that their relationship had changed, they talked as friends, sharing their lives.

"I married a woman I loved. But I screwed it up. I was too busy working to notice that she needed me. By the time I realized what was happening, it was too late. She was gone."

"How you make this mistake?"

"Her name was Suzanne. She was beautiful. I felt lucky that she would have me. I thought that we would always be together. But she needed more than just marriage. She wanted a family."

"So you had bambinos, Ted?"

"No, Miguel, we didn't. I was too busy with my work to have children. We had some bitter fights. I thought she would get over it, but I was wrong."

"That was not right. If a man and a woman, they have love, there should be children."

"That's true. Where were you when I could have used the advice? I was so into my work that I had no time for anything else. Eventually Suzanne found another man to give her what she needed. She has remarried and has a child now. I hope that she'll be happy."

"That is a sad story, Ted."

It was a sad story, but it no longer bothered him the way it once had. It occurred to Ted that this was the first time he had ever made this confession to anyone—and certainly the first time he had ever wished Suzanne happiness.

Miguel gave little time for solitary introspection. "Tell me another, Ted.

This time a happy story. About Canada, the one where you go sailing in a big boat."

Miguel was an avid listener. If Ted stopped or lost his place, the boy would prompt him. Some stories he made Ted tell over and over. "Tell me the story of how you come to Mexico. I like the jail part the best. Tell me how the señorita help you escape."

In turn, Ted asked Miguel about the Zapatistas. "This Revolution. Is there much fighting?"

"No, not so much. After we captured San Cristobal, there are no more battles."

Ted smiled at Miguel's use of "we" but let it pass. "These Revolutions are always violent. Like the Shining Path in Nicaragua. Do the Zapatistas attack government forces? Bombings, kidnappings, things like that?"

"Marcos teaches us that the way to victory is through '*fuerza no violencia.*' 'Strength not violence.' Zapatistas do not murder."

"This sounds too good to be true. A revolutionary who doesn't believe in killing."

"*Si*, Ted. He is too good. Don't worry. When I join the army, we shall kill many soldiers and all the pistoleros."

The boy's eyes shone in the dark. They were making each other happy. These were good times.

Rosa's tragedy was never far from Ted's thoughts. She always dressed in black and never smiled. Her life was a daily struggle. With only one arm, the simplest tasks were difficult. Chopping wood, drawing water, working in the garden—everything was managed but managed with difficulty. She coped, but with an attitude that said she would rather be dead like her family. She was waiting to die.

What must she do day in and day out alone in that little house? Spend each day in prayer for her dead? That was no way to exist. Ted greeted her daily, made small talk to show that he was friendly. Although her language was an Indian dialect, she spoke some Spanish and they managed to make themselves understood. She was polite but shared little of herself. She did not speak further of the massacre.

It was difficult for Rosa to hike the half-mile to the stream and to return carrying a yoke of heavy pails. The path was a rocky trail requiring strength, stamina, and two hands. She cursed as she climbed the steep path, stumbling often, spilling the water and having to start again.

Ted accompanied her to the stream one morning carrying his own empty pail. As usual she walked in silence. Rosa filled her buckets at the stream and stooped to shoulder the yoke. Ted gestured he would carry her load, and she should carry his single pail. She merely grunted, but he caught the suggestion of a smile.

Their trip to the stream became a daily event. They would walk silently side by side down the hill and then climb back burdened with the day's water. Ted didn't push things. He let the relationship develop on Rosa's terms.

Slowly, bit by bit, day by day, she warmed to him. It started with a simple "*Buenos dias*, Señor Ted," and a thank you for his help.

Her reserve slowly dissolved. One day when Ted and Miguel were with Rosa at the stream, she pointed to the pool from which they had been filling their buckets, and spoke in Spanish. Ted asked Miguel to translate for him.

She say, "The life of a campesino is like this water in the stream."

"Why is that?"

Miguel asked Rosa to explain, and then he said to Ted, "She say, 'Look at it run. See how it cannot choose where it flows, and must follow the channel. When the rain comes, the stream is full and brings life to the land around it. In times of draught the stream barely survives.'"

Rosa adjusted the pails on the yoke across Ted's shoulders. Miguel went on, "And she say that always the water continues on its journey, and in the end it arrives at the sea. There is nothing to regret in the flowing of a stream. It will always be as it is now; in the end there is always the sea."

"But she said the stream is like a campesino's life. I don't understand. How are they the same?"

They trudged up the steep trail as Miguel asked Rosa to explain. Then he said to Ted, "It is like this—we are the water in the stream. It is so for all of us. We must follow our set course in good times and bad. It does not help to complain that the rain does not come. All in good time, we will end up in the sea."

The words Miguel translated stayed with Ted all that day. He did not agree with her. Her philosophy went against everything he believed. He'd lived his life on the premise that a person could shape his or her own destiny, that anything was possible. But still the words were haunting—water in a stream.

He understood now the root of Rosa's stoicism. This is how she could accept her tragedy. There was no reason for grief—a person had no choice but to follow their destiny. She was water in the stream.

CHAPTER 24

EVERYTHING ROSA NEEDED SHE provided for herself. To live in Acteal, Ted and Miguel must learn to do the same. They had carried provisions on their donkeys, and Marcos had promised to check on them, but their supplies would soon be gone. They needed to learn to fend for themselves.

Rosa subsisted almost exclusively on vegetables. She grew beans and maize for tortillas in a small plot, a section cut out of what had once been a much larger field. Ted and Miguel went to work in her garden. Rosa grew enough produce to feed all three of them, and they came to an understanding—they would help with the farming and she would make tortillas and supply them with vegetables.

The plants grew like weeds. This was not what Ted had expected. Land reclaimed from the jungle usually produced meagre crops. But the opposite was the case here. It took all of their efforts to keep up with the growth and to harvest the produce. The garden could have fed many families without difficulty.

Ted liked the work. After a few days, his blisters hardened into calluses. Hard work with a hoe and spade agreed with him. He enjoyed the feeling of sweat rolling down his back and the sweet exhaustion that came with the end of each day. The black earth sprouted new life daily, and he admired the crops growing around him. He found himself whistling; sometimes he even hummed a tune. But for his thoughts of Bailey, he could have remained happily in Acteal.

One day he was hard at work, cleaning out weeds from a row of plants. Rosa was working close beside him picking beans.

"She taught us to do this." Rosa was looking the other way and her words took him by surprise.

"Who do you mean?"

"The American woman, the one you asked me about. She taught us how to make these fields so rich."

"Her name was Bailey. She was tall and attractive, long brown hair. Is that who you mean? Was she here when the village was attacked?"

"Oh, yes, she was here. That woman, she did many good things for us. She taught us to grow such fine crops. But then, on the last day . . . the last day . . ." She stopped. The stony Mayan reserve was back. She picked up the basket of beans and walked back towards her house. Ted stood in the field, watching after her.

———

It was early morning. Ted shouldered a basket of beans and started the short hike back to the village. Miguel met him on the way with two shovels in his arms.

"It is fine to dig in the dirt and farm like women," Miguel said, "but men, they should hunt. A boar would be a fine thing to kill. And it would give us much to eat."

Ted smiled at Miguel's Latino machismo. The boy was probably not yet thirteen, but already it flowed in his veins.

"Miguel, a boar is a large and dangerous animal. And we don't have any weapons. Besides, what would we do with two hundred pounds of pork?"

"Wild pigs are big, but they are not so dangerous. We killed them at home when I was a boy. The meat is smoked and lasts for a very long time. I will show you."

When he was a boy! When was that, last week? But Ted kept his mouth shut. He did not think for a moment that they could actually catch a wild boar. But, oh well. The principle was probably much the same as fishing. The challenge of catching a fish was the whole point of the sport. So they would try to catch a boar—and fail. Why not?

Hunting wild pigs was not as easy as casting a line. Miguel's plan was to dig a large hole—the boar would then fall into it and be captured. The plan was simple, but creating the trap was hard work and took two days of shovelling. Sweat poured in rivers from Ted's brow. *Digging holes in the ground in the tropical sun. I must be mad.*

The pit, when completed, was over six feet deep and lined with sharpened sticks pointing skyward. They covered the opening with thatch and vines. Miguel claimed the pig would not see the danger until it was too late. If it did not break its neck in the fall, or impale itself on the spears, they were to finish the job with lances from above.

Ted was doing his best at being a good sport. It was a lot of work, but Miguel was having fun and there was no harm to it. Surely, no boar was stupid enough to fall into this hole in the ground. He hefted his spear thoughtfully, playing the crafty hunter. This part at least was like fishing—sit around the pit for a while waiting for a boar to fall in. After a reasonable time, pack up your weapons, say something like, "maybe we'll have more luck tomorrow," and head home for dinner.

"Now we make the boar chase us so he falls into the trap," Miguel said.

"Whoa! You never said anything about this part. I thought that we just waited until one wandered by and fell in."

"Ted, sometimes you gringos are so stupid. A wild pig is very smart. He will not fall into a trap unless he is on a charge. When a boar sees something he doesn't like, he loses all reason. He flies into a rage. It is only then that we can kill it."

"So, Miguel, which one of us does the boar charge?"

It was not until afterwards that Ted considered the lunacy of what they had done. A business lawyer in company with a Mexican orphan taunting a long-tusked boar while armed only with pointed sticks. That will make a fine story someday over cocktails at the Pacific Club.

A boar had been raiding Rosa's vegetable plot. With a little scouting, they found it rooting in the bushes about fifty yards from their trap; they could hear it snuffling and tearing at the vegetation. It had no fear of humans. The village had been deserted for a very long time, and except for Rosa, who occasionally made noise to scare it away, it had never seen people.

Miguel started by throwing rocks at the bush in the general direction of the sound. The missiles fell harmlessly to the ground until they finally heard a splat and a grunt as one of them struck home. The rustling in the bushes grew ominously louder.

Ted had never seen a boar except at a distance. He had always just thought of them as large ugly pigs. But from ten feet away, a boar was the largest, scariest animal he had ever seen. Its flesh was brown and mottled and covered with bristles. Its tusks were nearly a foot long.

Ted took his cue to begin leaping up and down and making as much noise as possible. The boar swung its great head in his direction. The little yellow eyes hardened. It charged.

Miguel had warned him that wild pigs were very fast, but Ted was unprepared for its speed. He ran faster than he thought he could and clambered into the appointed tree. Miguel pelted the boar with rocks and yelled to attract its attention. It pulled up in a cloud of dust, snorted, and turned on him. Tusks down, froth blowing, it rushed in for the kill. Miguel stood his ground with his spear poised.

The boar did not see the disturbed soil in front of Miguel. The animal crashed through the leaves covering the trap and disappeared from view. There was a squeal of terror, an explosion of dust, and flying debris. Then silence.

Ted ran up with spear in hand. The boar lay in a lifeless heap at the bottom of the pit. Ted let out a whoop of joy. He embraced Miguel, and together they did a victory dance.

Rosa had heard the excitement and came running from her house to investigate.

"Rosa, come see, come see!" shouted Miguel. "I killed the boar for you. We are mighty hunters."

Rosa covered her mouth in astonishment. "I'm sorry, Señor Ted. I told him the boar was stealing my vegetables and wouldn't he do something about it. I thought he would just make noise to scare it away, not kill it. Miguel, I think you have gone loco!"

"I did it for us all," Miguel said. "The boar is dead and we have much to eat."

She graced them with a rare smile. "You are brave men to kill such a fearsome beast. I suppose now you would like me to cut it up and cook it for you."

Next came the hard work. The kill had to be butchered and removed before dark; otherwise, they would have to fight off every animal in the forest. Ted's skill in this area was confined to slicing a roast of beef at the dinner table. Quartering a huge, recently killed beast was a different matter. The three of them attacked the dead boar with knives, and a small saw. Twenty minutes later they were up to their armpits in slime and blood. In the heat of the day, the black flies feasted on the carcass; the air was thick with insects and the stench of blood and offal.

The jungle was alive all around them. It seemed to Ted that every carnivore for miles around was aware of the death and was waiting its turn at the carcass. The bushes rustled with movement. They were in a race to remove the choice parts to the safety of their houses before darkness fell. Ted had to abandon the great head to the scavengers. At another time, in another place, it would have made a fine trophy.

For dinner that night they feasted on pork. Rosa fried the choicest slices, and they ate until they could eat no more. Only then did she prepare an extra plate of food and take it outside. She placed it reverently on the roadside, knelt briefly in prayer, and returned to the house.

Ted did not comment until he and Miguel were alone. "What was that about . . . the extra food?"

"She is feeding her dead. It is her duty."

"But why only one plate of food?" Ted asked. "She lost her husband and two children. Shouldn't there be three plates?"

"No, her children's bodies were recovered. They were given a Christian burial. She takes them food only on *el Dia de los Muertos*. Her husband's body was never found, and so he is one of the wandering dead of Acteal. He must be fed until he can find his rest."

Ted had heard these references several times. First Marcos and then Ramone had told the same story. He was not sure how Miguel felt about the practice, and he did not want to offend him by ridiculing Rosa's beliefs.

"Do these unburied dead ever find their rest or do they wander forever?"

"They must wander until their bodies are properly buried. Or when they have avenged themselves on their killers." His words imparted a chill into the air. Ted decided this was enough on the topic for one evening.

———

The next morning the three of them were back at work smoking the boar to help preserve it. They hung pieces of meat inside a small shed over a smouldering fire. It was hot work, but the smoke kept the bugs at bay. Ted hummed as he hauled more wood for the fire.

Then from far off in the distance came the sputter of a small gas engine. They stopped what they were doing and listened intently. The noise grew increasingly louder as whatever was making it grew even closer.

Finally an object emerged from the trail below. It was a figure riding a small motorcycle. The vehicle was travelling at high speed and bounced over the small bumps in the trail. Before they had time to react, it roared up to where they stood and slowed to a stop.

The rider removed his helmet, revealing a tousle of black shiny hair. Ricardo's round face beamed at them. He jumped from the vehicle and embraced Ted. They had not seen each other since they parted company in Chihuahua.

"Greetings, amigos," Ricardo said. "Marcos sends his regards."

Miguel was enthralled with Ricardo's motorcycle. He trailed his fingers across the paintwork. He looked up at Ricardo expectantly and said, "I have never driven a motorcycle, but I am sure that I could learn."

"One day I will teach you," replied Ricardo, "but today I am on a mission from Marcos. The Subcomandante wants to know how you are faring here in Acteal. Have you found the answers that you seek?"

"No, not yet," Ted said. "But we are fast becoming the leading citizens of this village. And we have even become mighty hunters. Right, Miguel? We have killed our first boar."

Ricardo was suitably impressed as Miguel recounted their exploits. "*Es loco.* Don't you know it is dangerous to hunt such animals without a gun. Are you both crazy?"

Ted and Miguel grinned in unison.

"Marcos sent me to check on you. And as well I am looking for Ramone. He did not return after he brought you here. There is no sign of him or his donkey."

"He was fine when he left us here," Ted said. "He would not come all the way into the village, but headed back into the jungle the same way we came. He struck me as a competent fellow. What do you think could have happened to him?"

"*Quién sabe?* There have been army units sighted nearby. It is possible that he has been captured. Even worse, it may be Hernandez. He is no longer in Chihuahua, and his whereabouts are unknown. He has made inquiries about your woman friend."

Bailey had been constantly in Ted's thoughts. "How is she? Is she still with the nuns? Has there been any change?"

"There has been no word from the convent, but that is not unusual. The road is not good and they have no telephone. If you want, I can take you there—it is less than a day on my bike. Perhaps we may find some sign of Ramone on the way. I warn you though, it is not comfortable on the back of such a machine."

"What about me? I should come too," Miguel said.

"Not this time," Ted said. "You must stay here to protect Rosa while I am gone. And, Rosa, make sure he doesn't hunt any more boars while I am gone."

"He can stay with me," Rosa said. "But only if he obeys my orders and washes before dinner."

"If I am to stay with you, then I am to be the man of the house," Miguel said. "But I will share some of my boar with you."

"Then we have a deal," Rosa said. "You will protect me and I will cook the food."

Ted noted that, for the first time, Rosa was not dressed in black.

As they were about to leave, Rosa motioned that she wanted to talk to Ted alone. He asked Ricardo to wait.

"Rosa, what is it?"

"You are going to see the American woman, the one we spoke about days ago.

127

I did not tell you then. Her name, Donata—that was the name the villagers gave her, not her true name. Donata means 'gift from God.' It was a title meant to reward her for the help she gave to the village. Without her, we might have starved. The name, it pleased her very much. It was important to her."

"Thank you, Rosa, that may help. But can you tell me what happened to her on the day of the massacre?"

Rosa's expression changed, her face darkened. It wasn't clear whether it was too painful to discuss or there was a secret she was not prepared to share. "No, I cannot speak of it. There are things she must tell you herself."

There was no use pushing her for more. She would reveal what she knew in her own good time, or not at all. Ted thanked her and returned to Ricardo.

———

They set off with Ricardo driving and Ted on the back. The trails were not designed for motorized vehicles. On inclines too steep to either climb or descend, they got off and pushed. Even so, the pace was infinitely faster than travelling by donkey. Ted supposed that Ricardo was either displaying his skill as a motocross driver, or more likely testing his mettle. Ted's heart was in his mouth as the machine plunged through streams and leapt fallen trees. After less than an hour, his back was aching and his kidneys felt bruised. He did not dare ask Ricardo to slow down. This notion of machismo, which he had once ridiculed, was now a part of his life.

An hour into their journey, they found Ramone. His body was unrecognizable except for the tiny metal cross he always wore, still hanging from his neck. The animals had ravaged his body, but it was clear that he had been tortured and shot many times.

Ricardo's face was lined with anger. "What devils would kill a man like this and then leave him hanging from a tree for the birds to eat? And to shoot him so many times? Why would such a thing happen? Even our enemies do not behave in this manner. There should be some dignity in a man's death."

They cut Ramone down from the restraints and buried him by the trail. Ricardo crossed himself before the grave and said a prayer for Ramone's soul. He swore vengeance against his killers.

"You may rest easy, my friend. I promise that the ones who did these things to you will be punished. They will earn a warm corner in Hell for their sins."

They remounted the bike and continued on to the convent. Neither of them spoke further—words had no meaning. Ted retreated into his own black thoughts. Did the men who were searching for Bailey kill Ramone? He was oblivious to the jouncing of the motorcycle.

CHAPTER 25

THE CONVENT OF SAN CRISTOBAL could be seen from afar. Perched high on a hill, against the solid backdrop of the selva, it grew in size for an hour before their arrival.

The gates were open and Ricardo drove unchallenged into the main courtyard. They passed through deserted halls to the office of the Mother Superior. Magdalena's secretary was not at her desk. There seemed to be no one around. They had not seen anyone since their arrival.

"They must be at prayer," Ricardo said. "But they should have someone on the gates." He rapped on the door. "Be careful, my friend. Sister Magdalena has been known to bite."

From within the office a chair scraped the floor. Footsteps approached. The door opened a crack. Magdalena's face filled the opening.

"We are looking for Bailey," Ricardo said.

She looked to be in pain. "Away, get awa—"

The door was pulled open from behind her. "These nuns, they have no manners. Invite your friend in, Magdalena. I insist." Hernandez stood behind her with his pistol levelled.

Magdalena dropped her head. "There was no way to send word. Two days now. She is gone."

"Enough!" Hernandez put his hand under Magdalena's arm and pulled her into the room. "Now both of you, get in here."

"What do you mean she's gone? Gone where?" demanded Ted.

Hernandez jammed the pistol hard into his ribs. "Get in here! I'll ask the questions."

They were directed at gunpoint into the office. "Now leave us, Mother," Hernandez said. "I have matters to discuss with my guests."

"Forgive me," Magdalena said. "They are holding my children hostage. He has threatened to kill them." She glared at Hernandez. "You will not be granted the Lord's forgiveness. Hellfire awaits you."

"Save it, you old bitch!" Hernandez raised his hand. The nun stood her ground.

"These damned nuns are nothing but trouble. I think I should shoot a few to teach the others a lesson. What do you say to that, Sister?"

Magdalena turned her back on him and swept from the room.

Hernandez shot one last glare at her departing form and turned his attention to his prisoners.

"I am happy to see you both. Señor Somerville, that is your name is it not? I know all about your adventures in our country. Escaping from jail, and stealing a truck. Tch, tch. And then that affair of the murdered pistoleros. You have been busy. And Ricardo, my old friend. How goes the Revolution? Is Marcos still playing the strutting cock?"

"I am no friend of yours," spit Ricardo. "You are the bestia that killed Ramone."

Hernandez toyed with his gun, its muzzle pointing at the floor. "Ah, yes, your friend Ramone. He was most uncooperative."

"I'll kill you!" Ricardo was red-faced. With raised fists he charged across the room.

Hernandez side-stepped the rush and slammed the barrel of the pistol into Ricardo's forehead. Metal crunched against bone. Ricardo collapsed unconscious on the floor. Hernandez' lips turned up in a flicker of a smile.

Ted was speechless. Hernandez had been calculated in his reaction; he was not even breathing hard. He had known all along Ricardo would snap and had been ready for him when he did. This was a game for him. What was next?

"These peasants have no manners." Hernandez prodded Ricardo's inert body with the toe of his boot. "To attack me here in a convent of all places. When will they ever learn?"

"So back to you," Hernandez said. "You are looking for your girlfriend Bailey. I am as well. We have been hoping she may return. But if she does, she will not find you here. A pity, yes?"

"What are you going to do with me?"

"Kill you, of course. You are of no use to me." Hernandez held his pistol steady at Ted's head and moved around the room to a spot directly behind him.

He pressed the cold metal of the gun against Ted's right ear. "So what do you think death holds for you, gringo? Are you afraid?"

Ted's stomach clenched in spasms. His mouth went dry. He closed his eyes.

The click of the hammer was loud against his head. His world exploded with the roar of the gun.

The skin of his temple was scorched from the blast. The smell of burnt gunpowder filled his nostrils. Ted heard laughter above the ringing in his ears.

"Hah! What a brave man! You just pissed yourself."

Ted felt the wet warmth between his legs.

There was a pounding of feet and the door flew open. "What is it, Colonel? We heard a shot." Soldiers filled the small room.

"It was nothing," said Hernandez. "I was just demonstrating to our prisoner how it feels to die. A bullet past the ear is much like the real thing. I hope the Mother Superior will not be cross about the hole in her wall.

"But now, take them both away. I have shown the gringo a taste of how it is to die—he should experience the real thing. Take them to the forest. Execute them. But do it slowly. And be careful with the American. He might piss all over you."

The soldier tied Ted's hands behind his back, and a sack was placed over his head. He was yanked down a hallway, and fell down a short flight of stairs. Strong arms pulled him into the back of a vehicle, which immediately started and drove away. He lay against the floorboards, enduring the grind of the transmission. The truck bounced over uneven terrain. He was paralyzed with fear and self-loathing. Not only was he going to die, he was going to die a fool.

Through the burlap he was dimly aware of conversations among the soldiers.

"The colonel, he acts loco don't you think?"

"Careful, Pablo, such talk is dangerous. He would kill you if he heard."

"Yes, but to invade a convent and to abuse the sisters. It is not right. God will make us pay for this. It is one thing to kill these rebel scum, but the colonel talks of shooting the nuns."

"Yes, but it is a bad thing to be cut by a woman. I think maybe he has gone crazy in the head. We must be careful around him."

"Maybe some tequila would help our worries, eh? After we deal with these."

There were answering grunts of assent.

The truck slowed and crunched to a halt. The soldiers threw Ted bodily from the back. He landed painfully. The burlap that covered his face cut off all light, but he could sense the jungle all around. The odour of wet vegetation seeped through the cloth, along with the stench of kerosene. He could hear the sounds of his captors moving about and adjusting their weapons. There seemed to be four or five soldiers, one of whom was giving orders.

Ted was hauled to his feet. He could sense another person beside him.

"Ricardo?"

"Be brave, compadre," came the muffled return. "*Vaya con Dios.*"

Ted was pushed up against something long and hard, probably a fallen tree. His senses tingled. He was aware of every sound.

A soldier prodded him. "You are lucky tonight. Our commander ordered a slow and painful death. But he is not here with us, and torture is hard work. So I think that we will just kill you now. I don't think you will tell on us." There were snorts of laughter from the other soldiers.

The soldier backed away. "Line up. We will shoot them and then find a village with some tequila. On my count. Ready . . . Aim . . . "

Ted's eyes were screwed tightly shut.

A cry shattered the night, a high-pitched scream dying to a guttural rumble.

"Aaiiee! *Madre! El Jaguar! Los muertos!*" came panicked shouts from the soldiers.

All was confusion. Bushes were breaking; heavy boots tramped the ground. Something brushed by Ted's leg. Close by there was a scuffle, the scream of a man in agony. More running, shouts, gunshots, the sputter of fallen torches. The truck motor roared into life.

Shouts. "Wait, don't leave me!" and "Faster! Away from here!" With a grinding of gears the vehicle sped away.

The forest fell silent. The sound of the truck faded in the distance. Ted was dumbstruck. What had happened? Hobbled and blindfolded, he was unable to move or see.

He felt it, but not through sight or sound. Some other sense reported its presence. Something was there, large and menacing, very close. Its stink came to his nostrils. Ted felt savage eyes raking his body. It sniffed the air.

Oh shit! He felt its hot breath on his groin. He stopped breathing.

The beast withdrew. With barely a sound it padded away. Its movements were so quiet, he could not be certain it had really gone.

His breathing returned. "Ricardo. Are you there?"

There was a muffled response.

"Help me with these knots. They're not tight."

The soldiers had done a poor job of tying their hands. Standing back to back, they loosened each other's bonds. Ted removed the sack that covered his head.

It took a moment to focus. The scene about him was eerily silent. The soldiers had dropped their torches as they fled; the flames sputtered on the ground. The uncertain light made moving shadows. Ted's imagination created figures in the undergrowth.

The clouds swept away and moonlight illuminated the clearing. A dead soldier lay face up on the ground. His neck was a mass of mutilated flesh; the eyes were open and staring. His uniform had been shredded by the creature's claws, entrails protruded from the skin of his abdomen.

Ted shuddered. What creature could have done this? And why had it not killed them too?

"Come on. Let's get the hell out of here!" Ricardo pulled at his arm.

They ran down the mountain as if the devil were chasing them. In the uncertain moonlight, they slipped and scrambled over unseen obstacles. Tangles of blackberry bushes shredded their clothes and ripped their skin, but they were too terrified to care. The image of the dead soldier's bulging eyes drove them onwards.

CHAPTER 26

BAILEY TOOK THE LEAD AND strode into the jungle, drawn by the vision in her brain. The image was powerful and drew her onward, but the path was strange. She paused at the first fork.

Emilidia brushed past her. "This way, *Guardiá*. I know the way."

Bailey fell in silently behind the other woman. "*Guardiá?* Why do you call me that name?"

"Later. You will see. Come, *Guardiá*."

They hiked all night through a jungle black as pitch. There was no moon and clouds obscured the stars. Emilidia kept to the trail as if guided by some unseen hand. They headed ever upward.

The terrain was steep and the undergrowth dense. This was country where men seldom ventured. The trail was a rutted depression in the soil. In places it vanished altogether. They climbed rock faces and along switchbacks too steep for vehicles. Although Emilidia was probably fifty years of age, she walked with the step of a child. Her long plait of grey hair was Bailey's lone beacon in the darkness.

The rain forest was known as the Lacandon Selva. Ernesto had brought her here. It was one of his favourite places, and one that was important to the rebellion. After the 1994 uprising, remnants of the Zapatista army fled here to hide. Small villages were built in places secure from attack. Crops were grown under camouflage netting to avoid detection from the air. The impenetrable forest was credited with saving the rebel army so it could fight again.

To this point, Emilidia had been a silent companion. In the convent, she rarely spoke. Now she chanted in a low singsong cadence.

"The chosen one has come. She has come among us.

"Rejoice, rejoice. The world is new. The sun will rise.

"*La Guardiá de los Muertos* is among us. She will set us free."

Bailey was fixated on the vision of the eagle. The song was accepted without understanding; it provided texture to her thoughts. Emilidia repeated the same phrases until eventually Bailey's mind said them with her. "The chosen one has come, *la Guardiá de los Muertos*, rejoice, rejoice."

Bailey was intent upon her mission and the voices she heard calling to her. The voices were closer now; the words were clearer. She could make out the name that had been promised. "*La Guardiá, la Guardiá, la Guardiá de los Muertos.*"

———

The two women arrived at their destination after dark. The village was a collection of rough huts in a sheltered hideaway in the high jungle. They had been walking for over twenty-four hours without rest. Their strength of purpose had been sufficient to sustain them.

The settlement was in total darkness. A stranger would have missed it in the night or walked blindly into one of the buildings. Emilidia knew her way, and led Bailey to a structure larger than the others. Cracks of light could be seen through curtained windows. They entered without knocking.

The large main room had been converted into a chapel. It was lined with religious artifacts—crosses, carved figures of Jesus, some smiling, others in agony. The room was lit only by candlelight. Candles hung from the walls and the ceiling and the table that served as an altar. Rows of white tapers were set into the floor, lined up like penitents at prayer.

Flowers were everywhere in abundance. Bouquets and sprays of mixed blooms lined the altar. Petals were strewn about the floor. The air was filled with the odours of floral perfume, hot wax, and burning incense.

There were about forty people in the room, crowded towards the rear of the chamber, away from the light. They were softly chanting a dirge in some ancient Mayan tongue. At the front of the room, near the rows of candles, lay a young woman. She was prostrate, hands extended, face to the floor. From her lips came unearthly groans and shrieks.

The newcomers entered unnoticed. The ceremony continued until finally the worshippers became aware of their presence. One by one, the people stopped their chanting. The dirge died away and the people stared in silence. The praying woman rose and glided towards them.

"My sister, you have returned. We have missed you. Welcome." The woman and Emilidia touched in a ritual embrace.

Emilidia spoke in a strong and firm voice. "She has come, she is among us." She removed the hood of Bailey's shawl, revealing her roughly barbered head, covered now with a crust of dried blood.

The room reacted as one. Men and women together crossed themselves and kneeled. They began to chant, this time in Spanish.

"The chosen one has come. She has come among us. Rejoice . . ." The words were the same as Emilidia had voiced on the trail.

"*La Guardiá de los Muertos*," the sentinel of the dead. Bailey's mind caught the rhythm of the chant and repeated it with them. That was the name, the name that the dead had been calling to her. She understood her calling now. It was as Emilidia had said. She was *la Guardiá*—she was to be the sentinel.

Bailey knew of course the legend of the sentinel of the dead. When she first visited Mexico, Mayan folklore had fascinated her and she had read books and listened to the local shamans. *La Guardiá* was a priestess whose role was to watch over the souls of the wandering dead—people who died but could not be buried. In troubled times, such things happened often and *la Guardiá* was an important and revered deity.

A wooden bowl was raised to Bailey's lips. It was filled with a milky white liquid, bitter to the taste. She realized she was very thirsty and drank it all. She was immediately refreshed. She felt a sense of euphoria; the exhaustion fell from her body. Even the candles seemed to burn brighter. The murmur of voices became indistinct; she floated above the room.

A woman knelt before her and began to pray. This did not seem strange. With a sense of detachment, Bailey accepted the tribute as her due.

"We are the last people of Acteal. Those who survived escaped to this place. We have withdrawn from the world to pray for the souls of our dead. We have been waiting, waiting for the one that the legends said would set us free. It was prophesied that a white-skinned stranger, bald and bleeding, would be the one. She would become *la Guardiá de los Muertos* and we would be freed to return to our lives. The prophecy has been fulfilled."

Bailey's mind accepted this. It was the release she had been seeking. To guard the dead of Acteal—it was to be her redemption.

"Do you accept?" the woman asked.

"Yes," Bailey said. "I will set you free."

The women ushered the men from the room. They removed Bailey's robe and washed her skin, bathing her with warm cloths. They painted her body, covering her with a thick paste-like pigment. Then with long black lines, they traced her bones. Her face became a death's head.

At some level Bailey knew she had been drugged. Her mind would not focus, and she could barely form words. But she was happy, happy for the first time in years. This was what she had been waiting for. "*Guardiá, Guardiá.*" It was the name she had heard in her dreams.

Bailey did not resist as her skin was washed and then painted. She was being reborn. When her adornment was almost complete, she felt a transformation. There was a moment of awakening when Bailey ceased to be, and she became the goddess.

A necklace of human teeth was strung around her neck, and a sceptre of a skull perched on a staff was placed in her hand. A skirt made of raven's feathers completed her attire.

The congregation reassembled. Bailey was led to the front of the chapel, and the people dropped to their knees. They looked at her with faces full of awe and hope. The prayers resumed; dirges were intoned. The wooden bowl was passed from hand to hand. Bailey drank more of the white liquid. A chicken was slaughtered, and its blood was sprinkled on the altar. The ceremony continued long into the night.

One by one the people prayed before her. Their prayers were much the same and spoke of their dead families.

"*Guardiá,* I entrust to you the bones of my son Manuel."

"Care for the spirit of my husband Enrico. God rest his soul."

An old woman knelt in turn. "I entrust to you the soul of my son Ernesto. He died for our cause and for the love of a woman. Guard him well." Something in Bailey's subconscious stirred, and then was still.

"I accept the charge. I will guard him well," she said.

The ritual continued until dawn. With the sunrise, the people departed first from the chapel. They loaded their few belongings on pack animals and departed the village. The settlement was left deserted.

Finally, she was alone. Bailey slumped onto the chapel floor and slept among the still-burning candles.

———

When she awoke, it was dark. The candles had burned out. Food had been left for her, but she ate little. With the food was more of the white liquid. She drank it and the sense of euphoria returned.

Bailey had snatches of memory of the night before. She remembered some of the ceremony and the singing, and she knew who she was—"*la Guardiá*," the sentinel of the dead.

She walked alone into the jungle, glowing in the darkness. The paint that covered her skin was white only in the light; in the night it was luminescent. The eyes of animals were reflected in her light, and they drew back in fear. But they had no reason to fear her—she was the guardian not the hunter. She sought only her charges.

Far in the distance, the scream of a jungle cat split the night.

CHAPTER 27

THE MEN STUMBLED THROUGH THE NIGHT. They had little idea of where they were, and there was not enough light to see clearly. They were thoroughly scratched and bruised but too terrified to slow their pace. Towards dawn the clouds lifted, and they could see their way by moonlight. The trail became easier and they began to make good time, but they continued to be on high alert for any strange sounds. Was the creature somewhere behind them?

Ted caught his breath enough to speak, "What the hell was that?"

Ricardo was trying to sound brave, but Ted could hear the excitement in his voice. "A wild boar, I think. They can be very dangerous."

"But that roar. Pigs don't make that kind of sound. It had to be some kind of cat, maybe a cougar."

"No, we have no large cats," Ricardo said. "It must have been a boar."

Ted did not agree. He could still hear its cry—the sound had paralyzed him. It had been fixed on him; it had come right up to him and taken his scent. Whatever it was, he never wanted to encounter it again.

They were walking quietly, listening and watching. There seemed to be no one around.

Then a voice came out of a bush beside the trail. "My friends, you make as much noise as a buffalo crashing down that trail. Didn't anyone ever teach you how to be quiet?"

Ted threw himself to the ground. Ricardo grasped his arm. "Do not be alarmed. These are friends. Marcos! Come out and show yourself!"

The undergrowth parted, and Marcos stepped out in the company of seven other Zapatistas. The men were masked and armed with submachine guns.

"So where were you when we needed you last night? We could be dead," Ricardo said. "I hope at least you brought cigarettes." ·

"See what happens," said Marcos. "I send Ricardo on a little mission. Nothing too taxing. Just go to see how our gringo friend is making out and make some inquiries about Ramone. And what happens? He brings Hernandez down upon his head, almost gets himself killed, and then spends the night stumbling around in the jungle. Nice work, compadre!" The ritual banter of their greeting completed, the men embraced.

Marcos knew of the capture of the convent. "A message was sent to me when Hernandez arrived. I came as soon as possible. Last night we spotted an army truck coming down the mountain, driving very fast. I feared the worst. I am glad you are safe."

Ricardo recounted to Marcos the discovery of Ramone's body and Hernandez' admission of guilt. He said nothing about the attack of the creature in the night. Marcos frowned.

"Ramone was my friend," said Marcos. "He was among the first to embrace the cause. He was a brave man, and I will miss him."

"And Bailey's gone," Ted said. "She left the convent just before the soldiers arrived. She may have wandered into the jungle, but no one has seen her. She may have lost her mind. Anything might happen to her."

"We have no time for that," Marcos replied abruptly.

"Yes, but Bailey . . . "

"Bailey, Bailey, always Bailey! What would you have me do?"

"She's in danger, and we need to find her," said Ted.

"Gringo, I cannot be concerned with your friend at this time. As a result of her stupidity in attacking Hernandez, my good friend is dead. Two more are dead back in Chihuahua. The nuns are in peril. I have responsibilities. At this moment Bailey's sanity is not my most pressing problem."

This was a side of Marcos that Ted had never seen. To this moment he had been all charm and good humour. He had suspected as much—he had seemed too good to be true.

"More dead in Chihuahua?" asked Ricardo. "Tell us. What has happened?"

Marcos put his hand on Ted's shoulder. "The two old people who helped you escape. The army caught them. They were tortured and killed. The woman's hands were cut off."

Ted remembered the old woman well. She had bid them to "Go with God." He felt sick to his stomach.

"Understand then, compadre, why we must first deal with Hernandez. He is holding the nuns prisoner, and there is no telling what he may do. We must drive them out. As for Bailey, there is nothing we can do for her. She could be anywhere. I am sorry to hear what has happened to her, but I am not surprised. Many survivors of Acteal have become insane."

"What should I do then? What can I do to find her?"

Marcos was again the philosopher. "Go back to Acteal. There are things there that have never been spoken of, secrets that have never been told."

"Don't you talk to me in riddles, Marcos. I've been to Acteal. There is only one woman left in the village. I think she knows more than she will say, but she has told me little more than nothing."

"You gringos all make the same mistake. You think that the only way to find answers is to ask questions."

Ted was exasperated, "What else should I do?"

"When you understand the Mexican way, it will become clear to you. In Acteal the answers are waiting, and if you are patient, the knowledge will come. But for now we must deal with Hernandez. After, we will make inquiries about Bailey. Come."

Marcos had spoken before of "the Mexican way," but Ted had never understood his meaning. Was it a philosophy of life, a social convention, or just a manner of speech? It had a nice ring to it, but these snippets of wisdom were not helpful.

Ted said nothing more. He dutifully followed the band of Zapatistas back down the trail to the convent of San Cristobal.

CHAPTER 28

AT DAWN THE SOLDIERS GUARDING the convent were bleary-eyed. They had been a frightened rabble when they descended on the village outside the walls. Where normally they would have been riotous in their celebration and ardent in their pursuit of the local women, last night had been different. They drank tequila by the bottle, and they drank in silence. They drank only to forget the devil they had seen in the night.

They awoke slowly to aching heads and memories of bad dreams, each withdrawn into his own dark thoughts. They mirrored one another in appearance—soiled uniforms, unkempt hair. Some were splattered in their own vomit. One of them was muttering.

"We are damned. Our death has come for us."

The other soldiers looked away and ignored him.

"Don't you hear me? We are damned. Damned for all time."

"Shut up, Pablo! We all know what we saw. But to talk of it only makes it worse."

"It was a demon. You saw what it did to Diego. That was no creature of the jungle. It can mean only one thing. We are damned for all time. Why else would the devil come for us? It is all Hernandez' doing. We never should have come here, should never have insulted the Church."

"Shut up, you fool! You will meet your end sooner than you think if Hernandez should hear you. He may kill us anyway when he discovers we failed to execute the prisoners."

"What? You think they are still alive? The monster that came for us surely killed them."

The discussion was called to a halt by a gunshot. It echoed loud in the still of the valley. The birds fell silent. The soldiers scrambled for their weapons and assembled half-dressed at their positions on the wall.

"You in the convent!" a voice called out from the jungle. "We demand that you release the sisters of San Cristobal, by order of Marcos, Subcomandante of the People's Army of Chiapas."

The soldiers made no reply. The sergeant motioned for his men to remain behind the wall and ran to fetch Hernandez.

Minutes later Hernandez appeared at the edge of the convent wall. He held Magdalena by one arm. He held her in front of him.

"Marcos, is that you?" he yelled. "It has been a long time. I have been looking forward to this meeting. Come out where I can see you."

"Yes, Hernandez, it is I," called the voice from the jungle. "But I do not think that I should step out so you can shoot me. I have not lived so long by being stupid. But it is you who must come out. The convent is surrounded. You are out-manned and there is no escape. I demand that you surrender."

"Marcos, Marcos. You are such a fool. The sisters are my hostages. And I have no hesitation in killing them all. It is you who must lay down your arms and surrender. Or else I will begin shooting the nuns one by one until you do. Sergeant! Bring me the first of them. It is time we made an example."

A soldier pushed a young woman to the edge of the parapet. Her habit was in disarray and her head was bare. From the jungle below she alone was visible, silhouetted against the pale morning sky.

"Shoot her!"

"Hernandez, don't do this!" Marcos shouted. "Even you must have morals. You and your men will burn in Hell if you kill a nun!"

"Don't talk to me of Hell. I have already been damned twenty times over," Hernandez said. "Sergeant, carry out the order. Kill her!"

"You dare not do this!" Magdalena cried. "I forbid it." She took a step towards the parapet but was caught short in Hernandez' grasp. He held her about the waist with one hand over her mouth.

"Sergeant, do as I say. Shoot her in the head."

"But, Colonel . . . to kill . . . a nun. . . ," the soldier stammered.

The nun had her eyes closed and her head bowed. She fingered a crucifix. Her lips moved in silent prayer.

The soldier was slack-jawed. His forehead broke out in lines of perspiration. A tick began on one cheek. He looked back and forth between the nun and Hernandez. His eyes held a plea for Hernandez to change his orders. His rifle remained pointing downwards.

"Go on, shoot her! What are you waiting for? Fire!"

The soldier averted his eyes and did not respond.

Hernandez drew his pistol. "Refusal to carry out a direct order is mutiny. If you do not obey my command this very moment, I will execute you where you stand. Now shoot her!"

The soldier took one hand from his rifle and made the sign of the cross. He brought his rifle up to his cheek, worked the bolt, and aimed it at the nun standing ten feet away. His finger tightened on the trigger.

The soldier pulled the rifle back. He jammed the muzzle under his own chin. And fired.

The sound of the gunshot was muffled by flesh.

The nun remained unscathed. The soldier was momentarily suspended, as if he too was unharmed. In slow motion, he slumped to his knees. He toppled sideways off of the parapet and into space, his body cartwheeling as it fell.

The nun was the first to move. She pulled her cowl over her head and hurried from the parapet.

Hernandez' soldiers remained behind the wall. As seconds passed, one by one they rose from their positions with their hands in the air.

Hernandez railed. "Stop! This is treason! Pick up your guns and fight! Cowards!" The soldiers would not look in his direction.

Hernandez grasped the Mother Superior by the arm and dragged her away from the edge of the wall.

"Marcos, if you try to follow me, this woman is dead! My men may have deserted me, but I will kill this old bitch myself if you come any closer."

He dragged Magdalena by the arm down through the courtyard and into his jeep. He gunned the motor and propelled the vehicle out the gate and down the road. The jeep sped past Marcos' position outside the walls. The Zapatistas held their fire. Once clear, the jeep slowed imperceptibly. Hernandez leaned into the passenger seat and shoved Magdalena from the vehicle. She sprawled in the dust as Hernandez drove away.

A Zapatista rushed to help Magdalena to her feet. She seemed shaken but otherwise unhurt. Brushing dust from her dress, she called after Hernandez, "May you have a long life in Hell! God will have no mercy on your soul—I will have even less if I catch you myself!"

Marcos' men rounded up Hernandez' soldiers and bound them with their hands behind their backs. They stood in an irregular line for Marcos' inspection. They were a dishevelled and dispirited lot. They looked at the ground and would not make eye contact.

"What a sorry pack of thieves and murderers," said Marcos. "We would throw the likes of you out of the Zapatista army. Phew, and you smell like sewers! What should we do with you? Perhaps we should follow your example and convene an immediate firing squad."

The soldiers shuffled their feet but did not look up.

"You have committed murder, rape, and now even blasphemy. Were it my choice, I would sentence you to death. But in the new Mexico, we do not do such things. There will be a trial—you will be treated fairly. Your brothers and sisters will decide your fate.

"You should consider your crimes. It may go easier on you that you have deserted rather than obeyed orders to kill the nuns. You may want to tell how your commander made you do these terrible things. At our camp there are reporters who will be eager to speak to you, to make sure that you are able to tell your side of things to the world. Enrico, take them to our camp. And be gentle with them. I would not like to see any bruises when they talk to the press."

The prisoners were led away. Marcos watched them go, stumbling in their restraints. He mused about the possible headlines. "Federales captured while holding nuns hostage and confessing to killing unarmed peasants." He smiled, lit a cigar through the mouth of his balaclava, and walked into the convent.

Marcos sat in Magdalena's study. His eye was on the splintered wood in the wall behind her desk.

"She left suddenly," Magdalena said. "Another patient, Emilidia, left with her. Emilidia worries me. She practises the Mayan ways and talks of sacrifices to appease the spirits. We tried to exorcise the evil from within her, but we did not succeed."

"Do you know where they may have gone, Mother?"

"She belonged to a cult that meets in the highlands, near the old Lacandon trail. They may have gone there."

"I know it well," said Marcos. "I have hidden there many times myself. I will send someone to look for her, and I will leave two men here with you. I do not think that Hernandez will return, but if he does, they will deal with him."

Marcos rose and walked to the office door. "Ricardo, come here!" he called. "I have a job for you and your motorbike."

Hours later Ricardo located Emilidia's village. It was deserted. Doors stood open; the animals were gone. A flock of chickens had been recently butchered. He entered the chapel and found wilted flowers, burnt out candles, and something that looked like blood, or perhaps paint. On the floor was a wooden bowl, a whitish liquid still covering the bottom. Ricardo stooped and dipped his finger. He touched it to his tongue and grimaced at the taste.

"Opium."

Ricardo returned to find a message that he should meet Marcos in Acteal. Magdalena received him in her study, dressed in a simple wool tunic. The only sign of her office was the scapular at her neck. She was making entries in a large leather-bound book. He told her what he had found.

"It is as I feared," she said, putting the book aside. "I must come with you to Acteal."

"My orders say nothing of this," Ricardo said. "Do you think it wise? You have lived your life behind these walls, and the world is dangerous. We are responsible for this woman, so we will continue to search."

Magdalena picked up the leather book. "Do you know what is in this book? I'll tell you. In it are the names of the people for whom I am responsible. Bailey's name is in here, as is yours. You men think that only you can save the world and that it is too dangerous a place for the likes of me. Bailey needs more help than you can give her."

Ricardo did not answer and instead stood before her fingering his hat.

Magdalena pierced him with a glare. "It was from this convent that she escaped. You may be responsible for her safety, but it is her soul that is my concern. Do we understand each other?"

"Yes, Mother. Yes, anything you say. We leave for Acteal in the morning. You should prepare your pack animals."

"What is wrong with now?" she asked. "There is no reason to wait; we should leave at once. And once outside these walls, I am no longer the Mother Superior. My name is Magdalena. Learn to use it. I am quite looking forward to this trip—I have never ridden on a motorcycle."

CHAPTER 29

TED AWOKE THE NEXT MORNING feeling like he had not slept at all. The hike to Acteal had taken most of the previous day and well into the night. The trip had not ended when he closed his eyes. In his dreams he struggled up an endless hillside.

He recognized it before he opened his eyes. His nerves felt jangled, and a foul taste permeated his mouth. The symptoms were familiar, but it had been some time since they had come to visit. The best remedy was to keep his eyes closed until the feeling went away.

His black thoughts built on one another. Dead bodies in the jungle, firing squads, monsters in the night. Was he slipping into depression? It would be little wonder. He was without friends. The Zapatistas merely tolerated him. And he had been deluding himself about Bailey. He would never find her, and even if he did . . . and Miguel . . . He had probably robbed him and melted into the jungle while he was gone.

He wanted out of this damned place.

Marcos had insisted he hide in the jungle during the stand-off at the convent. He was not even allowed to speak to Magdalena or to accompany Ricardo. The explanation was something about not wanting him seen with the Zapatistas.

"If the army discovers you are with us, there will just be more trouble," said Marcos.

That was bullshit!

Now would they just leave him in peace? What was that damned hammering? It took a moment for the noise to register. It was not his imagination, it *was* hammering. Here in Acteal? This was not right. Here the only morning sounds were birds chattering in the treetops. He listened more closely and heard other domestic sounds—water splashing, someone chopping wood, people's voices.

Ted walked barefoot to the doorway. Ricardo had arrived late in the night and was sleeping in the main room. Outside he could see people moving about the houses. It looked like a scene from any little village. He shook his head to make sure what he was seeing was real. He called for Miguel.

Miguel came running at the sound of his name. He began talking even before he stopped for breath. "They came this morning, before the dawn, the people of the town, the people of Acteal. They have come back."

"Where have they been? Why did they come back now?" asked Ted.

"I don't know. Perhaps Rosa knows. I am going now to help her in the garden. She says we have much work to do to feed so many." Miguel turned and started out the door.

"No, stop, I need to know . . . " Miguel had already disappeared around the next house.

Ted dressed and ventured out. There looked to be between thirty and forty newcomers, about equal numbers of men and women. Women were at work in the abandoned houses, sweeping out floors and starting cook fires. At an adjoining house several men were on a roof repairing the woven matting. But the scene was far from normal. There was none of the usual bustle of a Mexican village, no neighbours calling back and forth. There were no children. The people attended to their tasks in silence.

"*Buenos dias,*" Ted said to the first man he met.

The man grunted and brushed past him. He tried again with the next person. And the next. They were equally unresponsive.

Ted's mood was becoming bleaker by the second. *What was this? A bunch of zombies? Maybe these were the walking dead everyone was always talking about.* He was fed up with people who treated him as if he did not exist.

Ted went in search of Rosa. He spotted her and Miguel from a distance. They were standing in an area recently planted in beans, engaged in a heated conversation with a heavy-set man. Ted could see the debate before he could hear it. Rosa was gesturing with her one arm and the man was brandishing a fist. Nearer, he could make out the subject of the dispute.

"My family has owned this garden for two generations!" the man shouted. "You are trespassing here! I say you should get off my land."

"Your land?" snapped Rosa. "You gave up your right to this land when you ran away four years ago! Anyhow, you and your lazy brothers never farmed this land. All of the real work was left to your mother, God rest her soul."

"Get off, I say! If you don't, I will throw you off." The man moved closer and was shouting into Rosa's face.

Miguel stepped between them. "Leave her alone! We have the right to be here."

Ted was still twenty feet away. He broke into a run. "No, Miguel!"

The man brushed Miguel aside with the back of his hand, and he fell into a row of beans.

"Mind your manners, bambino! Never speak to me like that again," the man said.

Emotions charged through Ted's brain. *That bastard! Pushing Miguel to the ground. Threatening him . . . Get him! Get him!*

His flash point was reached before he could cover the few paces between them. Ted pushed the man on the back as hard as he could. The man stumbled to one knee. He rose slowly to his feet, drawing a machete from his belt. "So this is what you want, eh?" The man swung the machete.

The swing was wild. Ted stepped back and picked up a long-handled spade. Ted was not afraid. All of his anger focused on this man. He wanted to kill him.

They circled. Ted was looking for an opening to swing the spade.

"Stop it! Stop it!" Rosa shouted. "There is no need for this!"

"Don't fight, Ted," Miguel cried. "I'm okay. He didn't hurt me."

Ted swung the spade. The man ducked. The machete sung past his ear.

"In the name of God, stop this! Stop it! Stop it this instant!" Magdalena stepped between the men. Her face was twisted in anger.

The man took a step back but did not lower his machete. Magdalena kicked him in the shin.

"You heard me, Abelardo. I said enough of this. Now put that knife down and get about your business."

"Yes, yes, Mother," the man said. He bowed his head and backed away. He slid the machete into his belt. His eyes were hard slits.

"And you, Señor Somerville," Magdalena said. "Go for a walk until you cool down. Afterwards I want to talk to you. Meet me in the village square at noon."

Ted felt like he was being scolded by one of his grade school teachers. He did not reply.

"And before we meet again," Magdalena said, "I also suggest you spend some time in prayer. Now excuse me. There are others here who need my care." She hustled off towards the village, her short legs pumping like pistons below the hem of her dress.

Ted stood in stunned silence watching Magdalena march away. What had come over him? Was he suicidal? Picking a fight with a man armed with a machete?

"Come," Rosa said. "I'll walk with you a while. Miguel, you take these beans back to the house."

They walked out to what had once been a field. The grass was chest-high in thistle and grass.

"You see, this was once all Abelardo's field," Rosa said. "His family had the largest farm in the village. Now it is all weeds. He has nothing."

"I thought that he was about to attack you."

"You do not understand. That was only a friendly discussion."

"Friendly?"

"Of course," she said. "He wanted to put in his claim on the garden, and I was disputing it. After a while we would have made an agreement. It is the Mexican way."

"But I saw him push Miguel to the ground."

"Miguel wasn't hurt," Rosa said, "and he should have known better. A boy must never challenge a man. Such things are bad for the machismo. No man would stand for it."

"I guess I have a lot to learn," he said.

They entered a grove of trees. "Here, sit," Rosa said. She motioned to a wooden bench. "Spend some quiet time. Let your mind have some peace. Let the land speak to you."

"Speak to me?"

"In time you will understand." Rosa left him without another word.

He supposed the trees were fruit trees. The limbs were short and thick, the leaves large and flat. He wondered what kind of fruit might once have grown here. Had Bailey pruned these trees, picked this fruit? He tried to imagine her laughter and the cut of her hair. She had been happy here once. Would she ever be happy again?

And what about him? He had turned into a monster again. What had he been thinking about? These people had been as open with him as any people in his life. They were warm, generous, loyal. And yet he had been ready to kill someone. Was he crazy? A lost cause? How did someone learn the peace that he saw in Rosa, or acquire the courage of Marcos or the enthusiasm of Miguel? Was he stuck forever as a burnt-out lawyer, stuck somewhere he did not want to be, forever trying to escape? Escape where and to what? To Canada? There was nothing for him there. There was nothing for him here.

The breeze rustled the leaves above his head. A woodpecker rattled a nearby branch. Starlings gathered nearby waiting to see if he had brought anything to eat. At the edge of the forest, a deer was feeding. In the background was the black-green of the forest. He could imagine a voice coming from the impenetrable undergrowth. If this was the land speaking to him, he did not like what it had to say.

"Don't come in here. You may die the next time you do."

"Spend some time in prayer," was what Magdalena had said. Ted could not pray. He wasn't religious. But he did think again about Rosa. Water in the stream. It was easy to think about but harder to believe. That he was just following a channel. There was no use in complaining. No matter what might happen in the end, he would run to the sea. He wished he could accept that. It would make life so much easier.

Ted rose to his feet, took one last look up at the fruit trees, and headed back to the village. "Bailey, wherever you are, keep safe." It was as close to a prayer as he could manage.

He found Magdalena in the area that had once been the village square. She was sitting on the ground. Several women stood around her. Magdalena's voice was raised in anger.

"This ceremony you speak of was devil worship! Have you no fear for your souls?"

The women looked cowed but did not respond.

"Speak up! Was there a white woman there?"

Again there was no answer.

"And another woman, one of you, Emilidia. Have you seen her?"

There was a glimmer of acknowledgement. Magdalena spotted Ted and shooed the women away. "Go now, but we will speak again, and next time I want some answers."

"Good afternoon, Mother," Ted said.

"Do not address me as Mother. You are not Catholic?"

Ted shook his head.

"I thought not. Titles are for inside the convent. Call me Magdalena." She patted the ground beside her and smiled. "Come. Sit."

The smile transformed her face into a cherubic mask. Dimples appeared in the corners of her cheeks, making her look almost merry. Her teeth were straight and gleamed white.

"How about if I call you Sister, at least for the moment?" he asked.

The nun nodded, but her smile was gone. "We have unfinished business. About this morning. How long have you been having these rages?"

Ted took a second to answer. He had not expected to be found out so quickly or so accurately.

"Yes, Sister, anger is a big problem. I've been doing my best to deal with it. I was getting better, but then this morning it overtook me again. This whole situation of being a fugitive and trying to help Bailey . . . and now this thing with Hernandez . . . I guess it got to be too much."

"Now, now. Everything will be fine." She gave him another radiant smile and touched his hand. "We'll work on it together. The Lord will help you."

Her touch lifted his spirits. He had confessed and she had forgiven him. Was it that easy?

"Now the reason for this talk," she said. "I have some news of Bailey, and it is not good. I grew to know her at the convent. She was secretive and much of what she said was garbled. I believe her condition is related to what happened here in Acteal."

"I've come to the same conclusion," Ted said.

"She is in great danger. Hernandez wants to kill her. He is the Devil himself, and will stop at nothing. But another peril is even more pressing. You have noticed these people act strangely?"

Ted nodded.

"They are all victims of Acteal. Some survived the massacre. Others were not directly involved, but lost entire families. In their grief they formed a cult to the dead and lived in the mountains. Many have become addicted to opium—they use it in pagan ceremonies. There is a woman, Emilidia. She was one of them until she too became a patient at the convent. She believed in spirits and talked of human sacrifices."

Ted felt a constriction in his chest. "Human sacrifices? You can't be serious? Surely that has nothing to do with Bailey's disappearance?"

"I fear that it may. Today the villagers told me of a ceremony in which the sentinel of the dead appeared to them. That is why they have returned to Acteal. Their description of this god sounds much like Bailey. I fear the worst."

Magdalena then told him about the discovery of the hair and the blood in Bailey's room.

Ted's mind boiled. He recalled Bailey's chanting and preoccupation with death. And now a pagan ceremony. Had she known all the time what lay in store for her? He had to stop her.

"But these people can tell us where Bailey has been taken. We must make them tell us!" Ted demanded.

"It is not so simple," Magdalena said. "Emilidia is a shaman, a holy woman.

She did not tell them where she was going, only that Bailey was the sentinel."

Ted was concentrating on every word. Mayan spirits, shamans, wandering dead—it was too much to take in at once.

"There was one more thing," said Magdalena. "Did Bailey ever tell you of her baby? A baby she refused to name?"

What? A baby? He thought he had known her. A month with Bailey and he had not known the first thing about her.

"I see you knew nothing of this. We'll speak again," Magdalena said. "I will see what else I can discover."

"What should I do?"

"Pray."

Ted found Marcos in the company of his Zapatista soldiers, inspecting the village. For the occasion, Miguel had donned his balaclava like the men and was strutting beside them like a bantam rooster. The villagers had become energized by the presence of their leader and his victory over the federales. They thronged around Marcos as he shook hands and made small talk.

Ted pulled Marcos aside. "I have news from Magdalena," he said. He related what he had learned. "Bailey is under the control of a shaman. We must find her before something terrible happens."

"Ricardo told me he found opium in the chapel," Marcos said. "Bailey was probably drugged."

"That must be what happened," Ted said. "But we must find her. When can we leave?"

"Find her where?" asked Marcos. "We have no idea where she is, and Chiapas is a very large place. There is no use in going anywhere until we have word on where she may be."

"But we can't just sit here doing nothing!"

"She will be found," said Marcos. "Messages have been sent to all of our villages. If she passes through any of them, we will hear. But in the meantime, there is nothing else you can do. You would do no good wandering around in the jungle. I must order you to stay here."

"Order?"

"Yes, order. Do you understand?" Behind Marcos' mask, his yellow-green eyes sparked fire.

Ted did not answer, but his face burned at the rebuke.

Marcos led Ted away from the others. He put his arm around his shoulder, and said quietly, "Understand, amigo. Running an army is not easy. Orders must be obeyed. And you must be more careful—you have made an enemy."

"Abelardo, you mean?"

"Yes, and he can be dangerous. He was in our army, but when his family was killed in the massacre, he took it hard."

"Marcos, I know I was wrong. What should I do to make it up?"

"It would do you no good to apologize. I have spoken to him, but you have offended his machismo. I told him to end this and he agreed, but you should be careful. He is unpredictable."

Marcos turned back to the others. He called Miguel over and patted him on the shoulder. "I will leave one of my best soldiers to protect you. Look out for him, Miguel."

"*Sí*, Subcomandante!"

CHAPTER 30

BAILEY REVELLED IN HER POWERS. She could run without tiring, and never knew thirst. Her enemies cowered before her; with a wave of her sceptre she could create terror. The beasts of the jungle were her allies and would do her bidding. She was a goddess. Now all that was left was for her to fulfill the calling—the lost dead of Acteal were to be her charges. She must seek them out.

Emilidia was with her. She was dressed in a simple white-hooded robe, her long grey hair hanging straight to her waist. Emilidia waited a short distance away, watchful, as if waiting for her mistress' command.

"*Guardiá*, I am here to serve you. I will prepare your way and help you to find the souls you seek. Drink this—it will sustain you." She handed Bailey a drinking gourd filled with the familiar white liquid. Bailey drank deeply and again she was refreshed.

They set out through the jungle, travelling ever higher into the mountains. The forests thinned and the steamy lowland jungles dropped away. They entered a land of huge rocks and cliffs. They were following a disused jeep track, the way barely discernible in the dark. It had been years since vehicles had passed this way, and trees had grown up in the roadway. They were forced to climb over mudslides and deadfalls. They walked through the night, yet Bailey did not feel fatigued. She felt as if she were floating on clouds. She could have journeyed to the ends of the earth.

The pathway ended at the foot of an immense rock face. In the moonlight, the edifice had been visible from miles away. From a distance, it looked like the head of a giant cat, a jaguar, its jaws snapping at the heavens. But up close its feline features disappeared, and it became just another rocky promontory seeking to escape from the clutches of the jungle. Dense greenery crept up the sides of the cliff; vines and roots ran halfway to the top as if tying it to the ground.

Emilidia knew the way and led Bailey up a short path to a cleft in the rock face. At the entrance were piled torches, ready-made for their use. The woman lit one for herself and handed another to Bailey.

They entered an underground world. Water splattered in dark pools. The dampness seemed to suck the air from Bailey's lungs. She felt as though she had been here before. This place held memories, bad memories. She caught an odour in the air. Could she smell tequila? And cigars? She turned back towards the entrance.

Emilidia beckoned her to follow. Her pull was powerful and Bailey obeyed. They climbed upward through a steep tunnel. The way broadened and they emerged into a large chamber. They entered the Temple of the Jaguar.

The floor was perfectly smooth, the air cool and damp. Emilidia lit a circle of torches that ringed the chamber. The flames made patterns on the stone. The cave was immense—neither the walls nor ceiling could be seen, and the dim light vanished into the distant gloom.

An immense stalagmite extended from the floor to the unseen ceiling. The pillar was decorated with ancient carvings, but the workmanship was well preserved. Gods were depicted riding winged chariots beneath a blazing sun. Next to the pillar was a circular altar, before which stood an oversize sculpture of a crouching jaguar. It was the centrepiece of the chamber and dominated the room. Its eyes were set with golden gems that reflected the light of the torches. It looked to be alive and ready to spring.

Bailey's eyelids had become impossibly heavy. Her limbs could barely hold her upright. Had she drunk too much of the white liquid? She needed to rest. Emilidia spread a fur cloak upon the stone tablet and helped her to lie down, covering her with another robe. Bailey reclined on her back and closed her eyes. As she drifted off to sleep, she was aware of words, a story being told.

"Far away, the jaguar pulls the sun in its fiery chariot from its birth in the east to its death in the oceans of the west. His eyes are flames as he lights the world for his people. The jaguar uses his life's blood to fuel the fire in his eyes and by the death of the sun the mighty beast is drained. He travels through the underworld in the darkness and then must once again draw the sun across the heavens. He must drink the strength of the earth to travel the sky, the blood of life replenished in his body. Only then is his life restored. You will be the donor, Giver of Life, the *Dador de Vida*."

At the edge of sleep something clanged deep in Bailey's subconscious. *Dador de Vida?* Her mind could not make the connection. The voice droned on and she slept.

CHAPTER 31

MARCOS AND HIS MEN PREPARED for their departure. The captured soldiers had been sent back to the main rebel camp, and Marcos was to be present when they were paraded before the media.

"Miguel, next time you can come with us," said Marcos. "For now you are to remain here."

"*Si*, Subcomandante," Miguel said.

Ted noted Miguel's wistful look as the brigade adjusted their packs and saddled their mounts. It would not be long before he would insist on going with them.

Ted had a quiet word with Ricardo. "Take care, Ricardo."

"Until then, be safe, compadre. And look out for this one," he said, ruffling Miguel's hair. "No more chasing boars with pointed sticks."

Ted was honoured by Ricardo's salutation. A compadre was a blood brother, both a friend and a protector in times of crisis. Marcos had made the same declaration weeks before, but at the time Ted had not realized the significance. Now he knew better. He saluted Ricardo in return.

"*Vaya con Dios*, compadre." They touched in the Zapatista embrazo of parting.

Ted handed his friend a letter. "This is something I have been meaning to do for some time. See if you can get it out for me."

"No problem," Ricardo said. He slipped the letter in his pack. The Zapatistas mounted their horses and turned up towards the jungle. Within moments they were gone.

Ted's letter had been prepared shortly after his arrival in Acteal, then revised and rewritten many times. The final draft now in Ricardo's backpack had been completed that morning after his meeting with Magdalena. Ted was afraid that it still said too little. He had not spoken to anyone from home since his telephone call to Bill Turcotte.

The letter was short on details as to where he was and what he was doing, in case it fell into the wrong hands. It just said that he was safe and would be back soon.

Along with the note to his friend there was another document, a resignation from his law firm. The decision had been a long time in coming, but his time in Acteal had cleared his thinking. Even if he made it home, Ted no longer wanted to practise law. Whatever he might do from now on, there would be no more sitting in offices dealing with other people's money. There were more important things in life—like gardening, or hunting wild boars.

He had also prepared an update of his will. He had felt strange writing it, considering himself still a young man. His own death had always been a distant future event. Here he was so close to it that he could almost touch it. There were times, alone at night, that he would shiver at the recollection of the guns and knives that had been pointed at him. In Chiapas, life was cheap and death was everywhere.

His previous will had been prepared after his divorce and had reflected his bitter state of mind. Now he left his beach house in the Gulf Islands to Suzanne. She had always loved it there, and for that reason alone he had denied it to her. Just to hurt her. Now she could have it.

The rest of his estate was to be put into trust, to be administered for Miguel's benefit. This clause had been included naturally without Ted giving the matter much consideration. Now in reflection, he realized the significance of the bequest. He had known the boy only a short time, yet he meant more to him than anyone else in the world. He smiled inwardly—Bill Turcotte would think that he had gone mad if he ever read it.

He was struck by the irony of it all. He would have to die to do the things he should be doing while he was alive. That was no way to do things. If he ever got out of here he planned to settle matters in person. The house to Suzanne, an education for Miguel—they were nice thoughts, but cheap. So long as he was stuck in Mexico, there was no danger of his having to make good on his convictions. Would he ever carry them through? He thought again of the water in the stream. Each person must follow the course that had been set. Time would tell.

———

Ted found Abelardo in the midst of repairing an abandoned house. He was working on the roof, tearing off the matted and rotten thatch, hacking and tearing at the decayed vegetation with his machete. Abelardo was naked to the waist and sweating in the hot sun. He was a big man, over six feet in height. Across his broad back ran a series of horizontal stripes. In places, the skin was bunched and broken, protruding in clumped white scars.

Ted did not call out a greeting or give any warning of his presence. Instead he climbed the side of the building and began pulling at the old roof materials. He threw several large armloads to the ground before the larger man saw him. Abelardo stood up with a start. Ted ignored him and continued to work. He could hear Abelardo's heavy breathing and sensed his closeness. He tensed for the attack. After a long moment in which nothing happened, he raised his head. Abelardo's eyes were boring into him. He made himself return the stare without flinching. His heart was racing.

After what seemed like a very long time, Abelardo grunted and went back to work. They continued to toil, side by side, without speaking, for the next hour. Finally, when the last of the old structure had been removed, the two men climbed down. The day was hot and muggy, and they were both drenched in perspiration. Back on the ground Ted did not know what to expect. He prepared for the worst.

Abelardo took him by the shoulders and pulled him close. "It is finished."

"Yes, it's finished. The old roof is off."

"No, I mean this thing between you and me. It is finished." Abelardo extended his hand. Ted's entire forearm disappeared in his grip.

"Good," Ted said. "Tomorrow I'll help you put the thatch on the new roof."

"And then we drink posh together."

CHAPTER 32

From across the field near Rosa's garden, Hernandez witnessed Marcos' departure. He held the binoculars steady, cursing under his breath. He was hidden in the edge of the clearing where he had been lying all morning.

Hernandez watched Ted and Ricardo as they embraced.

"Those two!" he cursed under his breath. He had ordered them killed. *Those traitors! How could he have trusted them?*

One of the Zapatistas was talking to a boy of about twelve or so, ruffling his hair in affection. After a time the small group of masked soldiers moved away up into the jungle. Hernandez spit in disgust. Marcos and his band of rebels—what he would give for a dozen loyal men right now.

Hernandez spent a time observing the village. There was no sign of other armed men. The village seemed totally unprotected, just like that day four years ago. They had thought then that huddling in the church would keep them safe. The memory brought a smile.

He had driven his jeep to within a few miles and then hiked in the rest of the way. After fleeing from the convent, he had doubled back. He had guessed correctly that Acteal was their destination.

For some reason the gringo had remained behind when the others had departed. He was working on the roof of a house. Hernandez thought he recognized the man he was with—even from a distance the scars on his back were visible. Perhaps that bitch would turn up here as well. He would wait.

The day progressed towards late afternoon, the shadows lengthened, the air cooled. There was activity in the square; people were gathering, cooking fires were lit. Large pieces of meat were placed in a pit in the ground—the village was preparing for a feast. As the sun was setting, a one-armed woman trudged towards the garden carrying a large basket. With her was a boy, the one Hernandez had seen earlier with the soldiers. A plan formed in his mind; this was too good an opportunity to miss.

The woman and the boy were chatting amiably, oblivious to their surroundings. "Rosa, why do we feed these people on our wild pig? They have not been friendly."

"So when do you learn? It is the way of life. When we have food, we feed our neighbours. When they have food . . . " She shrugged her shoulders. "We will see."

They stopped and began to pick beans from the vines, throwing them in piles in the basket. "Why are these people so strange?" asked the boy. "I have talked to many of them and they do not reply."

"I have known many of them from before the trouble, Miguel," she replied. "They were not always so. Perhaps a good bellyful of your pig will cheer them up."

"Yes, Rosa, I was tired of eating boar anyhow. I think that I should kill a deer next."

Hernandez had taken as much as he could stomach of this happy little domestic scene. He drew a long-bladed knife from its sheath and crept to the edge of the field of maize. The woman and the boy were working about ten feet away. Silence was important; he was alone and there might be guns in the village. He thought that he could take them both before they could raise the alarm. He might have to kill one of them, but the other would tell him what he needed to know. His mouth watered with something like hunger. He prepared to spring.

"Hey, Rosa! You and the boy!"

Hernandez pulled back into the brush at the sound of a voice. It was the scar-backed man, the one he had seen up on the roof earlier. He was standing a short distance away, shouting at the two people in the garden. Hernandez took in the long machete that hung from Abelardo's belt and thought better of his planned attack.

The boy reacted to Abelardo's approach. He moved in front of Rosa as if to protect her. "Stay away!" he shouted back.

The large man came closer, his hands open at his sides, palms forward. "Do not be afraid. I have not come to fight. I have come to help you with the beans. Let me take that for you, Rosa." He hefted the basket on his shoulder.

"What beans!" he exclaimed. "How do you grow them to be so big? I can barely lift them."

Rosa and Miguel shared a look. Rosa smiled. "*Gracias.* Tomorrow I will show you. Tonight we will eat together."

Miguel relaxed his defensive stance. "Yes, and I killed the boar."

"Ah, the hunter. I have heard of you." Together the three of them walked back to the village, Abelardo carrying the basket of produce.

Hernandez followed close behind, keeping to the shadows.

CHAPTER 33

TED GAGGED AT THE TASTE.

The liquid known as "posh" tasted like uncooked potatoes and smelled faintly of baking bread. Brewed in pots buried in the ground, it achieved a potent alcohol content. Ted found the taste to be vile, but it would have been impolite for him to refuse; it was the first overture of friendship he had received from his new neighbours. He feigned gusto as he took his turn at the bottle that passed from hand to hand. He was standing in a small circle of men.

"Have another drink, gringo. It is good, yes?"

"Yes, very good. Thank you," Ted said. He passed the bottle back.

"Have more. We have more."

Rosa and Miguel had come back from the garden in company with Abelardo. Ted was at first alarmed, until he saw the glow on Rosa's face. Abelardo was carrying her beans and at the same time receiving instructions from Miguel on the art of boar hunting.

"First you must dig a very deep pit and line it with spears."

"Ah, I see, but how do you make the boar fall into the trap?" Abelardo asked. He was baiting Miguel in a good-natured fashion.

"I used a gringo as bait," Miguel said, winking at Ted.

"Ah, very wise," Abelardo said.

A feast had been planned. Rosa decided they should feed the entire village on the remains of their smoked boar. She said that even preserved meat kept for only a short time and they should eat it before it turned bad.

Magdalena remained in the community. She was an enthusiastic organizer and directed the assembly of tables in the village square and supervised the preparation of the meal. The boar meat was wrapped in palm leaves and buried in a pit filled with hot coals and left to bake. The delicious smells of roasting meat filled the air through the long afternoon. The women worked over open fires, boiling pots of beans and baking tortillas, while the men stood in the shadows passing bottles of their homemade liquor from hand to hand.

When the sun set and darkness enveloped the valley, torches were lit. The glow of the flames added colour and movement to the scene. The baked meat was retrieved with great ceremony from the ground and carved with flashing machetes. The assembled guests made exclamations of pleasure and satisfaction at the amount and quality of the food and set to in a great clamour of eating and passing of plates. The bottles of posh found their way to the table and remained there despite Magdalena's frosty disapproval.

There had been a dramatic change in the people's behaviour. The same men who would not acknowledge Ted's greetings in the morning were now eager to talk. The bottles were pressed on him time and again as smiles cracked weathered faces.

"It is said that you are a compadre of the Subcomandante. Is this so?"

"*Si*, that's true," Ted said.

"*Bueno*, then we must have a toast. To the Revolution! Here. *Salud!*" There was no way of avoiding yet another swig of posh. The Mayans did not share Ted's concept of personal space. Conversations were conducted at close quarters, and to back away was considered impolite.

The liquor was fiery and Ted was soon feeling its effects, yet he dared not refuse the bottle when it was offered.

When the food was consumed and the dishes cleared away, the guitars appeared. The people of Acteal proved they loved to sing. The tunes were lyrical pieces about love, the beauty of the land, and the plight of the people.

There were satirical pieces aimed at politicians and how they would be damned to the inferno while the campesinos enjoyed their wives. The assembly sang the refrain with enthusiasm.

"*El Presidente* cooked his huevos in the flames!"

Some songs were performed as solos, a chorus of voices joining in on others. Many of the songs were familiar from the time Ted had spent travelling in northern Mexico with Bailey. They brought back fond memories, but still he did not join in.

Later in the evening Abelardo stumbled up to Ted. He threw his arm around his shoulder in a comradely fashion. "Amigo, you fight like a fiend from Hell. It is good we should be friends."

"But I am the one with the bandaged arm!" Ted was also slurring his words.

"It is only a scratch. It would be much worse if I had wanted to hurt you!" Abelardo punched Ted on his good arm and wandered away.

Ted extracted himself from the clutch of drinkers. His tolerance for alcohol was no match for theirs, and he had bad memories of his last headache from drinking tequila. A posh-induced hangover did not bear thinking about.

It was getting late. Ted sat with Miguel on their front stoop, watching the revelry. There was dancing, and some of the men had reached an advanced state of intoxication. Rosa was passing on her way home. Ted hailed her and she stopped to join them.

"This is good for these people," she said. "The men will not feel well in the morning, and the village will be very quiet until noon. I have learned something about your friend." She related much the same story as Magdalena about the Mayan spirit of the dead.

"Yes, I know all that. What happened to her after she freed the people?" Ted asked. "That's what I need to find out."

"She remained behind with a shaman as her servant. They would travel to the Temple of the Jaguar."

"Where is this temple?" Ted asked. "I must go there."

169

"It is an ancient place, far back in the jungle." Rosa's expression was unreadable. "Many years ago it was used to make human sacrifices to the jaguar god. I do not know what happens there now."

Ted seized Rosa by the shoulders. "Is that why she was taken there? Has she been taken as a sacrifice?"

Rosa recoiled at his touch and his tone of voice. Ted released her. "I'm sorry, but I have to know."

"These people do not know anything more. Their shaman, Emilidia, was the only one who ventured there."

———

Ted wanted to leave right away, saddle a donkey, and head into the jungle, but Miguel persuaded him to wait until morning.

"I will come with you, but we must have a guide. We would get very lost in the jungle if we leave now," Miguel said.

"Then go and find Abelardo—he will know the way. Find him before he gets too drunk. And tell him that we leave at first light."

———

Hernandez lay in hiding not far from Ted's doorway and heard every word that was said. His eyes hardened at the mention of Bailey's name. This had been worthwhile. He drew his knife and touched his thumb to its keen edge.

CHAPTER 34

THEY HAD THEIR DONKEYS LOADED and ready to leave before the first light crept over the mountains. The village was completely still, the people sleeping late after their feasting. Ted stood close to Rosa's cooking fire holding a mug of strong tea, impatiently waiting for the sun so they could get under way. His eyes stung from the lack of sleep.

Abelardo was an unwilling participant in their venture. By the time Miguel had found him, he was too far into drink to stop, and he and the other men continued to celebrate until they passed out in the square. As the dawn approached, they roused themselves and slunk away to their homes.

"He will not come. He says maybe tomorrow," Miguel said.

Abelardo was lying on the floor of his roofless house, snoring mightily.

"Come on, Abelardo, it's time to go," Ted said.

He growled but did not open his eyes. "Go away. Leave me alone."

"Stand back, Miguel," Ted said. He fetched a pail of cold water from the nightstand and dumped it on the sleeping man's head. Abelardo came up sputtering and cursing, his fists were up, ready to fight. He took one step towards Ted, stopped, and put his hands over the top of his head.

"*Caramba*, what time is it?" Abelardo said. "My head is going to explode! Come back later!"

"Come on, Miguel, grab an arm," Ted said. They each seized an arm and hoisted Abelardo to a standing position. "We have no time. You can sober up on your donkey."

"No, leave me. I die here. I cannot ride a donkey today."

Fifteen minutes later they were astride their mounts. Abelardo's face was ashen and his eyes were bloodshot, but he had recovered his spirits.

"You gringos are going to kill me," he said, the smell of posh heavy on his breath. "You think I am kidding? No, some day you will actually kill me." He urged his donkey towards the jungle's edge.

Rosa was there to see them off. She filled their saddlebags with tortillas and cooked boar.

"See if you can get word to Marcos and tell him where we've gone," Ted said.

"I will tell him, but he will not be pleased. This is a dangerous thing that you do."

She had words for Miguel. "Be careful. The jungle can be dangerous," she said. "Do as Ted tells you."

"Don't worry, Rosa. I will look after Ted. He is only a gringo, but with me he will be safe."

They were riding past the orchard towards the forest trail when they encountered Magdalena. She was sitting on a spotted burro.

"Good morning, Sister," Ted greeted her, "and where do you think you are going?"

"With you, of course," said Magdalena. "I told you I was here to see to Bailey's soul. I can hardly do that from Acteal. Come on, what are we waiting for?" She kicked her burro's flanks and broke into the lead.

They made their way into the jungle, the foliage closing in behind them. Within moments they were beyond all signs of civilization. Brightly coloured birds screeched from the treetops, and the undergrowth rustled with movement. Overhead a pod of spider monkeys challenged their progress by throwing bits of fruit, sticks, and feces. The missiles fell all about as the monkeys scolded the travellers not to come any closer. The travellers covered their heads and pushed on up the trail.

Abelardo clung sullenly to the back of his donkey. In response to requests for directions, he supplied a vague wave of his hand.

"Go back towards the convent. Wake me when we get there, and I will show you the rest of the way." He closed his eyes and appeared to fall asleep on his donkey.

They stopped to eat at midday by the side of a small stream. Abelardo dismounted from his donkey and lay down face first in the water. He drank for a long time. He got to his feet and shook the water from his hair.

Magdalena retrieved a parcel from her saddlebag and presented it to Abelardo. "Last night when you were drinking, you dropped something. I picked it up and brought it with me. Here, take it."

She offered Abelardo a full bottle of foaming posh. Its unmistakable odour of rotting fruit permeated the air. Abelardo stared at the bottle as if it was a venomous snake, wondering which end he should grab.

"Sister, I think you are just trying to punish a poor sinner," Abelardo said. "But if I must, I must." He took a long pull from the bottle. "Ah, yes, now I will live," he said.

Magdalena glared at him. "Will you never learn, Abelardo?" she said. She snatched the bottle back and poured its contents on the ground.

Ted stifled the urge to laugh out loud. Magdalena was glowering up at the big man who towered above her. Abelardo returned a sheepish grin, and seeming pleased with himself, threw his leg over his donkey.

"Come, Sister, we have many miles to go before the end of the day," he said.

They made camp that night just over halfway to the temple. They had been climbing all day and had left the rain forest behind. Their surroundings had changed. The trees were now taller and better spaced, great stands of giant mahogany towered above their heads. The roof of green that was everywhere in the wetlands was gone, and in places they could see the sky. The terrain tilted ever upwards until finally they could see the horizon and hills in the distance. The sense of oppressive closeness was gone as the air lost its humidity.

The wildlife was as abundant as in the jungles below. Howler monkeys screamed in the treetops, brightly coloured macaws squawked their ugly croaks, and the forest floor was alive with small rodents. Some distance away, they heard a crash in the forest that was probably caused by a boar or a startled deer.

Their camp was on a dry ridge just beyond the forest's edge. A small stream provided a source of water.

Their dinner simmered in a pot over a low fire—a mixture of beans, roasted boar, and hot chillies. Abelardo had recovered his appetite and was able to make light of his earlier distress.

"Sister, when you showed me that bottle of posh, I thought that I would die. You don't know how hard it was to take it from you. It was a good thing that you threw the rest of it away. I felt that close to death all day," he said, indicating a small gap between his first finger and his thumb.

"It would have been no more than you deserved," said Magdalena while stirring the stew. "I should have made you drink the whole bottle."

———

After they had eaten, they sat around the fire. Well above the jungle, the night was cool. Abelardo smoked a cigarette, staring silently into the flames, firelight highlighting the contours of his face. His skin was the texture of dried leather, cracked and rough. He was a hard man, a campesino of the highlands. He was unhappy. Except for his words with Magdalena, he had not spoken all day. Ted wondered what was bothering him.

"Tell us about the temple. Have you been there?" Ted asked.

Abelardo ignored the question and sat smoking his cigarette in silence. His refusal to speak hung in the air.

"The Jaguar's Temple, have you seen it?" Ted asked.

After a moment when the man again did not answer, Miguel intervened.

"Tell us, Abelardo, please. I have only heard of such a place. I want to know all about the jaguar."

Abelardo finally responded, although his eyes never left the fire. "No, I have never been in the temple—that was reserved for the priestess. But I know where it is. I have been close to the place. It can be seen from far away. It is a bad place."

"People here are always talking about bad places and evil spirits. What is so bad about the Jaguar's Temple?" Ted asked. "Isn't the jaguar one of your friendly spirits?"

Abelardo nodded solemnly. "Yes, the jaguar, he is our friend."

"Tell us about him," Ted said. "Do people still worship the jaguar?"

Abelardo took a puff on his cigarette. His face had a faraway look, and he lowered his voice to a hoarse whisper. Ted moved closer to hear.

"Long ago, before the conquistadors, the jaguar lived in Chiapas. He was the lord of the jungle and the god of my ancestors. He controlled the sun in the sky and ruled the animals in the forest. His name was *El Jaguar*, and this was his land. And the land was free."

Abelardo told the legend with a sense of religious fervour. A mixture of facts and superstition peppered his discourse. Three hundred pounds, eight-and-a-half feet long, ferocious, but the friend of the Mayans. There was no clear line between myth and fact. It was a story that had been told around many campfires.

"Then came the Spaniards who stole our land and enslaved our men. We were no longer free and were not fit to have the jaguar as our ruler. *El Jaguar* went away—he was gone from the land. Temples were built and sacrifices made to entice him to return. But he will not come again. Not until we are free will the jaguar return to Chiapas.

"You ask if we worship him?" Abelardo had become fervent. "You may as well ask if we love freedom!"

Ted had little interest in a tall tale of a mythical Mayan god. He wanted to know where Bailey had been taken and what they might expect to find in the morning, not to listen to a diatribe about the plight of the campesinos.

"Tell me of the Jaguar's Temple. What of this talk of sacrifices?" he said. "And why do you think Bailey was taken there? You know this shaman, Emilidia. What does she have to do with the jaguar?"

"This woman, Bailey, she and I, we have a history together," Abelardo said.

"What? You know her?" Ted asked. "Why didn't you tell me?"

"Look at my back," Abelardo said. He pulled up his shirt to display scars that crisscrossed his flesh. "This was done by a whip."

"I don't understand."

"You wonder why I am not happy to be here," said Abelardo. "See my reward for not minding my own business the last time I met this woman. She is trouble for me. And about the Jaguar's Temple I can tell you nothing more. Perhaps tomorrow we will both find out. For now, gringo, it is enough talking; it is time to sleep."

Abelardo climbed into his hammock and pulled the mosquito netting over his face.

Magdalena had sat apart but had been listening. She quietly unrolled a blanket and placed it over Abelardo. He was already snoring.

"What did he mean by that?" Ted asked. "Did you know that Abelardo and Bailey knew each other?"

"No, it is a mystery to me as well. In good time we will find out the truth. Join me in prayer." She made the sign of the cross. Ted and Miguel sank to their knees.

After prayers Magdalena left for her own bedroll. Miguel tugged on Ted's sleeve. "*El Jaguar* is a very fine creature. After we hunt for deer, we will go to look for a jaguar. We will capture him and bring him back to Chiapas."

"Go to sleep, Miguel."

———

Ted lay thinking. Bailey was connected to Abelardo; that was not a complete surprise—they had both been in Acteal at the time of the massacre. But what did she have to do with the marks on the man's back? That Abelardo was not prepared to speak of it made things even more bewildering. Ted was lost.

Maybe tomorrow he would find some answers.

CHAPTER 35

BAILEY TUMBLED THROUGH DREAMS on the edge of consciousness. A fire-breathing jungle cat chased her through a dark forest. She raced through the undergrowth, jumping to elude its snapping jaws. But it was gaining ground, getting closer every second. Her chest hurt. She was exhausted, and she could run no more.

From somewhere above her, a voice was calling, "*Donata . . . Donata—*" And there was a white light. She soared towards it, away from the pursuing beast, upwards, higher and higher.

Another dream followed, equally terrifying. A disembodied voice was speaking to her. The voice was familiar but she could not place it—a woman's.

"*La Guardiá de los Muertos* gives her blood to feed the jaguar. The jaguar will rule the land, and together they will keep her promise to the dead. There is pain, but it is brief. The glory of the sacrifice will live forever." The words resonated in her mind.

There was a final vision. It was of a young dark-haired man. He smiled at her and called her by name.

"Bailey! Bailey, Donata."

She knew the apparition instantly as Ernesto. In her dream she smiled, happy to have him returned to her. He looked as he had in life, handsome with a flashing smile and deep brown eyes. Bailey wanted to believe that he was still alive, but somehow she knew that she was only dreaming. Ernesto was dead.

He held out his hand and she took it. His flesh felt warm and real.

"Bailey, do not do this thing," Ernesto said. "You are not a goddess, you are a woman. This place holds only dangers. You were once Donata, our gift from God. You can be again. Do not be fooled—only death awaits you here. Run away. Run away."

Bailey made herself speak to him. In her dream it was difficult to form the words. "Ernesto, you must forgive me. Forgive me for what I did."

He touched her cheek with his hand. "What you did, you had no choice. You are forgiven. Return to your life." With a last sad smile, the vision faded. Ernesto was gone.

As the dream ended, she awoke. The morning light had touched her and driven back the demons of the night. Bailey's head hurt with a dull ache across her forehead. Her mouth tasted of cotton wool; her body complained of the night spent on a hard surface. But still the last dream left her with a warm glow. Ernesto's final words—she was forgiven. Bailey mouthed the words. "You are forgiven. Return to your life." It was comforting.

She sat up and looked about. She was in a huge limestone cave. The chamber opened to the east and the interior was bathed in the first light of dawn. The sun would rise directly at the entrance, flooding the cave with its first rays.

Bailey jumped with fright. *My God! What is that across from me?* At first she took the shape as a huge cat crouching at her feet. Its yellow eyes gleamed with menace. But it did not move. She caught her breath—it was only a statue, a stone rendition of a jaguar. The light was reflected from the golden gemstones set in the sockets of the huge head. Was this the snapping demon from her first dream? Her heart rate returned to normal slowly.

Bailey could not remember how she had come to this place. The surroundings were unfamiliar. Searching her memory was like looking through sheets of gauze—mists enveloped the past. There was the convent, the small room there, and she had been waiting for something. But then what? She was filled with foreboding. Ernesto's words returned to her, "Run away. Run away."

She became aware that she was all but naked. What were these garments? Teeth around her neck? A skirt of back feathers? And her skin. Arms, breasts, stomach, everywhere, she was covered with paint, a thick white, plaster-like pigment, on top of which someone had drawn a black skeleton.

And she remembered none of it.

Bailey got up from the rock shelf. She had been lying on a piece of porous stone slightly cupped in the middle, about six feet across. The material was carved in intricate patterns. Winged jaguars pursued the sun across the etched stone. It was discoloured, with irregular brown and black markings, as if someone had spilled ink. A chill gripped her. This was an altar. The carved jaguar, the inscriptions—this was an old Mayan temple. She shuddered. That meant the stains were . . .

Why was she here? She had a clear recollection of Ernesto's warning. "Only death awaits you here."

She seemed to be alone. She called out, softly at first, "Hello, hello, is anybody there?"

No reply.

She tried several more times, each time a little louder. The only answer was the echo of her own voice.

The cave was getting brighter by the second. The sun was about to rise, and the chamber would be flooded with light. It was a well-known Mayan design. This was a temple to the sun, a place where the priests worshipped the jaguar, the god of the sun. At the first light of day, sacrifices were made. People had died here to appease the gods. Despite the warmth of the morning, Bailey began to shiver. Alone in a ceremonial death chamber, the words of the second dream came back to her. "There is pain, but it is brief. The glory of the sacrifice will live forever."

She was getting out of here, and as fast as she could.

"Are you ready, *Guardiá?*" The words seemed to spring from everywhere at once.

"Who's there?"

Where there had been nothing moments before, now there was a shape. Far back in the cave, visible in the growing light, a figure in a white robe, head covered by a hood, glided towards her. A hand was extended, holding a drinking gourd.

"Drink this, *la Guardiá de los Muertos*. It will speed your journey."

She recalled Ernesto's words. "You are not a goddess, you are a woman."

"No, I am not *la Guardiá*." Her voice cracked with fear.

The figure continued to advance. "You seek the dead of Acteal. Drink the potion. The jaguar is almost here. He will lead you."

Bailey could barely command her mind to function. She shrank from the hand that held the gourd. She had some recollection now of drinking a bitter white liquid. Yes, something was coming back. Was this how she was brought here? Drugged? "Do not be fooled—only death awaits you here." Ernesto's words kept forming in her brain.

"Stop! Get back! I don't want to drink that, and I don't want this to go any further. Stop it! Whatever you're doing!"

The light was rising fast. The first rays of the sun had touched the entrance. Bailey had her back to the glow, but it was fully in the face of the cowled stranger. Her expression was glassy and fixed. Bailey recognized her.

"Emilidia! What do you want with me?" she screamed, as if words or reason would stop her. Bailey backed away towards the front of the cave.

Emilidia spoke. Hers was the voice from the second dream. "There is pain, but it is brief," she said. "The glory of the sacrifice will live forever."

Emilidia discarded the gourd and drew a knife, an intricately decorated weapon with a foot-long blade. She held it outstretched before her.

"It is not I who desire you, it is the jaguar. Your blood will make him strong. Together you will guard the dead of Acteal."

Bailey backed towards the entrance. She kept her eyes on Emilidia. The footing was smooth and her bare feet moved easily across the cave floor. She fought the urge to scream. There was no one to hear. Escape was her only option. Ernesto had said to run away, but run away to where? And how?

Her foot struck something hard and uneven—she had come to the entrance. She turned to run, but caught herself in time. The cave opened over a gorge, the rock wall falling straight down for hundreds of feet. She was balanced on the lip with nowhere to go. One more step would take her over the edge.

Emilidia was only steps away, her mouth serene yet determined, her eyes glowing with insane light.

Bailey caught movement out of the corner of her eye. She threw herself to the ground. The blade sliced the air above her head. She scooped dirt from the cave floor and flung it in Emilidia's face. The other woman wiped at her eyes. Bailey rushed her and grabbed her by both wrists.

Emilidia's arms were like bands of steel. Bailey stood face to face with her, struggling to hold both forearms. It was an unequal contest. Emilidia grimaced as she forced her arms together and broke free of Bailey's grasp.

"Stop it! Stop it!" Bailey screamed. "Don't you know who I am? We were friends!"

"You are *la Guardiá de los Muertos*. The jaguar desires your blood, and he shall have it."

Her back to the entrance, Bailey fought with a sense of desperation. She seized Emilidia's wrist with both hands and struggled for the knife. But Bailey knew it was only a matter of time. The other woman was stronger and equally determined.

Emilidia threw Bailey to the ground and lunged with the knife. "Drink deeply, Lord Jaguar!" Bailey rolled to one side. Sparks flew as the knife struck the ground where she had been. Bailey grasped for the hand that held the knife. Too late. Emilidia drew back her arm.

Bailey took a deep breath and waited for the end to come.

The light hit them. Released from the mists of the jungle floor, the sun's rays ignited the crystalline air. The atmosphere burst into a million sparkles. A spectrum of blinding colours filled the Temple of the Jaguar.

Emilidia's eyes lit up in wonder. She checked the blade in mid thrust. She raised her face to the sun, her lips drawn back in rapture.

Bailey caught Emilidia's wrist and yanked it towards her. Emilidia lost her balance. Her foot struck the lip of the cave, and she lurched forward into space.

The scream of "*Jaguar* . . . " floated up from the gorge. It was abruptly cut off.

Bailey scrambled to her feet and looked out the entrance to the forest far below. She could distinguish little through the glare. The forest floor was obscured by a canopy of trees. The jungle resumed its morning rituals; birds sang in the sunlight. In the distance, a pod of howler monkeys screamed.

She stumbled back inside the temple and sagged against the altar. She looked up to find the stone jaguar glaring at her. Its gemstone eyes sparkled in the sun.

CHAPTER 36

Six reporters gathered in front of a small hut, tape recorders and pads in hand. The correspondents were light-skinned and stood apart from the Mexicans. One was armed with a lightweight video camera. As Marcos approached the small group, two young women materialized as if out of nowhere, each taking one arm. The outlines of their lean bodies showed through their uniforms.

The reporters all tried to talk at once, thrusting microphones into Marcos' face. "Subcommander, Art Willis, *New York Times*, Gene Falk, American Press International, Pierre Lamarche, *Paris News*, Jose Perez, *Mexico City Journal!*" Their words were unintelligible. Marcos waited until the noise subsided before responding.

When he deemed they were ready to listen, he began. "I have asked you here today as witnesses. Two days ago I led a Zapatista patrol to the convent of San Cristobal. We had learned that the nuns were being held hostage by a death squad of the Mexican Army."

The reporters were scribbling madly, microphones extended, the one video camera rolling.

"At the convent we captured and took prisoner a squad of Mexican Army soldiers. One of their number committed suicide, but their commander escaped. We have brought them here. They have not been harmed, and we intend to turn them over to the civilian authorities. You have asked to see them so that there can be no suggestion that they have been mistreated, and we have agreed. You may question them if you like, but whether they choose to answer is up to them." Marcos turned to one of his soldiers and said, "Bring out the prisoners."

The door of a nearby hut opened and the dishevelled and downcast soldiers were herded out to meet the press. They shuffled their feet and stared at the ground. Their uniforms were filthy and they had not shaved. In spite of the cool of the morning, perspiration glistened on their faces.

"How did you come to be captured? Who is your commander? Did the government order you to occupy the convent? Were any of the nuns injured?" The questions came one after another, a chorus of voices demanding answers. No one asked whether the soldiers had been treated well by the Zapatistas. That was not news.

The prisoners stood mute. The press conference held no interest for them. Through demands, accusations, and raised voices they maintained a stony silence.

In frustration, the newsmen focused their attention on a soldier who bore the markings of rank on his shoulders. "Come now, corporal. You are the ranking soldier, surely you can speak for your men."

The corporal was a tall man with a moustache that had once been neatly trimmed. In other circumstances he might have been considered handsome. Perspiration ran down his slack-jawed face. His nose dripped mucous onto the hair on his upper lip, but he lacked the self-respect to wipe it away.

The American reporter was red-faced and aggressive. "Answer the questions!" He directed himself at the corporal. "We want to know what you were doing at the convent. Our readers have a right to know. Now what is your name?" He fixed the soldier with a steely gaze, notebook in hand, ready to record any response.

Marcos was about to step in when the corporal answered.

"My name is Corporal Pablo Pasquale, Mexican Army," the soldier muttered without lifting his eyes from the ground. "I am a member of the personal guard to Colonel Emiliano Hernandez."

"Tell us how you came to be captured, Pasquale," asked the American. His voice was softer now.

"Colonel Hernandez ordered us to shoot the nuns. We refused and surrendered."

The reporters smelled blood and began to talk all at once. "Where is Hernandez? Were the sisters harmed? What other crimes did you commit?"

Pasquale looked from reporter to reporter as if looking for somewhere to hide. "I will tell you. There is nothing more you can do to us. We are damned already." Tears ran down his soiled cheeks. "Hernandez offended the Church and brought the demons of the jungle down upon us. We have seen the thing that came for our souls. You ask us what evil we have done? There is no end to it. We have done the devil's own work."

The reporters were writing as fast as they could, but Pasquale was no longer looking at them.

"We have raped, killed . . . And not only men. Women, children, old people. We have ripped babies from their dead mothers' bellies and killed them with our machetes."

"And Acteal . . . We were there. We were the ones that massacred the people of Acteal. This is why the demons have come for our souls." Pasquale's knees gave way and he slumped to the ground.

There was a momentary silence. Before the reporters could recover, Marcos intervened. He placed himself between Pasquale and the media.

"That is enough. You have your story. This man is my prisoner; he has confessed to his crimes. That is a good thing. Leave him now."

Marcos drew Pasquale to his feet. He grasped him firmly by both arms and looked him in his face.

"You have much to answer for. It is not in my power to grant you forgiveness, but your actions today speak in your favour. I will tell the police that you saved the nuns from death by refusing Hernandez' orders. May God have mercy on you."

The soldiers were escorted back to their quarters. The other prisoners walked in a tight group around Pasquale.

The reporters were mad for more details, and Marcos obliged them as far as he could. By the next day, the news of the army's complicity in the Acteal massacre would be news all over the world. After half an hour of spirited questioning, Marcos concluded the conference with his own statement.

"As you can see, we have not harmed these men. It is not our intention to do so, although they deserve punishment. Presidente Fox has said that he wants peace with the Zapatistas and that he would have me come to Mexico City. I am sending these prisoners to him for trial. The way they are treated will tell us whether the government is serious in its offer of a solution. Thank you for coming."

Marcos walked alone back to his headquarters in the cueva. His mask hid his grim expression. It was at times like this that he doubted himself most. This parading of prisoners before the media was necessary—the world must know what was happening here in Chiapas. Already there were debates in the United Nations, stories in the foreign press, pressure on the government to make peace. But at what cost? The Revolution was becoming a sideshow. Events were staged for the press, complete with photo opportunities. Pretty women were placed at his side to make him appear more glamorous in the daily tabloids. He sometimes felt more like a circus performer than a leader. Exploiting prisoners was not to his liking.

Marcos was sitting down for his midday meal when Ricardo burst into the chamber. He was in the company of a young farmer.

"There is a message from Acteal. Bailey has been taken to the Temple of the Jaguar. Señor Somerville has left Acteal with a small party to rescue her. He asked that you be told."

"Damn that man!" Marcos exclaimed. "Why does no one do as I tell them? I ordered him to stay where he was and to leave the search to us. Hernandez is out there somewhere, and he is also looking for the woman."

He thought for a moment. "There is no other choice. Ricardo, we must go at once. Just you and I. The rest can remain here."

"Should you not remain with the prisoners? There will be much news of us delivering them to the police. As you have often taught me, 'the moment is everything.'"

Marcos began loading his pack. "Think of this, Ricardo. An American woman is lost in the jungle. She is probably in great danger. Even if she had not saved my life, I would have to act. Her rescue is important for the Revolution."

"I do not understand," Ricardo said.

"Think what the press will say if our people should sacrifice an American woman to a pagan god. All the goodwill we have worked so hard to create would disappear in an instant. That is why we must go at once. Do you understand?"

"*Sí*, Subcomandante. I am going now for our horses."

CHAPTER 37

AFTER OVERHEARING TED'S PLANS, Hernandez hiked to his hidden jeep and drove down the mountain. He had no need to follow Ted's party into the jungle—he knew where they were going and could intercept them along the way. Enough of this hiding in the bushes. Moving in for the kill, within reach of his goal, then being chased away. And all because those damned cowards would not shoot a few nuns. He hoped that Marcos had hung them all by now.

This was not like the old days when he commanded as many men as he wanted and they followed his orders without question. Acteal—now there had been a success. That was what manpower could accomplish. This business of killing one man here and a couple there was a waste of time. Only a large-scale victory could have the necessary effect. That would bring those simpering politicians to their senses, show them the truth of this conflict.

After the highlands the roads were good, and he was in the city of Tuxtla two hours later. He knew the men he was after—pistoleros, the same ones who had participated in Acteal. The men of the Red Mask were paramilitaries, government mercenaries, tough men who killed for money. Hernandez had enjoyed some great victories with these men, but some unpleasantness as well. "Paras" disliked following orders and had a natural hatred of all authority, including his. They were both useful and dangerous.

The Red Mask had fallen on hard times. This talk of peace made for little work for death squads. He would find them, talk of the old days, and plan one last offensive that would end it all.

He liked Tuxtla. The city was a stronghold of government support in Chiapas, and Hernandez felt at home here. He was among friends. Within an hour of his arrival, he sat in the back room of a cantina in the poorest quarter. Cigarette smoke filled the air, curling wisps of white in a cloud of haze. The overhead light was diffused by the thick atmosphere and gave the room and its occupants a soft glow they did not deserve. The men reeked of stale beer, nicotine, and body odour. An off-key marimba band played loudly in the next room.

Rugged-looking men surrounded Hernandez. They were big and unshaven—hard drinkers, all of them. Part of him despised them. They were a bunch of Indians. The only differences between them and the Zapatistas were political. But they were also vicious killers and exactly the men he needed. They would do anything for a price. The men of the Red Mask were without conscience; if they had been with him at San Cristobal, there would have been no problem in killing a few nuns. Hernandez bought bottles of tequila for the room. It was quickly consumed.

Their leader was Cerves, a heavy-set Mayan Indian. "So, Hernandez. Tell us, why did you call us here? We have heard that the fighting is over, that the government wishes to make peace. You people in the army have no more use for the likes of us." In spite of the free liquor, the man's tone was anything but friendly. He spat on the floor to emphasize his contempt for the military.

Hernandez knew he must choose his words carefully. If the Red Mask did not like his proposal, they might easily kill him just for entertainment. He understood them all too well—during an earlier mission he had been forced to use brutal means to maintain discipline. Some of the men bore marks from Hernandez' whip. They had long memories and some things would not be forgotten.

"This has nothing to do with the army. The politicians in Mexico City are fools and cowards. They believe that they can negotiate with Marcos. But we know better. The only way to deal with Zapatistas is with steel and blood!"

The men nodded in agreement. They liked this kind of talk just as he knew they would. Blood and money were the two things these Indians understood.

"Remember when those dogs defied the law and occupied our cities? Then

188

the men of the Red Mask were needed. Without you, the rebels would have had our women and our homes."

There was a murmur of assent.

"I have money to pay you. The work will be hard, but in the end you will be hailed as heroes. It is time this revolt was ended. When the government sees what we can accomplish, there will be no more talk of peace."

"What is your plan, Hernandez?" asked Cerves.

"Ask yourself, where was our greatest victory? It was Acteal. Am I not right? If the government had not lost heart, victory would have been ours. Now the campesinos have returned once more to the village. It is time we also returned."

The room buzzed. "*Si*, he is right! We should go back. Finish the job! Death to the Zapatistas!"

"We are with you, Hernandez," Cerves said. "So long as your money is good. How much do we get paid, and when do we attack?"

"The pay is five hundred American dollars to each man, half in advance. We strike on the Day of the Dead. That is a fitting occasion to send the people of Acteal to meet their ancestors."

"Where will you be until then, Hernandez? How can we be sure that you will bring the money?" Cerves asked.

Hernandez put his face close to Cerves'. "It is a personal matter and none of your affair. As to your money, remember whom you are dealing with. Do not question my orders, now, or ever!" He glared about the room, meeting each man's eyes in turn. He was satisfied only when each of them averted their eyes.

Hernandez tossed back his drink and stepped out into the night. *Damned Indians!* He had best keep his gun handy.

CHAPTER 38

AFTER A NIGHT IN A CHEAP HOTEL, Hernandez drove back up into the jungle along a narrow track. He was in position long before the party from Acteal had completed their first day's travel. He had time to reconnoitre the Jaguar's Temple before dark.

In the cave itself he found little of interest. There was evidence of recent habitation—some cooked beans and discarded garments—but nothing else. There was no sign of Bailey.

He circled the rock face from the outside, looking for a campsite. He found Emilidia's remains at the bottom of the gorge beneath the temple. The body had been smashed by its fall onto the rocks, and already ravaged by animals. He peered up at the cave entrance. *Throwing people out of caves onto the rocks—these Indians did have some interesting customs.*

The expedition from Acteal would probably be somewhere on the trail leading from the rain forest. If he headed in that direction, their paths would inevitably cross. He hoped that Bailey might have moved back down off the heights and be with them by the time he arrived. He took his machine pistol and a light pack and set out on foot. It felt good to be hunting—his finger itched for a kill.

He found their camp just before dusk. They had pitched hammocks on a rise on top of a limestone ridge. As he was watching them through his binoculars, he accidentally dislodged a rock and startled a tapir, a large stupid creature with a turned up nose and long legs. The animal crashed away through the forest. Hernandez cursed and remained still. The sound of the animal's escape would have carried for miles. After a moment when nothing happened, he relaxed.

The fools. Not posting a guard. They were making this too easy.

Hernandez huddled in a blanket on a low tree branch. He had passed countless nights in similar circumstances and the dark and jungle noises had long ceased to bother him. Tonight, though, was different. He neither saw nor heard anything, but he had a sense that he was not alone. Some *one* or some *thing* was watching him. The feeling stayed with him and he could not sleep. He moved out at the first glimmer of light.

In the last minutes of darkness, Hernandez approached the camp. He deemed the big man with the machete as the only threat and would attack him first. With him out of the way, the others would be easy—he could kill them at his leisure or use them as hostages.

Abelardo was suspended in his hammock between two trees. The others were some distance away, spaced unevenly up the ridge. Abelardo lay on his back, breathing evenly with mosquito netting covering his face. Hernandez crawled the last few feet on his belly until he was immediately under the man. He placed his machine pistol on the ground and drew his knife.

As Hernandez rose from his crouch, Abelardo grunted and tossed in his sleep. He was muttering, the words almost inaudible. "*El Jaguar, El Jaguar.*"

Hernandez pulled the netting aside to expose the man's throat. The blade's edge gleamed in the early light. A sound intruded on his concentration, out of place and seeming to come from everywhere at once. It started as a vibration, a low rumble below his range of hearing, and increased in volume and pitch until it seemed to shake the ground. Hernandez had heard such a sound only once before, made by a caged lion. A guttural growl, as if the beast had been plucking its vocal chords one by one.

Hernandez turned his head. At that moment Abelardo's eyes snapped open. His hands reached from the hammock, seizing Hernandez' wrist.

"Aieee! *Bandidos.* Help!"

They wrestled for control of the weapon.

Heads poked from hammocks. "Wha. . . ?"

Hernandez abandoned the struggle. He dropped to the ground and retrieved his machine pistol. Abelardo had the knife and was struggling to free himself from the hammock. He was too late. Hernandez sprayed him with a burst of automatic fire. Abelardo's body jerked with the impact of the bullets. He fell to the ground with one leg still entangled in the netting. His body lay still.

The others scrambled to their feet. Somerville, the old nun, and the boy from the village. A smile crossed Hernandez' face.

"So, Sister, you again! You should have stayed out of my business. All of you, hands in the air. Move over here! Now!"

"What have you done to Abelardo?" Miguel screamed. He stared at the body. "What have you done to my friend?"

"Abelardo, so that was his name?" Hernandez said. "He will be sleeping late today."

Miguel held a pocketknife in his hand. He charged. "You killed him! You killed Abelardo! I'll get you!"

"Miguel! Stop!" Ted shouted.

Hernandez turned his gun towards the boy. The distance was less than twenty feet. He flicked the lever to single shot and brought the weapon up to fire.

Ted caught Miguel from behind and tackled him in the dust. They wrestled for the knife.

"Don't be stupid," Ted said.

"But he killed my friend. I must . . . "

"Must what? Get yourself killed? Give me that."

Hernandez separated them with a few well-aimed kicks of his boots. "This is very touching. Now get up with your hands in the air before I shoot you both."

Ted tossed the pocketknife in the dust before Hernandez' feet. He dusted off his clothes as he rose to his feet. He held Miguel by the shoulder. The boy was twisting in his grasp.

"I'm looking for the girl. Where is she?" snapped Hernandez.

"We know nothing," Magdalena said. "Leave us."

"Do you think I would believe anything a lying nun says? How about the two of you? Where is she? Or do you want to die like your friend over there?"

"You're going to kill us anyway," Ted said. "Why would we tell you anything?"

"So, big talk from the gringo today. Haven't pissed your pants yet? Let us see how brave you are. Do you know what happens to a man when he is shot in the gut?" Hernandez levelled his machine pistol at Ted's stomach. "No, I didn't think so. With medical care such a wound might be treated. But here, here it is fatal. You may live for a few days, your companions may sacrifice themselves in trying to save you, but you will die. A slow, painful death. Let's start with that."

Hernandez fired a single shot. Ted's shirt puckered as the bullet hit. He looked confused. He groped his midriff and raised a hand sticky with blood. His eyes were fixed on Hernandez as he sank to his knees.

"Now the rest of us should talk," Hernandez said. "If you are to have any chance of saving yourselves, you must tell me what you know. As you can see, I am serious."

Miguel fell to Ted's side. Magdalena knelt in front of him and unbuttoned his shirt. A large red stain covered Ted's abdomen. Blood was oozing from a small hole just above his navel. Ted's eyelids fluttered shut.

"Leave him, Sister, he'll be dead soon whatever you do. And you will be too if you don't start cooperating."

The nun paid him no attention and held a kerchief against the wound. Miguel was screaming, "Ted! Ted! Open your eyes!"

Hernandez clubbed Miguel across the side of the head with his weapon. He collapsed to the ground.

Damned kid. I'll have to kill him too just to shut him up.

He worked another bullet into the chamber. Magdalena was probing at the wound in Ted's stomach.

Might as well finish them both.

The sound he had heard earlier interrupted his aim. Only it was much closer. And more distinct. He recognized it now as the throaty growl of a large animal. Hernandez aimed his weapon into the nearby bushes.

But then there was another sound, a more regular rhythm superimposed over the first. It became louder, more distinct. It was the thudding of hoof beats, horses coming at a gallop from the jungle below. And they were very close. Hernandez lowered his weapon and withdrew into the undergrowth.

Retreating to his jeep, Hernandez cursed his bad luck. Made to run again; turned away when he was so close. Even so, it felt good to kill that meddling gringo. It was about time he was out of the way. But he regretted not killing the nun and the boy as well. They could identify him.

Hernandez drove his jeep back down off the mountain. As he replayed the killings in his mind, he realized his penis had become fully erect. It chafed pleasantly against his clothing. Was killing the only thing that could excite him now? He imagined capturing Bailey and killing her slowly. His organ throbbed and his mouth watered.

CHAPTER 39

BAILEY WAS PANIC-STRICKEN. She had to get out of this place. She looked for anything she could use as clothing. She found the fur robe she had slept in and some pieces of cloth. For sustenance she found a small bag of beans and some tortillas.

She fashioned a sarong from a piece of cloth and wrapped it around her waist, throwing the fur cloak over her shoulders. She discarded the black feathered skirt and the tooth necklace, disgusted by the touch of them. In her search she also came across a sceptre, a human skull fastened to the end of a staff. She shrank from it. Who would carry such a thing?

She found the rear entrance to the cueva and minutes later emerged into the sunlight. She felt a sense of relief to be away from that place. The morning was brilliant. She was standing on a rock outcropping overlooking a lush expanse of jungle. As far as the eye could see, the foliage extended like a vast green ocean. The air was full of the morning calls of a million birds. The same rays that had saved her life only minutes before warmed her now. She took deep breaths and finally stopped shuddering. She was alive.

Her painted skin was garish in the light. She would not be clean of that place until the physical evidence had been removed. She needed a bath.

In the selva, water was everywhere. It flowed in streams, rivers, and torrents, channelling the abundant rainfall to the lowlands. From where she stood, a waterfall could be heard in the distance, the cascade crashing against the rocks below.

Bailey followed the sound, seeking its source. She descended from the summit, following a track that seemed of recent origin. The trees had not yet regrown, and the way was visible. Overhead, howler monkeys set up their usual din of screeches and lamenting cries. They were unnerving to the ear, sounding like all the demons from Hell were about to ascend. But their protests were all show. When they broke into sight, they were exposed as furry little simians with etched faces and inquiring eyes. Bailey was happy to see them; so long as they were not alarmed, she was safe as well. They accompanied her down the path to a place where a stream poured from the cliffs above.

The waterfall dropped a hundred feet to a pool below. The basin was only fifty feet across, a small liquid oasis in a sea of jungle. The tall trees hid the sun; the sky was visible as a small square of blue directly over the falls. Bailey wasted no time in plunging in. There were no dangers in the waters of the selva. She dropped her garments on the bank and waded into the bone-chilling waters. The white pigment dissolved and swirled away in the current, and the pink of her skin re-emerged. The pasty whiteness left her arms and breasts; her nipples resumed their deeper tint, now erect in the chilly waters. Some areas needed to be scrubbed with sand before they gave up the last of the whitewash that had been her second skin.

She was about to wash her hair when she caught her reflection in the pool. A hairless creature stared back at her. She stopped and touched her fingers to the top of her head. From somewhere overhead came the screech of a large bird. The memories came flooding back. With staggering clarity, she recalled everything—the convent, her self-mutilation, the ceremony. She sat down with a splash.

Her initial response was disbelief—how could this have happened? How could she have done this to herself? Her scalp was covered in healing scars. Bristles stuck into her hand where her thick brown hair had once been. She remembered Hernandez and her attack on him. She clamped both hands to her head and began to rock back and forth.

She sat naked in the shallows for ten minutes, then twenty. Finally the chill of the waters broke into her thoughts; she shivered and rose from the pool. She could not sit here in the middle of the jungle feeling sorry for herself. Her head was clear, and her mind was more focused than it had been in some time.

And Ted was very much in her thoughts. She recalled the things she had said and the way she had behaved. Bailey needed to atone for many things; she needed to get back.

She dried herself and dressed as best she could in the rags and furs. She fashioned a turban to cover her damaged skin and to protect it from the sun. Placing her belongings into a bag slung over her shoulder, she set off down the jungle trail. The howler monkeys heralded her passage through the undergrowth.

It was a day later, just after dawn. Bailey had spent the night in the crook of a rubber tree and was stiff and sore. It had been uncomfortable but better than sleeping on the jungle floor.

She was lost. Without a compass she had spent an entire day walking in circles. She had ended up back at the waterfall where she had started. Today she would keep the sun on her left shoulder. One good day of travel should see her out of the forest. Her destination after that was unknown. She had to find Ted.

She ate some of the dried beans and adjusted the turban on her head. Ten minutes later she stood at a fork. Which one had she taken yesterday? She no longer remembered, and she could not see the sun through the trees. She chose a trail at random. A rattling noise in the distance brought her to a halt. After a minute the sound was repeated but only once. A sharp crack, it stood out from the sing song clatter of the jungle. A gunshot.

She ran towards the sound.

CHAPTER 40

Darkness. Hernandez with the gun. Miguel! No, no! The muzzle spitting fire, the searing blow to his abdomen that stopped his breath. The light faded and was gone. Deeper and deeper into blackness he tumbled. To sleep. To die.

A jaguar was eating him. Devouring his stomach, ripping at his entrails. The pain engulfed his innards where the beast ripped his flesh. No, there were no jaguars. They had gone away. It must be a dream. He was dead.

A ceiling, white plaster. Hands, faces. Sleep. Don't wake me. Return to darkness. The ceiling again. He saw faces from his life. Miguel, Marcos. Was this his coffin? These his mourners? Mind won't work, keeps slipping away, back into the dark.

The ceiling again. Now odours with the light—iodine and lavender. More faces and now voices too, calling to him. "Wake up, Ted. Ted, open your eyes." How could he do what they demanded? He was dead. The pain was worse than ever, his midriff alive with flames. He did not think it would be like this. His mouth was full of cotton wool, his brain stuffed with cobwebs. The vision of the white plastered ceiling came more frequently.

The dream ended, and he awoke in a room. Above his head the ceiling was cracked white plaster. There was a figure with him, cloaked in white. Was this an angel bending over him? But as his vision cleared, he recognized the woman as a nun. She looked into his eyes and hurried away. Within moments there was another face. This one smiled at him.

"Ted, don't try to talk," Magdalena said. "You have been shot. You nearly died."

Shot? When? His brain would not work. *Shot?* It came back. Hernandez, the camp. *Miguel!*

"Miguel?" He wanted to shout the question but it took several attempts to form the word. It came out as a hoarse whisper. The effort drove a lance of pain through his body.

"He's fine. Don't worry about him. He's just outside and will come to see you when you are feeling a little better. Don't try to move around. The bullet was deep, and we don't want the bleeding to start again."

She smiled at him. "You are a brave man. You saved your son's life."

He remembered. She did not understand. It had nothing to do with bravery. He wanted to tell her that it was not like that at all, but he did not know the words to express it. It was just that Miguel was about to be killed, and he had to save him. Bravery had nothing to do with it. Anyone would have done the same.

She had called Miguel his son. He mouthed the word several time silently. *His son.* He liked it. Exhausted, Ted closed his eyes and lapsed into sleep.

He awoke minutes or perhaps hours later. The memory came again. After only a glimpse of the white ceiling, he remembered. He was alive—somehow he had survived being shot. He wanted to see Miguel.

The boy was his first visitor. He was escorted in by Magdalena, who gave him strict instructions. "You may only stay five minutes. Don't ask him to talk—he is very weak."

Miguel was beaming. "I was afraid that you were dead. You have been sleeping for three days."

Ted made his mouth form words. They came out in a croak, and Miguel had to lean closer to hear. "What happened? How did I get here?"

"Hernandez attacked us. He killed Abelardo then tried to shoot me. You saved me."

"That's the last I remember," Ted said. Even the slight movement of his jaw drove waves of pain through his body, taking his breath away. Must be more careful.

Miguel took Ted's hand. The touch pleased him.

"After he shoots you, Hernandez was to kill me, and the sister too, I think. I was hit on the head with his gun and saw nothing. Then Marcos and Ricardo came, and Hernandez ran away. Sister Magdalena is nurse. She save you. After we carry you here, to convent.

"Bailey, she hear shots and come. She waits with me outside."

In spite of the pain, Ted had to know, "Is she here now? Can I see her?"

"No, Sister say that only me today. Tomorrow she will come." With that, the door opened and a stern-faced Magdalena showed Miguel out.

"You've had him talking, haven't you? For not obeying my orders, I have a punishment for you. The brass in the rectory needs polishing. Now off with you!"

The nun lifted Ted's coverings and examined his dressing. "He has been so worried; he's been driving us crazy until we knew whether you would live or die. We'll put him to work now and let him burn off some of his energy. He can come again when you are stronger. There will be others here to see you. Get some rest now."

"Live or die?" Ted considered the concept briefly before he returned to oblivion.

It was morning. The white plastered ceiling was brighter, and he could hear the birds saluting the day. From somewhere in the convent he smelled food cooking. He realized that he was very hungry. Ted felt better than he had the day before, although his midriff still pained him at the slightest movement.

He had a visitor. She was wearing a baseball cap. It took him a moment to recognize her. Bailey looked so different. The thick brown hair was gone and her face was thinner. He remembered the smile—he would never forget the full lips and the silver-grey eyes.

She held Ted's hand. "Hi. Welcome back. You scared me." Bailey did not remove her hand and continued to caress his skin. More than her appearance had changed. The delirium seemed to be gone. He smiled.

Ted was unable to form words. After all the worrying and searching, he could not think of what to say. He just continued to smile. A tear formed and ran down his cheek. He was happy.

"I heard the shot. I was lost in the jungle not far away. When I arrived,

Marcos was already there. It was terrible—we thought you were dead. I'm glad you're alive." She leaned over and kissed him on the lips.

Bailey pulled away. "I must go. Magdalena threatened me with purgatory if I tired you. We will have lots of time together—I'll come again tomorrow."

She gave him one of her best smiles. "Everything is going to be okay."

The next day he felt better again. Magdalena lifted the restriction on visitors and he had company most of the day. Miguel parked himself by the foot of Ted's bed and left only when shooed away by one of the nuns. The boy made no attempt to conceal his delight at Ted's return to health. He chattered away happily and provided the missing details of the aftermath of the shooting.

"Hernandez was to shoot all of us, but then there was a noise. First it sounded like something fierce, but then it was horses. Marcos and Ricardo came and Hernandez ran away."

"How did I get here?" asked Ted. "I have no memory of anything until I woke up here."

"Ricardo, he built a sling with poles, and he and Marcos carry you."

"All this way? How did they manage?"

"Magdalena, she said that you could not ride a horse, it would kill you. Marcos is very strong. I will be like him some day."

"Tell me about Bailey."

"She came soon after Marcos. When she saw what Hernandez had done, she cried. I think she likes you," Miguel said with a sly smile. "She held your hand for a long time."

"How does she seem?"

"Not like before. She much better now. But her hair is all gone. They say she cut it off."

Marcos and Ricardo arrived in the early morning. They were dressed for travel in broad hats and black denim and carried packs. They were subdued as they sat by Ted's side. Even Ricardo lacked his usual irreverent edge.

"You are tough, gringo," said Marcos. "But you were lucky to have Magdalena with you. Sadly, there was nothing she could do for Abelardo."

"You saved my life. Thank you, compadres." The two men nodded imperceptibly.

"What happened to Hernandez?"

"*Il bastardo!*" Ricardo said. "He is a coward. As soon as he heard us coming, he ran away. He had a jeep hidden by the trail. We do not know where he is now, but we will find him. He will pay for this."

"I have seen Bailey," Ted said. "She seems much better. What happened at the Jaguar's Temple?"

"I do not know, and she will not speak of it," said Marcos. "She appeared about half an hour after we found you. She was as you see her—the condition that afflicted her had vanished. I asked her where she had been but she did not answer. It is a mystery. But it is no secret that she cares for you, my friend. You should have seen how she behaved when we thought that you would not live. I would have such a woman mourn for me."

Marcos rose to his feet. He squeezed Ted's shoulder. "But now we must go. There are important matters in the wind. There is talk that I may be invited to Mexico City. It would be a great day for our cause. You will be in hospital for a while, but arrangements have been made. You will be well cared for."

Miguel stood in the doorway, looking after Marcos. He said solemnly, "The next time, I go with them."

Bailey had been waiting outside the door until the Zapatistas left. She met the men with a nod and a word of greeting as she came into the room.

The morning sun created a square of light in the middle of Ted's room. Bailey entered the room like a diva onto a stage. Ted would have applauded if he could. He could think of little else except her parting kiss from the day before. He wanted her to kiss him again.

Bailey's features seemed more pronounced—eyes darker, lips fuller. She was wearing a brightly coloured dress that showed her legs to advantage. Why would that be? It took him a moment to understand—she was doing this for him.

Ted let out a long breath. He liked the way she looked. He liked it very much.

The only jarring detail was the straw hat on Bailey's head. It was unbecoming only because of what it concealed.

The scent of her lavender perfume reached him from across the room. He recalled the odour from his time in oblivion.

"Bailey, come in. I like the dress. Sit down." Ted felt awkward in his speech. It was as if yesterday's small intimacy had changed everything.

"Hello, Ted. Hi, Miguel." She sat in the one empty chair, sweeping her skirt under her. It was a feminine gesture, natural, yet strangely provocative. Ted's eyes followed her every movement. An uneasy silence filled the room. Neither could begin. Miguel saved them.

"Señorita Bailey, you look beautiful today. I have never seen you look like a woman before."

The remark broke the tension and made them laugh. Ted stopped at the warning twinge from his chest. But it was enough—they both started talking at once.

"Ted, how are . . . "

"Bailey, I'm . . . "

"Sorry, you first . . . "

"No, you . . . "

"Ted . . . "

"You two are driving me crazy. Sister told me to polish the brass in the rectory. I will be back in a while." Miguel launched himself to his feet and was out the door.

Miguel's departure made them both uncomfortable. They sat in silence for a time before Ted was able to venture the first words. "Yesterday, I'm sorry my brain wouldn't make my mouth work."

"No, don't say that. I was happy that you could open your eyes."

There was a further uncomfortable silence before Ted could ask the next question. "Bailey, you seem better . . . From before you went to the convent, I mean. What happened to you?"

She rose and walked to the window, her back to him. "I was kidnapped, but I escaped." She stood looking out the window at nothing. Her voice had assumed the same distant note that he had heard many times before. Ted did not believe her. She might be better, but there was something more going on here. For the moment, Ted let it be. It felt good just to have her back.

There was a knock on the door. Bailey straightened her dress and adjusted her hat, although neither was in need of attention. She was acting like a teenager caught by her parents at some mischief. Ted could not imagine what had come over her. The knock was not repeated. The door opened and Magdalena came into the room.

Ted had known Magdalena only outside of the convent. She had been on a first-name-only basis and downplayed her role as Mother Superior. But here she was different. She was in charge—it showed in her manner of dress, her bearing, and her speech. The black and white habit with the broad collar signifying her office brooked no arguments. Her word in the convent was law.

Magdalena was her usual bundle of energy; she bustled about the room, plumping pillows that did not need attention, and rearranging the blinds at the same time as taking Ted's temperature. When she was satisfied that her personal touch had been imparted to the room, she got down to the purpose of her visit.

"I think that by tomorrow you will be well enough to travel. I have ordered an ambulance from the hospital in the morning."

"Why am I going to a hospital? I am feeling much better."

"You have little curiosity about your condition. The bullet lodged in the mass of muscle below your lungs. It did a good deal of damage. I was able to remove the bullet, but there was much bleeding. We have been treating you with sulpha to help prevent infection, but your injuries are more serious than we can deal with here. There has been blood in your urine and there may be internal damage. You need to be taken to Tuxtla to see a doctor."

Ted suddenly felt queasy. Bleeding inside? He had not considered he might still be in danger. After all, he had been feeling stronger every day. Bailey gave his hand a squeeze.

"There's nothing to worry about. I'll be coming with you."

The prospect of some time alone with Bailey lifted Ted's spirits, but he was exhausted from his visitors. He had a desperate need to sleep. His eyes closed while Magdalena and Bailey were discussing the details of the next day's journey.

CHAPTER 41

THE AMBULANCE ARRIVED IN THE early morning. Ted's condition had worsened overnight. He had not slept much and was feeling feverish. He had heard the horror stories of Mexican medicine and his imagination ran wild. Was he doomed to die slowly of infection, or be butchered by an incompetent surgeon? In the dark hours before sunrise, Ted played mind games, trying to convince himself the pain was only in his imagination. Nothing helped.

He was carried in a litter to the waiting vehicle. Magdalena and Bailey were at his side. They emerged from the shadows of the convent into the sunlit piazza where the ambulance was waiting. The driver was sitting with Miguel in the shade of a tree. He stood up and ground his cigarette butt under his heel.

"I have been telling him I should ride up front," Miguel said. "Tell him what a good driver I am, Ted."

"Run along, Miguel. And don't let him drive too fast now," Magdalena said. Ted smiled through the pain.

Magdalena saw Ted off with a blessing. She called Bailey to the side.

"My child, I have been watching you. While we waited to see if Ted would live, you visited the chapel often. You have learned how to pray again?"

Bailey seemed embarrassed at having been caught. She looked down without answering but nodded her head.

"Good. I thought so. Do not be ashamed—anyone can pray. Remember that sometimes when we pray, miracles can occur. Who is to say whether he would have lived without your prayers. Faith can be a great comfort to you in times of need."

"Thank you, Mother. I will try to remember."

The ride to the hospital was about forty miles, but from the rear of the enclosed ambulance they saw nothing of the surrounding countryside. Descending from the highlands, the vehicle bumped and rocked down steep grades on a rough gravel road. Hairpin turns separated the many switchbacks. The ambulance stopped frequently to avoid unknown hazards.

The interior was close and uncomfortable. Ted experienced each hole in the road as a jolt of pain. He was covered in a thin film of perspiration. He clenched his jaw and kept his eyes closed, willing the ordeal to be over. Bailey dabbed the moisture from his brow and kept up a soothing monologue.

"It's just a little further now. We'll be there any minute. You'll be fine."

After what seemed an eternity, they entered a paved roadway. Half an hour later the ambulance slowed, announcing their arrival in Tuxtla.

The rear doors to the ambulance opened directly into the hospital. A doctor met the ambulance and after a brief examination directed orderlies to take Ted to his room. He felt faintly lightheaded but made the effort to smile and assure Bailey that he was okay.

Ted overheard Miguel in conversation with their driver. "The next time I should drive the ambulance. I am a good driver, except for steep hills. There you will have to show me."

"I will let you drive as soon as you are tall enough to see over the wheel," the driver said. "See you later."

The hospital was a small stuccoed structure with interconnected hallways. They entered through the lobby, past food vendors and curio stalls, and into the patient wards. From his gurney, Ted saw only arched ceilings and a succession of bare electric bulbs. Characteristic hospital sounds—intercoms and hard heels clacking on linoleum floors—were replaced here by the creak of ancient wood under soft-soled shoes. There was a hubbub of voices and much activity. It sounded like a day at the market, with antiseptic smells mixed with the odour of live chickens.

Ted was moved into a stationary bed. His room was small with a rounded ceiling and double doors, looking over a plaza below. Its orientation insulated it from the commotion of the hallways. The windows were open and a fresh breeze cooled the room. The chamber had the feel of a bedroom in a private residence.

After his doubts about Mexican medicine, the accommodations were a pleasant surprise. With the trip over and a comfortable bed, he felt slightly improved. His chills had passed, and his last urine had been pink rather than brown.

When they were alone, Miguel announced he was leaving. Ted was taken by surprise.

"You say I should be a soldier," Miguel said. "It is time now. I must learn to shoot a gun so I can kill Hernandez."

Ted motioned Miguel to come closer. He struggled to sit up in bed. "You can't go. It's much too dangerous. You are not old enough."

He tried to think of reasons to make the boy stay. But Miguel was determined. The boy's jaw had the set it acquired when his mind was made up.

"Have you talked to Marcos about this?" Ted asked.

"*Si*, when he was at the convent. He said I could come as soon as you were safe at the hospital."

"How will you get to his camp? It's far from here."

"The ambulance driver is a Zapatista. He will take me most of the way."

There had been a time when Ted had encouraged Miguel to stay with Marcos. That seemed like a long time ago.

"Shouldn't you go back to Acteal instead? Rosa will be worried about you, and she needs your help."

"Rosa and I talked before we left. She knows it is time for me to be a man. Don't worry, I will see you again soon, and I will visit Rosa." He picked up his pack to leave. He touched Ted on the forearm. "Get well, compadre."

"Yes, compadre, and you take care. Do as Marcos says. . . ," Ted called after him. But Miguel was already sprinting down the hallway, the sound of his footsteps fading quickly away.

They experienced another interlude of awkward silence. Bailey busied herself opening their bags and sliding clothing into drawers.

"He will be fine," she said. She was folding a towel and facing the other way. "Miguel can look after himself, and I don't think Marcos will expose him to any danger. He likes the boy."

"I hope you're right," Ted said. "I didn't expect to be this worried."

"You'll see him again soon enough," Bailey said. "You'll only be in hospital for about a week. I am going to be your nurse."

Nurse? This was the first he had heard of this. He was tired from the journey and wanted to rest but this announcement brought him wide awake. He did not want her to nurse him.

"Why you? Doesn't the hospital have staff?"

"That's just it—it doesn't. The hospital has doctors and some nurses, but patients are responsible for their own housekeeping, food, and some medicine. That's why there are extra beds in the rooms. Family members move in to provide care for sick relatives."

There was an extra bed in the room. He only now understood its significance. A week in the same small room with Bailey. If only . . . Even so, the prospect pleased him.

"Are we safe?" asked Ted. "What if Hernandez finds out we're here?"

"Marcos has sent two of his men to stand guard. There will be someone outside the door at all times. And you're here under an assumed name—for the next week you are Señor Diaz, a businessman from San Cristobal."

Doctor Alvarez arrived within the hour. He was an earnest young man with short hair and thick-rimmed glasses, dressed in surgical scrubs with a stethoscope around his neck. He exuded an air of busy competence. He examined Ted's wound, wrote something in a chart, and ordered an x-ray.

Again Ted was wheeled through the hospital but this time with Bailey pushing. Dr. Alvarez was back almost as soon as the procedure was completed.

"Señor Diaz, the surgery is not complicated, but there will be some bleeding. The bullet passed through the muscle, just below your lungs. You are lucky to be alive."

He traced his finger along Ted's abdomen. "You see the bullet struck you here. But it was a small calibre. It did not damage any organs, and then it lodged here."

"What about the blood in my urine?" Ted asked. He had a good feeling about this doctor.

"That is why we perform surgery. It is probably just a nick of the bladder, and if so, we can repair it easily. We operate first thing in the morning."

"How will I pay you?"

"Don't worry, Señor Diaz," Alvarez said, pronouncing the name deliberately, "it is already taken care of. Marcos and I, we have a little understanding." He gave an abbreviated version of the Zapatista salute, turned, and left the room.

The surgery was a success. Alvarez was proven to be correct in his diagnosis. He visited Ted and gave him the good news.

"Five days, a week at most in hospital, and you will be fine," Alvarez said. "There was some bleeding and we need to guard against infection. It will be a while before you can ride a horse, but most other activities are okay as soon as you can tolerate them. I'll check on you once a day, but for now just take it easy. With such a pretty nurse you should have a pleasant stay." He winked at Bailey and was on his way to his next patient.

Ted felt better almost immediately. Half of the pain had been in not knowing what was wrong and imagining the worst. Now that he had been told he would recover, he planned to do so quickly.

"Here, roll over, I need to change the dressing," Bailey said. It was the second day after surgery, and Ted was now able to move without undue pain. He had been pushing himself. Since the first day, he had refused the chamber pot and had made his way to the washroom without assistance.

"That looks much better today," she said. "How does it feel?"

"Better, much better," he said. "Here, I can do that myself."

"Just stay still," she said, dabbing at the incision. Her fingers were cool against his skin. He drifted in her touch.

Bailey was his nurse, but theirs was like no professional relationship Ted had ever experienced. She tended his dressing, slept in the adjoining cot, and arranged for all of their daily needs and did so without any outward indication that anything had changed between them. But things had changed, and Ted felt it in every touch, every movement.

Although the relationship had not been defined, Ted knew exactly how he felt. He could not take his eyes off of her when she walked across the room; he listened for her breathing at night. When she left the room on an errand, he counted the minutes until she returned. He ached for her touch—her fingers on his skin felt like ice and fire all at the same time. He longed to touch her, to kiss her; he imagined making love to her. Did she feel the same way? He hoped so.

Most times it was hard to remember that he was in a hospital at all. There was none of the usual hustle and bustle. No visits from nurses, orderlies, or social workers. It seemed that every patient's well-being was left to their family. The rooms were like small private residences, into which visitors entered only with permission. The sounds of children at play came from the hallways, and cooking smells filled the air. Once a day Dr. Alvarez would arrive, announcing his presence by a knock on the door. He would give Ted an antibiotic, check his wound, provide words of encouragement, and then depart. For the rest of the time, he and Bailey were alone.

They had long conversations but talked mainly of unimportant things. The subjects were as irrelevant as the words they spoke. The real communication was in the silences. But even so, some topics remained out of bounds. Bailey bristled at any mention of Acteal. On one occasion, Ted started to describe the experiences he had there with Miguel. Bailey got up without a word and left the room.

Ted knew enough not to ask again how Bailey came to be lost in the jungle, or what had happened at the Jaguar's Temple. She'd lied to him once. He had no doubt she would do so again. There were still secrets that Bailey was not prepared to share.

He chanced only one inquiry. There was an issue that had nagged at him since Magdalena had raised it. He waited until Bailey was in a particularly good mood—she had just won a hand of cards.

"You now owe me twenty-five pesos. With that and the money I won yesterday, I'll soon retire a rich woman."

"Do you mind if I ask you a question?" Ted asked. "There was something that Magdalena told me . . . "

"What's that?" She levelled her eyes at him. Her smile faded.

Ted should have heeded the warning but instead he blundered on. The last of her good humour drained from her face.

"She told me that you had a baby soon after you left Mexico."

"That's a goddamned lie." Her jaw was trembling.

"Bailey. . . ?"

"We have nothing more to talk about." She dumped the cards onto the floor. She slammed the door as she left the room.

Bailey did not return until the next morning, and then came bearing his breakfast. She behaved as if nothing had happened. No explanations were given, and Ted did not broach the subject again.

Ted told himself this whole situation did not make sense. He knew it could not continue for very long. They were living together in a hospital room, and yet were unable to discuss the events that brought them here. Bailey never even alluded to the fact they were in Mexico. There was no mention of what they would do when Ted was released—where they would go or how they would escape. On the other hand, between them, things were good. For the most part, Bailey seemed to be happy, as happy as Ted had ever seen her.

Through it all, time took on a comfortable pattern. The hours were filled by rambling discussions that did not suffer from their lack of depth. It was as if they had just met, and were discovering each other for the first time. They talked of books, food, sports, art—every subject imaginable except Mexico.

"What's your favourite Beatle's song?" he asked.

"'Lady Madonna.'"

"I knew it. Guess mine."

"It's probably 'Hey Jude.'"

"Have you been reading my mind? What else do you know about me?"

They found they were alike in many ways. They shared similar tastes and held the same views on many issues—wine (red from Australia), art (the Impressionists; Renoir in particular), food (Italian), and even baseball (anyone but the Yankees.)

The pauses in their conversations spoke volumes. They could communicate through nothing more than a look. They would sit quietly for hours without speaking. Ted remembered the sense of connection he felt the first time they met. It had not been his imagination.

On the fourth day after surgery, Bailey brought a large bowl of steaming water to the room. She set it beside Ted's bed and began to peel back his bed covers.

"What do you think you're doing?" Ted pulled the covers back over his chest.

"It's time for a sponge bath. Just lie still."

"No, that's all right. I'll do it myself," he said. "Just wait outside."

"Stop being so sensitive." She pulled the covers down again. "And besides, it's in my job description. Just relax."

There was a husky burr in her voice that stopped any further protest. Ted relented and closed his eyes. He lay back on the bed, leaving his body to report the progress of the bath.

She unbuttoned his gown to the waist and began to wipe his head and upper chest. The sponge moved in a circular motion, stimulating and warming the skin. He was lulled by the sensation and relaxed to her touch. The sponge dipped and dived, defining the contours of his face, washing his eyes, his nose, and his lips. Down to the shoulders, into the armpits, carefully skirting the dressing over the wound, Bailey hummed as she worked, a tuneless but soothing rhapsody. Ted floated in the moment.

She lifted the bottom of his gown and folded it over his midriff. He was naked except for the cloth folded over his groin. He felt the roughness of the sheet through the skin of his penis. Was he becoming aroused? He did not dare to move, or to open his eyes.

She started with the extremities, and washed the toes on each foot. The cloth slid languorously between his digits, sending shivers of pleasure up his legs to his groin. He breathed slowly through his mouth trying to recall the feeling of a cold shower. He could visualize the tenting of his sheet.

Bailey gave no indication that anything was amiss. She continued to work her way up his legs. His knees, then his thighs felt the delicious swirl of the warm touch.

Finally she touched him. It was only a pass of the sponge as she wiped his lower belly below the gown. The fabric no more than touched the end of his penis. A low gasp escaped his lips, an involuntary escape of air. The movement of the sponge stopped, as did her humming.

"Sorry, I didn't mean to . . . " she said.

"That's okay. I like it."

"You better finish the rest yourself," Bailey said. She dropped the sponge on his chest and rearranged the sheet across his legs. She left the room on an invented errand, leaving Ted to finish washing. On her return she said little. They spent the rest of the evening in relative silence.

The tension was palpable. The air was so thick they could barely make eye contact.

That night Ted lay awake for hours. He could hear Bailey's breathing. It was shallow and uneven—she was not asleep. Was she thinking of him as well? For the hundredth time, he thought of making love to her. His mind pictured an unhurried, warm, and loving union.

The room was illuminated by indirect light from the courtyard below, leaving the chamber bright but without colour. He heard her sigh and the bedclothes rustling. Bare feet padded on the wooden floor, and all at once she was with him. The cool warmth of her naked body stretched against his skin.

"Be still," she whispered in his ear. "Leave this to me."

He was instantly aroused.

"I can't do much to help," he said. Ted had an overwhelming fear he could not perform. What would she think of him if . . .

She pressed him back on the bed, removing the covers from his body.

"I said, be still. Leave this to me," she said, her voice husky.

She knelt over him, supporting her full weight on her arms. She slid her body up his, brushing her breasts against the full length of his chest.

"Touch me," she said.

Bailey arched her back, filling his vision with the roundness of her breasts. She pressed a nipple to his mouth. Ted took the hardening bud in his lips, teasing the tip with his tongue. She moaned in response.

"Touch me," she said.

His hands explored her smooth, firm flesh, finally probing between her legs. She was already moist.

"Yes," she said. "Like that, yes. Touch me there."

The lovemaking was all of her design. Ted was a willing but limited partner. She gave the instructions and he followed. It was not at all like he had imagined. Bailey was like moving fire against his skin. She moved up his prone body, avoiding his wound, and positioned her thighs astride his head. She lowered herself to his lips.

"There, kiss me there."

Bailey made noises deep in her throat, little cries of pleasure. "Yes, there. Just there."

She moved her hips, first up and down and then side to side, directing the attention of his mouth with the movements of her body. She ground herself onto his lips and tongue.

She reached back and cupped his penis in the palm of her hand. His flesh burned with her touch.

"I want you now," she said. She pulled away and slid down Ted's torso until they were face to face. She kissed him once on the mouth. Sitting upright, she straddled his hips and guided his penis inside her.

She sat above him in the semi-darkness. Light from the window played across her body. Ted covered one breast with each hand, caressing the nipples with his palms.

She moaned in response.

"You're beautiful," he said.

"No, don't say that. Tell me you want me to fuck you."

"Fuck me, Bailey. Fuck me, please."

She raised herself until they almost parted, then lowered her hips, burying him completely—long languid strokes, each one making Ted feel he would melt from the heat. She quickened her pace, and drove against him faster and harder. Ted was lost in the sensation of his penis moving inside her. She was sitting upright, perspiration running between her breasts, ramming her hips against him. Their union made a slapping sound, audible even over the roar of his breath and blood rushing in his ears.

She shuddered and froze. They clung together, and their breathing reached a crescendo.

The entire building seemed to shudder. *Never before, never before like this.*

"You okay?" She kissed him on the lips. "I didn't hurt you?"

"I think you might have killed me. But don't take that as a complaint."

After a time, she rose quietly from the bed. Ted lay in a warm and languid stupor. It had been like a dream, like some out-of-body experience. Sex had never been like that, not even in his imagination. Completely drained, he slid into a warm slumber of pleasant dreams.

The next morning Ted woke as if emerging from a trance. It took an instant to summon up the memory of the night before and to realize it had really happened. For a few minutes he simply lay there, not wanting to open his eyes. Behind his eyelids he could visualize the way she had looked, her body above him, straddling his hips. He wanted to hold onto that vision, to burn it into his memory and have it always.

It had not been at all like he had imagined. He had expected a warm romantic interlude. Bailey had been carnal, almost savage. Still, it had been wonderful. He wanted to tell her so.

Bailey was busying herself in the washroom, and it was a few moments before she appeared.

"Hi there. You look beautiful this morning." Ted gave her his best smile.

The smile was returned but without enthusiasm. Her reply was a toneless, "Good morning."

"Come here," he said. "We should talk."

"No, not now. There are things I have to do this morning." Her voice seemed tight.

"Is this about last night?" he asked. "There's nothing to be embarrassed about. I wanted to do that as much as you."

"No, it's not that," she said. "The sex was great. It's just been a long time." She paused looking down at her bag. "I didn't plan that you know. It just happened." She turned away without making eye contact. She picked up her bag to leave.

"Planned or not, it was great . . . I love you," he said. The words hung in the air.

"Don't say that! Don't even think it!" Bailey had her back to him. She continued walking towards the door.

"What?"

"Don't you get it?" Bailey whirled to face him. "There is no love in this world for me. Not from you, not from anyone!"

"What's wrong? I thought last night you felt the same."

"Is that it? Because some woman makes love to you, then you own her?" Her face was a hot mask.

"No, not at all. You've got it all wrong."

"Look, Ted, let's forget about last night and about what you just said. You'll be out of here tomorrow. I'm fine now, so you can go back to Canada and get on with your life. Now excuse me. I've got some things to get at the market." She left without looking back.

Ted sat alone in the sunlit room. He did not know what to think or what to do.

CHAPTER 42

BAILEY HAD DRESSED IN HER USUAL ATTIRE of slacks and open blouse, topped by the mandatory straw hat. Examining herself in the mirror, she saw that the scabs on her head had healed and the hair was growing back nicely. In a few more weeks there would be enough to comb and form into some kind of style. *Good!* She was sick and tired of the damned hat. Bailey donned a pair of dark sunglasses to complete her ensemble.

She had to get out of here—she needed time to think. Too late. He was up. He wanted to talk. That big smile. *Carry it off, Bailey, just for a few minutes. Don't let him see what you're thinking. Don't say it, please don't say it!*

Damn, he said it. "I love you."

That smile, that puppy dog look. *Couldn't he leave well enough alone? Tell him what you think.* "I'm out of here," she said, slamming the door. The last thing she saw was the bewildered look on his face.

Bailey stormed out of the hospital and was almost in the town square before she stopped to catch her breath. *What do I think I'm doing? What had that been about last night?* She stopped into a cantina and ordered coffee. She toyed with her cup.

She had not lied to Ted about last night. It had not been planned. That in itself was something new. Sex was usually an orchestrated event. She used it as a kind of currency, a commodity with which to pay her debts or to get the things she needed. Sometimes the offer of sex had been enough. It had worked with Fuentes, Marcos, even Hernandez.

Sex for sale. So what did it make her? She did not care—that was just who she was.

There was no way she could get involved any further with Ted. It had already gone too far. She had slept with him. Slept with him—hell, she had practically killed him. What did she think she was doing? Playing some kind of game, that she was normal, that everything was all right? It was only a matter of time before she plunged again into the abyss. There was nothing else to do—she had to get out now. Otherwise, she would destroy Ted too.

She pulled a piece of paper from her bag and wrote a short note. It was terse and said much less than she felt, but it had to be done. In it she told Ted that she was not coming back, that she needed time to herself. It made no promises, and there were no hints of deeper feelings. Bailey hated to write it; she knew how he would feel when he read it. But it was for the best. She folded the paper, addressed it to Señor Diaz at the hospital, and paid her waiter to have it delivered. Bailey went on her way.

She had expected writing the note would put an end to things, but it failed to have that effect. She didn't feel relieved—if anything she felt worse. It was not over. As she picked her way listlessly through the market, she continued to think of Ted. Last night had been different. Things had changed; there was no point in denying it. Once she would have made love to him and considered it part of a bargain, his payment for rescuing her. But it had not been like that at all.

It had started with the sponge bath. Maybe even before that, she had felt the tension between them. It had been only a matter of time. The bath was an excuse. She used the pretence that it was one of her duties. That was not the real reason. She had wanted to do it; she had wanted to touch him, touch him all over. It had been an amazing experience, watching him with his eyes closed, enjoying the sensation, his erection growing under the bedclothes. It was no accident when she had finally touched his penis. His gasp had muffled her own intake of breath. That night she had to have him. One moment she was lying in bed waiting for sleep to come, and the next she was naked, making love.

It had been another of her reckless acts. They could easily have ripped out all his stitches. But that had been part of the thrill of it. He was on his back, barely able to move. She had been on top, in control. It was fantastic. Her orgasm had been so intense, there had been nothing like it since . . . since she made love to Ernesto that last day in Acteal. That must have been what had scared her.

Insight came to her in a flash. What a fool she had been! She was running away at the very moment she should be staying. What had she been afraid of? Was it commitment, or that Ted would get too close to her past? Whatever the reason, it was not a good one.

That damned note. Why did she write it? What must he think of her now?

She would make it up to him. Apologies were not enough, but she hoped he would understand. It was time she stopped lying, both to Ted and to herself. She was already at the market—her impulse was to buy them something nice to eat and buy a present for Ted. Everything would be all right. Bailey felt both happy and foolish at the same time.

Tuxtla was a trading town, its market large and lively. The entire plaza of the old city was filled with rows and rows of stalls. People shoved and shouted, vigorously negotiating prices. Bailey pushed her way through the crowd. She had a smile on her lips.

The Day of the Dead was approaching and the market was busier than usual. Vendors sold sugared figurines shaped into tiny skulls and skeletons. Children begged their mothers for the ghoulish treats. No one seemed concerned by the bizarre imagery. In adjoining stalls, other merchants sold religious artifacts—crosses and flowers fashioned into wreaths.

Bailey wandered from stall to stall, examining articles and chatting to the vendors. She had decided on a shirt for Ted, something he could wear when he left the hospital. She fixed on one in a smooth blue silk—he would like that. After some ritual haggling and the exchange of a few pesos, the shirt was wrapped and in her bag. Bailey next visited the food stalls, looking over the cooked specialities. In the midst of making her purchase, she looked up. She had a premonition that someone was watching her.

He was three stalls away, separated from her by dozens of people. His back was to her, and all she could see was that he was tall and dark-haired. He turned as if sensing someone was behind him. His cheeks were sallow, his moustache carefully groomed. His was the face that haunted her dreams—Emiliano Hernandez.

He had seen her. A flash of recognition crossed his face. Hernandez scowled and shouted, the words inaudible over the noise of the crowd. He seemed to have others with him. He was directing, pointing at her. Bailey dropped her parcel and ran, racing headlong through the market, knocking over baskets and trays. Behind her she heard shouts of anger and surprise. Her mind reeled. How could he have found her? People were in her way, blocking the aisles between the stalls.

Bailey crashed into a man, sending him sprawling. She leapt over him and found an open path. She was getting away, increasing the distance from her pursuers. She heard cursing in her wake. The edge of the market was close now, the hospital not far beyond. There was safety there—Marcos' men and Ted. A man running beside her now, one row of stalls over. He called for her to stop. A clay pot exploded beside her head.

The gunshot brought screams. There were cries of panic as people dove for cover. Tables were overturned, baskets of vegetables were strewn on the ground. It became harder to run, too many people in the way. She ducked under a table piled with clothes and then scrambled on her knees from stall to stall. Bailey could no longer see any pursuers. Perhaps they had lost her. She hid under a vegetable cart and could see nothing but legs. People rushed everywhere. In the distance a siren sounded. She must move. The police would not protect her.

She was now near the edge of the market. Only one row of stalls separated her from the alleys of the city and safety. Again she rose and ran. Behind her she heard angry shouts, but she had a lead. They were not as close. Bailey was racing for the first buildings of the old city, not far away now.

She was almost there. A narrow alley ahead. Down that alley and she would be safe. More gunshots, but they were further away. Bullets whizzed above her head. A few more yards. Faster, faster. Her heart hammered; her lungs gasped for air. Twenty feet . . . ten . . . Her feet went out beneath her and she fell, sprawling in the dust. A man stepped out of the shadows. Someone was on her from behind; strong hands gripped her arms. She felt a pinch of steel to her neck and an explosion of pain at the back of her head. And then darkness.

———

Hernandez was overjoyed at his good fortune. He still had contacts, and he had heard that the gringo was still alive. They told him of his survival and transportation by ambulance. The news had maddened him. Inquiries had been made at the hospitals, but there was no sign of a Señor Somerville. He ordered his men to keep looking.

His encounter with Bailey was more than luck. His men had been watching the square for days with no results. That morning he had been present as well, supervising the purchase of supplies. Suddenly, there she was, four stalls away. Her appearance had changed; she was wearing dark glasses and a broad straw hat, but he would have recognized her anywhere. For a brief moment it had looked like she might escape, but there were too many of them. She had been captured without serious injury.

Now that he had her, things would be perfect. There was a little drama he wanted to re-enact. For it he would need a cast of players, her friend Ted for one. And he would again enlist the people of Acteal. But they were to be bit players. Their only role would be to die.

Hernandez realized that he was hard again. This would be so sweet.

CHAPTER 43

AT FIRST TED WAS MORE ANGRY than worried. This slamming out of rooms whenever she didn't like something was becoming an annoying habit. But he simply could not wait for her to return. Fifteen minutes later he was dressed.

He called for one of the Zapatista guards outside his door. "Juan, I'm going out."

"You should stay inside, señor. Is dangerous. There are many men in the square."

"I don't care," Ted said. "I'm going to look for Bailey. You can stay here if you like."

"No, we come with you," said the young Zapatista. "Lean on my arm."

The three men emerged from the alleyway on the edge of the market. Ted was moving awkwardly, taking care with each step. The Zapatistas were on either side of him, ready to support him if he stumbled, their eyes scanning the crowd.

"There are too many people here, señor. We will never find her."

"Keep looking," Ted said. "She is here somewhere."

There was sudden chaos on the far side of the market. People were running, knocking into stalls and overturning tables. The sound of angry cries was audible over the hubbub of the crowd. The distance was too great to make out any details.

"Come on, let's get over there," Ted said.

"Wait, señor . . . " the Zapatista said.

Ted pushed into the crowd. His progress was blocked at every turn; the market was thronged and it was impossible to travel with any speed. He pushed several people to the side, to cries of protest.

The first gunshot created pandemonium. Screams rose all around him. Where people had before been merely in his way, now they were charging towards him. It was impossible to move towards the source of the sound. Ted was knocked from his feet and lay against the wall of a vegetable stall. Sirens sounded from several directions.

"Come, señor, we must go!" One of the Zapatistas pulled Ted to his feet and half carried him towards the edge of the crowd.

"Stop, stop! I need to go back there." He struggled to escape from the man's grasp. "Bailey's out there somewhere. She may be in trouble."

The Zapatistas ignored his protests and pushed through the crowd with Ted between them. Five minutes later they were back in the hospital room.

Ted was furious and railed at his guards. "Don't you understand. I have to go back, I have to . . . "

He spied the note on his bed. It had not been there when he left.

It was short and to the point. She was not coming back; there was to be nothing more between them. Good luck and goodbye was all it said. Ted's shoulders sagged. The Zapatistas stood silently watching him.

"I'm sorry," Ted said. "I won't be needing you anymore today." He closed the door behind the men as they left the room.

He sat the rest of the day brooding. He had been so afraid that something had happened to her, but now . . . He re-read the note for the hundredth time. What had gone wrong? It was when he had said, "I love you." He could still picture the look on her face in response. When would he ever learn? Some things with Bailey were just not that easy.

He slept poorly, the empty bed across the room a constant reminder that she was gone. More than just gone—this time he had a feeling she was not coming back.

The next morning the doctor removed Ted's sutures and discharged him from hospital. He was reluctant to leave. He held to the flickering hope that any minute she might walk back in the door, bearing his breakfast, and that this would all be forgotten. But he was just fooling himself. If she wanted to find him, she would know where to look. He was going back to Acteal.

By noon Ted was ready to leave. He needed a new shirt and had one of the guards make a purchase for him at the market. On a whim he asked the man to look for a blue one.

They travelled in an open jeep. After the days of confinement, the sun on Ted's face and the warm breeze whipping against his skin helped to lift his spirits. On such a beautiful day it was hard to feel sorry for himself, but still he would have gladly traded this ride for another trip in an ambulance with Bailey.

They passed miles of golden fields ripening in the sun. The land looked rich—there would be a fine harvest in Chiapas. Strangely, not all the fields were verdant. Some of the land looked abandoned. Fences were falling down and the sod was unbroken. He thought this peculiar—the neglected land looked much the same as the cultivated acreage. Ted asked his companions for an explanation.

Of the Zapatistas, Juan was the more talkative. "This land, it belongs to the hacendado. They do not need the land or the crops it can produce. The owners live in Mexico City, some even in America. They just leave the land to rot."

"Why don't they sell it?" Ted asked. "Couldn't this land be used to feed the campesinos?"

His companions broke into bitter laughter. "Ha, it seems the gringo suddenly understands the Revolution!"

Juan gestured across the planted fields up onto the mountainside. "See over there. Those are the fields left to the campesinos."

In the distance Ted could make out slopes so steep and rocky they could hardly be described as fields. Crops were planted on hillsides that rose directly upwards. Irrigation was impossible and the scrawny plants were wilted and parched. Rough shacks adjoined the small holdings. Large numbers of women and children were working the fields.

"You see, gringo, this is what it is all about. The hacendado owns most of the good land, but they don't use it. But they will not give it up, because land is power. So the campesinos are left to farm dirt and rocks that would not even feed a goat."

"So you intend to take back the land by force?" Ted asked.

"*Si*, and with blood if we must. Even if we die in the struggle, it is better that way than to starve a little at a time."

Ted's arrival at Acteal was bittersweet. It felt good to be home (he thought of it as his village now), but strange not to find Miguel waiting for him. He met Rosa at the door to her house, and she embraced him. There were tears in her eyes.

"I feared you were dead," she said. "The last word we had was that you were to be taken to the hospital for surgery. There has been no news. I have been worried." Regaining her reserve, she stepped back from the contact.

"Where is Miguel?" Rosa asked. "I thought that he was with you."

"Miguel has gone to join Marcos. He told me that you already knew. There was nothing I could do to stop him."

The surprised look on Rosa's face told him she had known nothing of the boy's plans.

"That little brat," Ted said. "Wait till I catch him."

The antidote to depression was work, and as soon as Ted was able, Rosa had him busy in her garden. He was not capable of heavy labour, but he was fit for weeding, and he spent long days on his knees among the beans. It helped to keep busy. The perspiration rolled off his back in the hot sun, and his hands were occupied with the repetitious ripping of the weeds. The work dulled the ache, but it also gave him time to think.

A thousand doubts crowded his mind. What should he have done differently? Should he have confronted her, told her that he knew she was lying, demanded the truth about Acteal? Had he backed off too quickly when she refused to talk about her baby? Or should he have kept his feelings hidden? He bent to his work with a will, the blisters that formed on his hands the punishment for his stupidity.

CHAPTER 44

MIGUEL STOOD BEFORE MARCOS for inspection. He was proud of his new regalia—the black denim shirt and pants that served as the uniform of the Zapatistas. His most ardent wish was to be given a gun, even an old one. He hoped this was why he had been summoned to the leader's private quarters.

"You look very fine in your uniform, Miguel," said Marcos. "Although you will have to grow into it a little." The clothes had been cut for an adult and on the boy's slight frame, the shoulders sagged halfway down his arms and the cuffs were rolled up over his boots.

"Thank you, Subcomandante. When can I shoot a gun?"

"And what would you do with a gun, little one?" Marcos asked.

"Kill Hernandez of course, Subcomandante. He murdered my friend Abelardo, and I have sworn revenge."

"Well, well, so you are to have revenge? I should tell you about this thing, revenge. If everyone should kill to settle every wrong, soon there would be no more people left."

"Yes, but . . . "

"Enough, I have a special assignment for you. It is something that only you can do. But it will mean not wearing your uniform for a while. You will have to go back to your old clothes."

Miguel's face fell. He had so hoped to carry a gun. And now he was being asked to give up his fine new uniform. This was a blow. His old street clothes were little more than rags, good enough to run through the streets of Chihuahua, but he could not think why he should wear them now.

Miguel straightened his shoulders and did his best to be a soldier.

"*Si*, Subcomandante. I will do as you say."

"Come over here," said Marcos. He unrolled a map on his desk. "Let me show you exactly what I want you to do. See here, this is the city of Tuxtla . . . "

"*Si*," Miguel peered at the map, alive with interest.

"And this is the way . . . "

Marcos huddled with the young boy, speaking earnestly and drawing diagrams on the dusty surface. Miguel nodded his head. "*Si*, I can do that. And then what do I do?"

Miguel's eyes widened at the response. "A pigeon? You would let me take one of your birds?"

Marcos handed Miguel a small cage containing a single pigeon. "Take good care of him, little one."

Only a soldier on an enterprise of great importance would be trusted with one of the carrier pigeons. There was no more reluctance on Miguel's part. He stood to attention and delivered a crisp salute before leaving.

Marcos had one more order, "When you get back to the camp, tell Ricardo I would like to see him for a moment."

"*Si*, Subcomandante." The boy saluted again.

CHAPTER 45

BAILEY AWOKE TO INKY BLACKNESS. She was bound, her wrists tied behind her back, but her head was bare. She was in a dark room, a closet, or perhaps a cave. The ground beneath her was cool and damp. A soft breeze carried the odours of mould and decay. With a sick feeling she realized she was in an underground cave.

She tested her bonds—they were made of thick twine tied with tight knots. It was impossible to loosen them even a little. Any movement made the cords even tighter, and they dug painfully into her skin. After a few minutes of struggle, she was covered in perspiration but had made no progress. There was no use. She waited in the dark, dreading what lay in store for her.

Bailey had no memory of anything after she was captured in Tuxtla, but she remembered all too well who had been in the market. She was in Hernandez' power. She steeled her mind, trying to stop her imagination from running wild.

Her vision adjusted to the darkness, and she was able to distinguish her surroundings. This underground cave was similar to the one that Marcos used as his headquarters, but much smaller. The chamber showed signs of recent use. Empty bottles and tins littered the floor. She caught the stench of rotting garbage. Dim light filtered through a passageway. Bailey could hear men talking, but distance and the walls of the cave muffled the words. The voices were getting louder now, the words more distinct. Someone was coming. She closed her eyes.

Heavy boots tramped on the stone floor as several men entered the room. The kerosene of their torches added a pungent aroma to the air. Someone kicked her in the ribs, and she gasped for breath.

"Ah, she is awake. Open your eyes, bitch. Open them before I peel off your eyelids."

Bailey recognized Hernandez' voice. He was standing two paces away holding a torch over his head. There were two pistoleros with him. She could smell alcohol on their breath.

"What do you want with me? Why am I here?" Her words were a croak.

Hernandez reached out and grabbed her face. He squeezed her cheeks between his thumb and his fingers and brought his face very close to hers. She felt a sharp pain where he held her, but it was his words that made her blood run cold.

"Finally you are afraid. Good, you should be. I brought you here to kill you." His voice was a snake's hiss; spittle ran from the corner of his mouth. The blast of his tequila-scented breath made her want to gag.

"And not only you. I am going to kill everyone you care about. I have been planning your death for a long time and it will not come easily. Your friend Ted, he too will die. I have already killed him twice and still he lives; he is like a cat with so many lives. But this is his last. I will make him watch while I set my men upon you. As you know, my pistoleros have a taste for white women. After they have had their fill of you, they will start to cut off little pieces. You are not the only one who can use a knife. They will start with little things—a finger, a toe, an ear. But soon they will take off larger pieces—a foot, an arm, perhaps a breast. And we have drugs to ensure that you will be awake for every second of it. In the end you will beg me to kill you, beg as you have never before. But first we go back to Acteal . . . " Hernandez' face was flushed. His eyes bulged with insane fury. His two companions stared off into the distance.

Bailey closed her eyes to shut out Hernandez' face. Her body tensed in anticipation of the agonies to come. Phantom pains shot through her limbs as he described her dismemberment.

And she was to be taken back to Acteal. It would happen there. Just like it had once before. She was no longer listening. The floor beneath her was no longer solid; the air shimmered. Hernandez ranted on, but his words were no longer clear. His mantra, "Kill you, kill you, kill you, kill . . . " were the last things she heard before she slipped away.

Bailey felt something stirring within her. Something deep inside was coming to the surface. She was no longer a prisoner in the cave—she had gone somewhere else in her mind.

Bailey opened her eyes. It was the same cave but another time. Soldiers and pistoleros surrounded her. They were lounging against the cave walls, throwing dice and drinking from bottles of liquor. Further back in the cave there were gunshots. The smell of burnt gunpowder came to her nose. There was a scream. A man was begging for mercy. A shot was fired and the voice was stilled.

Bailey was wrapped in a sheet. She was naked beneath it. Her face hurt where she had been slapped, and her lip was split and bleeding. She tasted blood in her mouth. What was she doing here? More shots, another scream. She remembered now.

They had brought her in a jeep. The soldiers were killing the men. They were killing Ernesto.

"Stop!" she cried. "Don't do this! No! No!" The shooting continued. Her mind ran out of words, and she simply screamed in protest.

There was a soldier in front of her. He slapped her. "Quiet, bitch, or you will be next!" Her face stung with the sudden pain.

They had not tied her—Bailey's arms and legs were free. She sprang to her feet and ran for the entrance. Strong hands caught her. They pulled her to the floor. She felt the weight of a man on top of her, pressing her into the ground. Her coverings were torn away, and she was exposed to the men who held her down. She felt hands on her buttocks, others squeezing her breasts. She screamed at the sudden pain between her legs. Bailey writhed in their grasp, but they were too strong.

A gunshot was fired at close range, deafening in the enclosed space. Rock dust and small pebbles dislodged from the cavern ceiling rained down, making it difficult to see. Everything stopped—the groping hands withdrew. The pistoleros choked and coughed on the polluted air.

Hernandez was holding a pistol. "Stop this! We still have use for this one. Afterwards, if you have the energy, you can have her then. You can screw her to death if you want. But for now leave her alone, and give her back her cover. I will need her when we arrive at the village. Bring her out in half an hour along with her boyfriend. We will have some entertainment."

The men muttered but obeyed and wrapped Bailey in the sheet. Her wrists were tied, but she was left alone. The men played cards and smoked cigars, whiling away the afternoon.

———

It was late and getting dark. Bailey was seated in an open jeep. Her face was swollen; her cuts had stopped bleeding but there was dried blood on her lips. She had been crying for hours.

She had seen Ernesto being loaded into a closed truck. That he was still alive meant that there was still hope. She tried to call out, but the words would not come. Ernesto had seen her—their eyes met briefly before he was thrown into the back of the vehicle. The distance to the village was covered in a short time. Along the way, soldiers and pistoleros adjusted and loaded their weapons. They had donned masks and looked primed for battle.

The village of Acteal was as she had left it—rows of neatly kept houses, each with its tidy yard and bit of garden. A few lamps could be seen through windows, and torches flickered in the yards. Without electricity the hamlet was ghost-like, almost invisible in the dark. One building stood out from the rest like a bright oasis in the blackened jungle, illuminated by a host of candles. From within came the low murmur of voices and the chant of hymns. The people were at prayer.

The convoy of vehicles pulled to a stop in the square adjoining the church. The pistoleros formed up in small groups, loading and checking their weapons. The night air was alive with the clash of metal upon metal, bolts slamming home, bullets being levered into chambers. Then everything stilled. The men waited quietly, smoking cigarettes.

Hernandez stood in his jeep and pulled Bailey to her feet by the arms. "Bring out her Indian lover!"

Two pistoleros pushed Ernesto to the back of the covered truck. His arms were bound and his feet tied together. A hard shove propelled him from the vehicle and onto the ground.

"Bring him here! Closer, I want to see his face."

Ernesto was prodded into a standing position with the barrel of a rifle. His features were barely recognizable. Blood ran down his forehead from a cut somewhere above his hairline, and he looked as if his nose had been broken. His eyes were clear, and they smouldered with hatred.

Hernandez examined him briefly. Then without warning he hit him with a backhand blow across the face. Ernesto stumbled but did not fall.

"This one has no respect." Hernandez paced in front of Ernesto, removing his thin leather gloves. "He does not understand that of all his friends he alone has a chance to live. The rest are dead. You understand that, do you not? The only reason you are still alive is this woman. She alone can save you."

Ernesto spoke through damaged lips. "Leave her out of this. She is not involved."

"Ah, but she is. She chose to dirty herself by sleeping with dogs. Now it is only right for her to decide which of you animals shall live and which shall die." Hernandez' lips twisted in an icy smile.

"Here is your choice, señorita. A military court has convicted your lover of high treason. The sentence is death. His conspirators have already been executed. But I can be merciful, and it may be that he is not guilty. Perhaps it is the people of Acteal, those wretches in the church, who are the true enemies of the state."

Hernandez brought his face close to hers and lowered his voice. "Come now. It is important that you tell us—is it he who is guilty or is it they? If it is the people of the village, then you and your lover may go free with the thanks of the government of Mexico. Otherwise we must carry out the sentence of the court."

Bailey was petrified. It was not for her to decide. Hernandez was only playing with her. But she also knew he would make good on his threat. The other men were already dead—Ernesto would be killed unless she did something. Perhaps she could save him. Perhaps there was a real choice to be made. The violence and confusion had numbed her brain; it would not respond. She stood mute, shaking with fear.

Ernesto was struggling with his captors. "Don't do it, Bailey! They will kill me anyway." A blow to the back of the head dropped him senseless to the ground.

"Which will it be then?" Hernandez demanded. "Who will you choose to save?" He pulled his automatic from its holster and placed the barrel against Ernesto's forehead.

Bailey was paralyzed. She could not let Hernandez kill him. Surely the army was only after Zapatistas—they could have no quarrel with old men, women, and children. This could not be happening.

"Choose. This is your last chance. On the count of three I will fire. One . . . two . . . "

"No, it was them! It is they who are guilty!" She pointed wildly at the church. "They are all Zapatistas. They have been plotting . . . they have guns . . . they have . . . " It was as if someone else was uttering the damning words. Was this her voice she was hearing? She could not be saying these things. They were not true. It did not matter—she would have said anything to stop Hernandez from pulling that trigger.

Hernandez smiled in satisfaction. "Thank you, I thought as much." He put his pistol back in the holster. "Put this criminal back in the truck! We can deal with him later. Now burn the church!"

The pistoleros lit kerosene torches and tossed them onto the roof of the chapel. The building was constructed of wood and grass thatch—the dry materials ignited immediately, and within moments flames towered into the air. A ball of fire and heat erupted from the building. The doors to the chapel flew open and people poured out coughing and choking. Some were already on fire as they fell to the ground, rolling to smother the flames. There were screams and confused shouts. The killing began.

The machine pistols chattered and spit, their muzzles creating bright flashes in the night. As the worshipers burst from the burning church, they were greeted by a maelstrom of bullets. Women with babes in their arms stumbled and fell. Some died while running, landing in shapeless heaps. Old men, too ill to run, stood waiting until the bullets found them. Others approached the pistoleros with their hands in the air, seeking to surrender. They slumped down with mouths open, as if astonished by their own deaths. The running and screaming continued; the scene was chaos, a glimpse into Hell. Some of the fleet seemed about to escape, only to tire and lie down upon the ground. The hammering of the guns continued until finally there were no more running forms in the smoke. The dying flames backlit a pile of bodies, some still moving and whimpering in pain.

The pistoleros drew their machetes and moved in among the fallen. The bright blades shone in the reflected light as they rose and fell. The cries began anew. Hands were raised in supplication as the knives struck time and again. Somewhere in the melee a machete cut into a belly and a fully formed fetus was held up as a prize.

There were shouts of excitement from the attackers, mixed with pleas for mercy and the wail of children. After long minutes, movement ceased, the last anguished voice was silenced. The only sound was the panting of the men, out of breath from excitement and exertion. The pistoleros were covered in gore, their pant legs wet to the knees in blood.

Bailey could not accept the reports of her senses. She could not bear to watch or to hear, but she could not turn away. She recognized her friends as they fell. Pedro, Maria, Luisa. All dying now—their blood spilling onto the ground. She felt their eyes as they raised their hands in futile attempts to plead for mercy and to protect their children. They seemed to be looking directly at her, as if they could see her through the smoke. Their pleas were directed at her. Their imagined last words were burned into her brain. "You betrayed us. You killed us. Our blood is on you." Bailey wanted to close her eyes and shut out the horror, but this pageant had been staged for her. It was her duty to witness.

Bailey's mind finally could accept no more. A sense of unreality overtook her. She saw the people fall; she knew they were dead. But her brain would not accept this. It told her they were only resting. They would soon rise again and be alive and unharmed. Such evil could not exist.

The pistoleros stumbled back to their vehicles. One fired a short burst of fire at an imagined movement. A machete swung in one last arch. The men were smiling, clapping each other on the back. Exhausted but happy, they accepted the proffered bottles Hernandez had waiting.

"Well done. Well done." Hernandez congratulated each man as he arrived at the vehicles. There were hugs and comradely laughter. Empty bottles were thrown among the still bodies.

The small caravan bumped along the dirt track back to the cave. The pistoleros' work for the night was over. They drank and sang lusty songs. The man sitting closest to Bailey pulled her to him and plunged his hands and fondled her breasts. He met with no resistance—her face was fixed in a vacant stare.

In the cave they raped her, but she was already past caring. Bailey was aware of the weight on her stomach and movement within her. She was struck time and again, but the pain was as nothing. Her mind drifted. When would they kill her? Might it be soon? She hoped so, as one after another spilled his seed inside her bleeding thighs. She did not care. There could be nothing more terrible than what she had already seen and done. She should die quickly.

They killed Ernesto. The pistoleros thought it would provide fine entertainment to have him watch as they raped her. They tied him to a chair. Ernesto glared at them with contempt and refused to speak. Finally they made Bailey watch as they slit his throat, and cheered as he choked on his own blood. They threw his body into the pit with the others.

Towards dawn the pistoleros tired of their sport. Bailey had not responded to the atrocities committed upon her. The men had been brutal, and she had suffered at their hands. Her eyes were closed and swollen; blood oozed from between her legs. She was no longer appealing, even to drunken pistoleros. She was bleeding somewhere inside, and her breathing was laboured and shallow.

A pistolero drew his knife and pulled her head back to expose her throat. "No, don't waste your energy on her." Even through the pain, Bailey could recognize Hernandez' voice. "She is not worth the cleaning of your blade. Leave her to die in the dark with her Indian lover."

They left her. The pistoleros extinguished their torches and set fire to stacks of brush piled in the cave. They mounted their vehicles. Voices took up drinking songs as they pulled away.

She needed to die. Her body screamed for release. She choked on the thick smoke from the fires, but she was beyond physical pain. The long sleep of death beckoned. But not here, not in the dark like a rat. She should die in the sun, where the wind would blow away the stink of this place and the rain would mix her body with the soil.

She had lost all feeling in her legs and could not stand, so she crawled on her hands and knees. She dragged her body along the ground with her hands, past the fires that licked at the walls. She must get out.

Finally, she was in the light. She lay on the warm ground, waiting for death to take her.

Hands were on her body. Were they back again to finish it? Had they not had enough? But the hands covered her with something soft; she felt herself rising into the air. Was this what death was like? Was this God? Surely He would not have come for her. The air against her cheek felt warm and the birds sang in the trees. But the pain was still with her, the agony in her mind more terrible than the injuries to her body.

Abelardo was her saviour. The Zapatista soldier had been travelling a seldom-used trail on his way to Acteal for Christmas when he had chanced upon Bailey's naked body. He carried her the five miles to the nearest help—a police station set up by the government to monitor Zapatista activities. For his act of charity, Abelardo was arrested and beaten. He had expected as much—he was wearing a rebel uniform.

Bailey was rushed to a hospital for treatment. The police interrogated Abelardo for twenty-four hours, using the bull whip as their instrument of persuasion. They could prove nothing. He stuck to his story that he had found the injured woman and that he knew nothing about Marcos and the rebellion.

After Abelardo had received his first sixty lashes, a messenger arrived bringing the news of a massacre. The police had no more time to torture a lone bandit, so they let him go. He was thrown from the police station with his skin hanging in ribbons. His Christmas with his family was spent with a shovel at their graveside. The scars on his back were a constant reminder of his wife and his children, and of the woman he had found in the jungle.

CHAPTER 46

THE VILLAGE WAS PREPARING to celebrate the Day of the Dead. The streets had been swept and decorated with flowers. Baking smells wafted through the air and parties of labourers were at work in the churchyard, straightening tombstones and weeding the graves. The crowds in the market were in a holiday mood. An outsider would never have guessed at the macabre nature of the upcoming celebration—that the village was about to celebrate the slaughter of family and friends.

Ted wondered at the contradictions but said nothing. Although he could now think of Acteal as his home, he was not a campesino. Thousands of years of culture and history separated him from his neighbours and there were many things that remained outside his understanding. It was not for him to judge the Day of the Dead.

Stalls had opened in the small central square, making the village look like any Mexican market town. Local craftsmen displayed their wares—carvings, paintings, artifacts. Itinerant peddlers had arrived in the village with goods and delicacies not normally available in Acteal. The campesinos lined up to purchase chocolate-covered skulls and pastry skeletons. Offerings of fruits, vegetables, crated chickens, and tethered goats gave the scene an air of normality.

Rosa was a changed person. This was the first time that she would actually celebrate the Day of the Dead in Acteal since the death of her family. As the day grew nearer, she smiled more frequently and seemed increasingly at peace, as if she truly were about to visit with her husband and children. She hummed as she worked. Ted volunteered to spend extra time in the garden, freeing Rosa for sewing and preparing her ceremonial wreaths.

Two days before the festival, Magdalena arrived, travelling with three other nuns. She set up court in Rosa's home and called the neighbours together. Five or six villagers stood uneasily in the small house as Magdalena announced that she was staying for the events, paying homage to the dead.

"There has been enough devil worship in this village. We should respect the dead but remember that the first of November is also a sacred holiday, the Day of All Saints. As this village has no priest, I am here to represent the Church. There will be services in the churchyard tomorrow evening." The Mayans looked down at the floor as she lectured, but no one talked back.

After the others had left, Magdalena and Ted greeted each other warmly. Her official duties over for the moment, she was once again the energetic little woman who insisted on the use of her first name. Ted forgot himself and put his arms around her, pulling her close. He realized his error and began to pull away—there must be a prohibition against hugging a nun. Magdalena grabbed him firmly by the shoulders and drew him closer.

"I'm not made of glass you know," she said. "It's good to see you. How are you?"

"Fine, I'm fine, really. Getting better."

Magdalena's eyes narrowed. "It's Bailey, isn't it? Something is wrong. Tell me about it."

"She's gone. She left me in Tuxtla."

Magdalena took his hand in both of her own. "How? I cannot believe that she would do such a thing. She seemed so devoted to you when you left the convent. Are you certain that something hasn't happened?"

"The morning she left we had an argument, and then she did not return. She sent a note. I hoped at first that she would come back, but now . . ." Ted's shoulders sagged.

Magdalena smiled sadly. "Do not lose heart. She may return. I think that she cares for you. But you know that she is very troubled. It may be that she is afraid to be too close to another person. Love scares her."

"Then you think there is a chance she may return?" he said.

"In everything there is a plan," said Magdalena. "And I believe that the Lord means for you and Bailey to be together. It may just take a little time."

Ted found comfort in Magdalena's words even though he could not make himself believe them. A plan? Like the water in a stream? It would be nice to see the world in such simple terms.

The next morning there was a commotion in the village. Marcos arrived alone and without apparent means of transportation. He wore his black uniform and balaclava. The people thronged to the square to hear him speak. Marcos stood on a stool in the street and addressed the assembly in a loud voice.

"Amigos, I bring you greetings. You have won the respect of Zapatistas everywhere. In Acteal, we are winning the Revolution."

Marcos was a charismatic speaker and the crowd warmed to him instantly. He spoke as if to each person individually and was constantly making eye contact. Applause and cheering broke out from the campesinos.

"How is that, you say? How are we winning? I will tell you. We are winning just by your being here. The government, the Red Mask, they sought to kill you, to destroy the village of Acteal. But your presence here today means that they have failed—you came back."

The speech was interrupted by more cheering.

"And by coming back, you have won. The government knows now that they cannot defeat us with bullets. We will simply come back."

Shouts of "*Viva Zapata!*" and "*Tierra y Libertad!*" came from the crowd.

"So that is why I am here today. Where better in all of Mexico to celebrate *el Dia de los Muertos* than in Acteal. And I know that in being here, I am also helping to win the Revolution."

There was applause after every sentence.

"Our friends from the press, they have asked if they could come as well to witness this sacred event in this place. I told them no, not this year. This year is for the people of Acteal and the ones that we remember. Perhaps next year we will let them put us on TV." There was laughter at the last remark.

"So now, let us get ready. The first celebration of *el Dia de los Muertos* since the massacre should be one to remember!" Marcos drew his pistol and fired shots into the air.

Ted pushed through the crowd to speak to Marcos, but before he could get close the Zapatista had disappeared. Ted was unable to find anyone who knew where he might have gone.

The population of the village had grown. The word of the return of the first residents had spread all over Chiapas. The news had attracted other campesinos to return from exile. People who had escaped to other villages learned of the resettlement and rushed back to reclaim their homes.

The upcoming festival had drawn Mayans from the surrounding countryside like a magnet. Where else in all of Mexico was there more to mourn or more dead heroes of the Revolution to remember? Over two hundred people waited for the dawn of the Day of the Dead in Acteal.

CHAPTER 47

THE MEMORY OF WHAT HAD HAPPENED that night had never been forgotten. She had hidden it from herself, confined it to a small space in her brain and locked it up tight. But it had always been there, trying to get out. She had never been without the weight of it.

In the beginning it had been a defence mechanism. Pretend that it had never happened. The choice had been to either do that, or to go completely insane. The psychiatrists had encouraged her. "You must get past the guilt. Put it behind you or it will destroy you." So she had tried, and for a time she had been successful. The massacre had taken place, but she had not been there. She was a victim, but not a participant. She repeated the mantra over and over until she started to believe it. Slowly, Bailey started to function again, and life went on.

But all the time the memory was striving to escape from its little locked space. It tried to sneak under the door, cracks of light that had seeped into her consciousness. Visions had haunted her dreams, and then her waking hours as well. Now it was out. And it was in control of her.

Bailey started screaming. There was no thought behind it; the resurfacing memories were too terrible to bear without giving voice to the pain. Her cries filled the small space.

The pistoleros were at first amused by the din, but quickly found it distracting. Threats were followed by cuffs but to no effect—Bailey continued to wail. The men had been forbidden by Hernandez to mistreat her, so they finally stuffed rags into her mouth. Bailey was shoved into a small chamber at the back of the cave to await her fate. The area had been used as a latrine and the stench of urine permeated the air. Garbage littered the stone floor.

Bailey was oblivious to her surroundings or to the bonds that held her. Her mind was back in Acteal four years before, reliving the massacre time and again. The events had been suppressed for too long. She endured the vivid recall. Her nostrils smelled the gunpowder and her ears were full of the screams of the dying. Her eyes were blind with tears.

After Mexico there had been the hospital near San Diego, a place she had remained for almost a year after the attack. Almost nine months after her return to the United States, Bailey had delivered a baby. It was a girl. She had been counselled to have an abortion but refused; she insisted on continuing to term. Her doctors thought her pregnancy was a result of her rape by the pistoleros. She did not tell them the truth.

She had known all along the baby was Ernesto's. From the moment of conception, she had felt the quickening. It was to be a surprise for him, their love child. Now this new life was all that was left; she could not let anyone kill his child. When she went into labour, Bailey imagined she would die, like her mother before her. The thought had pleased her—death in giving life.

She awoke disappointed to have survived the ordeal; it was not supposed to be this way. When the nurse showed her the wrinkled infant, she made her take it away. Bailey never saw her daughter again. One look at the eyes had been enough. They had been Ernesto's eyes—they were accusing her, damning her for her choice. The next day Bailey signed the forms renouncing her parental rights.

She had refused to give her daughter a name. She had no right to burden her child with a name that she would bear for the rest of her life. Her adoptive parents, whomever they might be, should be the ones to name her—it would help to make the baby theirs. Bailey had a name in her mind, although she had not revealed it to anyone. She thought of her daughter often by that name. Her name was Donata.

Eventually Bailey had been released from hospital. The trance-like state had slowly lifted, and she learned to live life a day at a time. Bailey had not gone back to work; there was no possibility of her ever returning to Mexico or to aid work of any kind. She lived on her inheritance, a life without complications. She never thought of Acteal.

Now she was destined to relive the horror of that night. Hernandez intended to finish what he had started and kill the survivors of the original massacre. And again Bailey was to have a starring role in his theatre of death. There was nothing she could do to stop him. She was bound and gagged, unable to move, incapable of even harming herself.

There were loud voices outside her chamber. "Throw him in there with the woman!"

There was a thump as another body was thrown to the ground beside her. The new prisoner was bound like her. He was small, a boy perhaps. His face was streaked with dirt and there was blood running from his nose. She recognized him.

"Miguel!"

Guards posted near the camp had spotted something. There had been movement in the undergrowth, and they thought at first they had spotted a boar. Close up, the creature was identifiable as a street child, dressed in rags. The boy had led the pistoleros on a spirited chase and then when cornered had spat and scratched like a demon. Miguel had been knocked unconscious by the stock of a rifle across his face. His nose was bloodied, and probably broken, but he was otherwise unharmed.

Hernandez had been delighted when the body had been carried into the cave and dumped onto the floor. This was the boy he had seen in Acteal, the one who had been travelling with the gringo in the mountains. This was getting better and better. He would find a role for him as well in his upcoming drama.

"He is not to be touched," he commanded, "and neither is the gringo whore. And no drinking before the raid. Any man who disobeys me will be shot."

Bailey heard Miguel sobbing as he lay beside her. He was mumbling, words she could barely make out. It sounded like nonsense. He kept repeating that someone had killed his pigeon.

Bailey struggled to bring her emotions under control. She could not allow herself to wallow in self-pity. It was right that she should die, but now Miguel was involved as well. She had to find some way out of this, anything that might prevent Hernandez from following through with his plan. Nothing came to her. Her situation was hopeless. In desperation she began to pray.

In the adjoining chamber the pistoleros were playing cards, drinking, and talking loudly. Their words came to Bailey through the passageway.

"*Bastardo!* Who does he think he is? He says we are forbidden to drink before we attack."

"Eh, Paulo, just one will not hurt. Here, it will steady the nerves."

"And that bitch back there, we should have some fun with her while we wait. But no, Hernandez, that high and mighty prick, he commands us to leave her alone. The men of the Red Mask take orders from no one."

"Even so, we take his money. Here, more tequila."

"Yes, one more, take one for yourself. When this is over, we should rid ourselves of him. What do you think? Hernandez will take all the glory for himself. We will be forgotten like the last time."

"*Si*, you are right. We are nothing to him. All he cares about are his foolish games of death."

"Maybe we should make him get his hands dirty, kill a few campesinos himself. Bullets can go wild. Anything can happen."

There was a growl of assent. "Drink up! To the Red Mask!"

Bailey listened to the exchange and the toasts and the drinking that followed. So they hated Hernandez. What good was that knowledge to her? These men were animals—they would rape and kill as eagerly as their commander. She continued to pray, seeking inspiration. Bailey had prayed before, but this time was different. This time she was calling on God.

CHAPTER 48

"ROSA, TELL ME OF THIS Day of the Dead," Ted said.

Rosa looked up from her weeding. "It is the most important day of the year. The dead arise and visit with the living. I will see my children again."

"Come on, Rosa, you can't really believe that. That the dead actually come back to life?

"It is not just belief. It is real," Rosa snapped. "Even the nuns participate. Sister Magdalena may tell you it is all superstition, but she will be there in the churchyard at midnight. You will see." She turned her back on him and began working at the far end of the garden.

Ted bent his head down over his hoe and reminded himself to keep his opinions to himself.

The village hummed with activity. The women stoked their wood ovens, preparing special foods to place on the graves. The men tidied the graveyard and wove bunches of flowers into trellises and wreaths. Marigolds were the flowers of choice, yellow being the favourite colour of the dead.

Ted's role in the preparations was to pick as much ripe produce as possible for the various feasts, and he worked from dawn until dark. The work was good for his body and for his mind—it left him little time to dwell on Bailey. His health was returning and his wound was almost healed.

The main event of el Dia de los Muertos was to take place in the cemetery. The graves were already festooned with flowers and long tapers were set before each one, ready to be lit. The procession began as dark fell.

Torches made of oil-soaked rags lined the route, bathing the scene in a flickering orange light. The smell of burning kerosene filled the air; black smoke drifted above the flames.

Women carrying baskets filled with marigolds led the procession. They threw the leafy blooms underfoot, creating a yellow carpet for those who followed. Grieving mothers bore plates of food to set on the graves. Amongst the mourners marched Magdalena and the other three nuns. They held small white crucifixes and their lips moved in quiet prayer.

Costumed revellers dressed as spirits and demons, and Mayan gods ran back and forth, blaring horns and clapping sticks. Fireworks were set off. Missiles exploded in the air as the procession marched round and round the tiny cemetery. The tears of grieving mothers were mixed with revelry and the murmured prayers of the nuns. Candles were lit on every grave. The parading celebrants were bathed in their flickering light. Meals were set near the tombs to entice the spirits to awake and join the living.

Ted felt out of place. He was not open to the supernatural, and did not believe anything he had been told about the raising of the dead. Devils, rockets, food placed on graves—it seemed to him his friends were making fools of themselves.

But as time passed and the festivities continued, Ted came slowly to understand. Bit by bit the incongruous parts of the ceremony began to fit together. *El Dia de los Muertos* was a contradiction. It seemed to be both a party and an occasion of public worship, solemn and boisterous all at the same time, a pagan ritual and Christian worship co-existing. But for the people of Acteal, every part of it was real—the eyes of the participants shone with genuine tears of grief and merriment. At this very moment they believed themselves to be touching the spirit world.

At long last, he thought he understood what the Mayans were about and found that he agreed with them on many things. These were simple people whose hold on the real world was tenuous and uncertain. Death could come suddenly and from many directions. It was a comfort to both feel the touch of the other side and to celebrate the thing they feared the most.

Ted stayed in the background and tried to remain as inconspicuous as possible. He still felt himself to be an outsider, and these people should have their day without being distracted by him. But although he did not participate, he began to feel the power of the moment. Life was transitory, death inevitable. To die was simply to move from one dimension to another.

The Mayans believed that death was not to be feared but to be welcomed, even celebrated. What was important was that the journey through the present state be made worthwhile. They were right—they had been right all along. It had just taken him a long time to see it.

Ted began to feel lightheaded, somehow intoxicated by the celebration around him. He knew the mourners were seeking to touch the other world, but he had not expected the same reaction in himself. Now, in this otherworldly setting of a torch-lit graveyard in the middle of the night, Ted let his mind wander where it would.

His thoughts strayed naturally to the two men who had been killed since his arrival in Chiapas—Ramone and Abelardo. He had not known them well, but their deaths had touched him. It was right that he should think of them, perhaps even mourn their deaths in his own way. But the experience was more than that. He could feel their presence nearby, almost hear them whisper to him. He felt their strength, their courage, and their certainty in a life hereafter.

Ted sat slightly apart from the others. Nothing like this had ever happened before. How could he be sitting in a graveyard deep in conversation (*were they really speaking?*) with two dead men he had barely known? He told himself that this was all superstition; the voices he heard were just figments of his wild imagination. Or perhaps there had been something in the food.

But he could hear the voices clearly, even if their messages were obscure. There was a voice, he thought it to be Ramone's, counselling him that he must not "choose." What did that mean? "Choose?" "Choose what?" he asked the voice in his head, but there was no response. There was a second voice; this one he recognized to be Abelardo. How was it that he could identify voices that his ears did not hear? This voice told him about strength and courage. "Strength is not in the arm, but in the heart." Again the message made no sense.

Whatever the meaning of the words, the presence of the spirits (if Ted could believe there really were spirits with him), gave him a warm and secure feeling. There was nothing uncomfortable about this dialogue; it was not in the least frightening. The spirits of these men were visiting him for a reason, and he would need their messages one day. Ted listened to the voices, shutting out everything else around him. The hours passed. It was in the wee hours, just before the first light of dawn, when they left him. It was a palpable leave-taking—Ted could feel the warmth of their embrace as they departed. Their last message was one that lingered: "Strike true. Do not be afraid. We will be with you."

Ted sat deep in thought, trying to make sense of what had just occurred.

CHAPTER 49

THE DARKENED CHURCHYARD was suddenly flooded in cold white light. The celebrants all froze where they stood, illuminated in stark relief. The cemetery was surrounded on all sides by vehicles, their headlights shining inward. There were some shouts from the people, a single scream, and then a gunshot followed by a voice amplified through a bullhorn.

"*Atención! Atención!* Do not attempt to escape. Anyone who does will be shot! Everyone gather here in front of me. Now!"

A man standing in the front seat of an army jeep was giving the orders. As Ted's eyes adjusted to the light, he could make out four covered trucks. Pistoleros were standing beside the vehicles. Their machine guns pointed into the crowd.

Caught by surprise in their mystic revelries, the people were unable to do anything other than obey. They shuffled nervously towards the entrance to the cemetery. Graves stood abandoned, their tapers still flickering but now untended. The prancing devils and ghosts that had been animated moments before were now subdued, as if no longer certain of their immortality. They gathered around the source of the shouted orders.

"My name is Colonel Emiliano Hernandez and these are my loyal followers of the Red Mask."

A gasp went through the crowd. Somewhere a woman screamed. The headlights reflected eyes opened wide.

Magdalena pushed to the front of the crowd and up to Hernandez' jeep. Her face was flushed with anger. "How dare you come here. And of all days—the Day of All Saints. You have no business here. Leave us immediately."

Hernandez sneered a half-smile. "Your orders are for your novitiates, Sister. You have no power over me and my men. We are here to settle an old score. It has to do with your friend Bailey."

"You will have to look elsewhere because she is not here," Magdalena said. She stood with her hands on her hips, glaring at Hernandez.

"Ah, but she is," Hernandez said. He heaved the figure next to him to her feet. Her hands were bound and the gag around her mouth obscured most of her face, but her close-cropped hair was recognizable. She was wearing the same clothing as when she left the hospital in Tuxtla.

Ted rose from where he sat and strode to the front of the crowd. He stepped in front of Magdalena.

"I'm here," he said. "Now let her go."

Even as he spoke the words, Ted realized that something had changed. There was no rage; this was not one of his explosions of anger that allowed him to confront his fears. And what was even more surprising was that he was not afraid. And for once he should have been—Hernandez was an armed psychopath who meant to kill him. For the first time in his life, Ted faced his fate with calm resolve.

"Señor Somerville," Hernandez said. "How nice to see you. I have another of your friends here to see you."

Hernandez motioned to one of his men who picked up a body and threw it into the dust in front of the vehicle. It was a boy, bound by the wrists and feet. Ted ran forward and rolled the body over. Miguel's eyes were open and blinking.

"What do you want with the boy, Hernandez? Let him go."

Hernandez smiled. "Certainly, anything you like. The choice is yours. I will trade your friends' lives and even your own for those of the villagers of Acteal. One word from you and the three of you are free to go. Or if you choose otherwise, I will kill your two friends and leave the village alone. Either way, I have no quarrel with you. You will not be harmed. Your friend Bailey, she made this choice once before and as a result she is still alive today. Tell him about it. Tell him about the choice you made." Hernandez ripped away the tape that held Bailey's gag in place.

The words boiled from Bailey's lips. "Ted, he's lying! He means to kill us all. Don't choose. It will destroy you. Ted, his own men hate him. They want to kill him."

Hernandez clapped his hand across her mouth. He held her tightly, preventing further attempts at speech. She squirmed and kicked in his grasp but was unable to escape.

Hernandez seemed only slightly ruffled. "Perhaps the señorita does not wish you to play our little game, but what about the chico? Bring me the boy."

Miguel was yanked to his feet. His face was filthy and he was bruised about the mouth and nose. But his eyes were clear. "Ted, do not choose for me. Miguel is Zapatista. I am ready to die. Save the village."

"What do you think, señor?" Hernandez asked. "Do you believe your friends that they do not wish to be saved? Can you let them die? And what do you owe to these villagers? They are nothing to you, just a pack of rebel criminals. Do you think that they would save you if the choice were theirs? Of course not."

Magdalena shouted at Hernandez. "This is an obscenity. Let them go. In the name of the Church I command it."

"You command nothing, Sister. Tie her up; gag her. I want no more from her."

The pistoleros obeyed. Two men seized the old woman firmly but gently and tied her hands and taped her mouth. Her eyes flashed daggers at her captors.

Ted thought suddenly of Marcos. He had not seen him all day. Was he still in the village?

Hernandez was still holding Bailey in front of him. "Now choose, señor. The boy will die first." A pistolero levelled his machine pistol at Miguel.

Ted was resolute. He had made his decision—Bailey had given him the inspiration he needed. There was no need for delay. The river must run its course, and in the end there would be the sea. There was no other way.

"No, Hernandez, it is time for you to choose," Ted said.

"What do you mean, it is time for me to choose? I am in charge here," Hernandez said.

Ted was icy calm. His voice did not break, and there was no anger in his tone. "No, Hernandez, it is you who must choose. Listen carefully, and I will explain. On the one hand, you can fight me. I intend to kill you. You will have the right to defend yourself with your own blade. Or if you choose, you can order your men to shoot me down where I stand. But if you make this second choice, your men will know you for the coward that you are. They will no longer obey your orders—you will be as good as dead. Now choose. Either I will kill you now, or your men will kill you later. Perhaps with me you have a better chance."

The eyes of the nearest pistolero widened behind his mask. He nodded. Other gunmen inclined their heads in agreement.

Hernandez' eyes followed the subtle gestures. "No!" he shouted. "It is you who must choose who shall live!" His voice had risen a half-octave.

From behind Ted, a figure wearing a feathered headdress drew a hunting knife from his costume. Without a word, he pressed the weapon into Ted's hand. The pistoleros did not intervene. Ted held the gleaming weapon in front of him and pointed it at Hernandez. They were about ten feet apart.

Hernandez was standing in the jeep still holding Bailey. Now he threw her aside, and she fell with her face pressing into the earth. "God save him. I beg of you," she said.

Ted's concentration was on what lay ahead. He was calm, his senses acute, his emotions were under control. He saw what lay ahead as clearly as looking into a glass of water, and he both accepted and welcomed his fate. If he died, he died. He circled Hernandez, drawing closer by the step.

"Enough of your games of death, Hernandez. Now choose. Draw your knife or tell your men to fire. Make your choice before I kill you."

His brain told him this was suicide. His body was still weak, only days out of the hospital. Hernandez was an expert and had killed with a knife many times. But none of this mattered. Ted was not alone—he felt the spirits within him. He sensed Abelardo's strength coursing through his arm; Ramone's knowledge and courage stilled his heart. Their voices urged him to be steady and to strike true. The knife felt natural in his hand, the blade balanced, his arm strong. He could visualize the spot on Hernandez' chest where the knife would slide easily between the ribs. The man's heart beating within his chest was his target. Hernandez was as good as dead. There was no doubt in his mind.

"This is ridiculous!" Hernandez unbuttoned his holster and began to draw his pistol. "I have no intention of fighting you. You are not worth the blood-stains you would leave on my clothes. I will deal with this myself."

"No! Leave your pistol where it is." Cerves' words were coarse and loud. "The gringo has spoken well. We think it is right that you should make this choice."

Hernandez looked up in surprise. Cerves' machine pistol was pointed menacingly between his legs.

"It would be good sport for us to watch you in action, Hernandez, to see if you are really as good with a knife as you say. Or are you afraid of the gringo? Do you want me to kill him for you?" Cerves' words were slurred and his voice had an angry edge.

"*Remember me, Hernandez?*" Ted said, in fluid Spanish. The words came from his mouth but not from his brain. Ramone's spirit was speaking through him. "*You laughed when I promised that you would pay for my death. You strung me from trees for the animals to eat. It is time now for you to atone. Draw your knife—your death awaits you.*" There followed an oath that Ted did not understand.

Hernandez may have seen something in Ted's eyes, or he may have recognized the message in his words. Or perhaps it was the angle at which Ted held the knife or the sureness of his step. Hernandez' hand moved towards his own knife, then stopped. The sneer on his lips faded. His eyes darted, shifting back and forth frantically from the approaching knife to the pistoleros with their guns pointed at him. Perspiration ran down his face in the cool night air.

"Kill him!" Hernandez' voice broke as he screamed the order. There was no reaction from the pistoleros. Their machine guns remained at the ready, but no one moved.

"Kill him now! I command you!"

Ted was almost on him. Hernandez' jaw was trembling. He made no attempt to defend himself but continued to scream for his men to shoot, his voice becoming louder and more desperate by the moment.

"Kill him! Kill him!" Hernandez shrieked.

The screams ended as Cerves smashed Hernandez across the back of the head with his rifle butt. Hernandez collapsed to the ground.

Cerves removed his mask and with disgust on his face he spat on Hernandez' prone body. He worked a bullet into the chamber of his rifle and pointed it at Ted's chest. "That was good sport, gringo. You have saved us some trouble. Now, adios."

"Stop! Drop your weapons!" A voice called from beyond the circle of light.

The pistoleros whirled to face the darkness.

"By order of the People's Army of Chiapas, I demand you to surrender! You are surrounded."

Cerves turned his weapon from Ted and fired towards the sound of the voice. There was a shot in return. His weapon fell from his hands and he grasped his shoulder. Blood oozed from a wound beneath his hand. The other pistoleros looked about in confusion. Nothing moved in the darkness that surrounded the circle of light.

There was movement from the crowd. The devil figure whipped off his headdress. Under the first mask was another—a balaclava. Yellow-green eyes shone out from the slits. Marcos held a pistol in his hand.

"Drop your weapons! Now! Down on the ground or I will order my men to kill you where you stand!"

A pistolero swung his machine gun up. Marcos shot twice and the man fell backwards. The others dropped their weapons to the ground and slid to their knees. They raised their hands over their heads.

"Quick you, tie their hands. Use their belts." Marcos motioned to the campesinos. The pistoleros were bound with their hands behind their backs, their boots tied together with their shoelaces.

Marcos bent to untie Miguel's hands.

"They killed the bird before I could send word. I am sorry, Subcomandante. I failed you."

"No, it is I who have failed you. I should never have sent you into such danger. You have Ricardo to thank for your safety. He convinced me that he should follow and keep track of you. While you were spying on the Red Mask, Ricardo was watching you. You have done very well Miguel—you have made me proud."

Ricardo had come in out of the dark and was inspecting the captured pistoleros.

"Is it only the two of you?" Miguel asked. "Just the two of you captured all of these men?"

Ricardo was wearing a cocky grin. "It was something I learned from Marcos, to do with an empty bottle and the art of deception. If you believe in your ability to defeat a foe, anything is possible."

Marcos gave him the congratulatory salute of the raised closed fist. "You worried me when you shot that pistolero. I did not think that you were a good enough marksman to only wound him. I was afraid that you would miss and hit me."

"Actually, Subcomandante, I did miss," Ricardo said. "I was aiming for his head."

The villagers had freed both Magdalena and Bailey. They were huddled together, the nun cradling the younger woman in her arms. Bailey cried softly while Magdalena whispered to her in a soothing voice.

———

In the confusion, Hernandez had been forgotten. He was lying on the ground with his eyes open; he did not appear injured. Like a rodent frozen before a snake, his eyes were fixed on the knife in Ted's hand. Ted held the long knife with its point aimed at Hernandez' heart. The others gathered about.

"You chose badly, Hernandez. Now prepare to die." Ted spoke softly, like a parent to a delinquent child, regretting the punishment he must administer.

Hernandez' face expressed the terror that was now his only emotion. All life had gone out of him, and he was unable to defend himself. He began to babble, to beg for his life.

"Please, no, I was only following ord—"

Ted placed the point of his knife to Hernandez' throat. "You embarrass yourself. The souls of those you killed demand you should die. Your victims died bravely—you should learn from their example."

"No!"

The voice stopped his hand.

"Leave him," Rosa said. "The right to deal with Hernandez is mine. It was my husband and children he killed. I have the right." She was carrying a machete dropped by one of the pistoleros, eighteen inches of gleaming steel.

Her eyes were hard as she repeated, "I have the right."

Ted's concentration was broken. He looked to Marcos.

Marcos considered briefly before rendering judgement. "Sometimes it is necessary to do hard things. And yes, Rosa has the right."

Ted stepped back. He threw the knife into the darkness.

"Bind his hands, and hold him up. Everyone should witness this. Even them," Rosa said, indicating the bound pistoleros. Hernandez' hands were tied behind his back with his belt as Ricardo held him in a standing position. He was whimpering, tears running down his face. The odour of feces filled the air around him.

Rosa held the machete blade down. She pressed the point into the soft flesh of Hernandez' abdomen, hooking it under the waistband of his pants. She drew the machete straight down. Hernandez shrieked. Ted flinched and looked away.

Ted looked back to find Hernandez unscathed. The razor edge had sliced through Hernandez' trousers and shorts, rending them to the groin. Rosa pulled at the remains of his garments, dropping them around his knees. He was revealed naked to the waist.

Rosa examined Hernandez, looking closely at his genitals. He was now buckling at the knees; it took all of Ricardo's strength to hold him upright. Rosa spoke in a voice that smoked with hatred.

"Tonight I visited with my husband and children. This is the retribution that they seek."

She reached with the machete between Hernandez' legs. He screamed in terror at the touch of the metal on his skin. With the flat of the blade she lifted his penis, now hanging limp and bent. His scrotum was a mass of jagged white scars.

"See," Rosa said. "Look at the butcher who would have killed us all. He is not even a man. He has no *cojones*. For this thing I have only scorn." Rosa raised Hernandez' penis higher so that everyone could observe the deformity.

"Come closer. There is nothing to fear from this eunuch." The people crowded round. Men pointed at the emasculated flesh, muttering to each other. Some stooped down and made to look beneath Hernandez' groin. Women covered their faces but looked from behind open fingers. There were exclamations and chuckles, derisive laughter. The bound pistoleros spit in disgust and looked away.

Hernandez' face collapsed into tears, and sobs wracked his chest. His legs would not support him and Ricardo let him fall to the ground. He grovelled at their feet, dirt mixing with his tears. He emitted mews like a stricken cat.

"Untie him!" Marcos said. "His punishment is not to be death. Our cherished dead do not desire his company, least of all on *el Dia de los Muertos*. Instead he is to be banished from this place. Let the jungle decide if he should live or die."

Ricardo hoisted Hernandez to his feet, untied his hands, and propelled him towards the jungle with the flat of a machete laid across his backside. He stumbled away, falling, tripping, half running, half crawling in the near dark. Illuminated in the vehicle headlights, his bare buttocks gleamed below flapping shirttails. There was laughter and catcalls from the people of Acteal.

"You're just letting him go?" demanded Ted.

Marcos held Ted firmly by the arm. "Rosa has finished what Bailey began. She has taken from him his machismo. Without it he is already as good as dead. He will not bother us again."

As Hernandez reached the edge of the jungle, there was movement close by in the undergrowth—a fleeting suggestion of a large shape, its features indistinct in the darkness, just a flash of spotted tawny hide dissolving into a flowing form. After only a moment, it too was gone, and Hernandez' running, scrambling form was swallowed by the jungle.

The people turned away to their respective gravesides. Candles were relit, wreaths of flowers straightened.

Then screams came from the jungle. "Aarrrrgghhh! Help! Help! No! No! Aaaieeeah!"

Ted's muscles clenched involuntarily from the terror and pain the sound implied. Surely only the devil himself could wring such cries from a living being.

But no one turned to look. The villagers, the pistoleros, even the nuns continued about their business.

The cries ceased.

CHAPTER 50

THE CELEBRATION CONTINUED until dawn. The ritual prayers were said, the food left uneaten. The traditions of thousands of years went unchanged by the night's events. Life was too brief and death too all embracing.

The circle of bound pistoleros was only a minor distraction. Inebriated campesinos stood over them and opened their trousers.

"Red Mask, we piss on you."

In the soft pre-dawn light, the churchyard was an otherworldly place. Tapers burned down to a few inches as the last prayers were said at the tombs. The families quietly packed up the uneaten offerings and stole away to their homes. The ground was stained yellow by the marigolds trampled into the soil.

Ted had gone to Bailey after Hernandez had been dispatched. She was sitting quietly with Magdalena's arm about her shoulder. Her cheeks were wet with tears, but she was no longer crying. Ted took her hand, but she did not react. She seemed far away, her thoughts in some other place. He held her hand until she returned.

She smiled. It was her old, sad smile. He had always wondered what lay behind it. Now he knew.

"I'm sorry about the note. I was coming back, but he caught me."

"I understand."

"I remember it all now. It all came back to me—the killings, what I did, everything." Her eyes met his. The tears welled up again.

Magdalena took her arms from around Bailey and brought her to her knees. "Pray with me child. It will help. Can you pray now?"

"Yes."

"Then say with me, 'Our Father who art in Heaven, hallowed be Thy name, Thy Kingdom come . . . '"

They remained together in the churchyard until daylight spread across the valley. Bailey's lips mumbled in prayer, her eyes tightly closed, hands clasped before her. Finally she slumped down exhausted where she knelt. Ted and Magdalena supported her back to Rosa's home and put her to bed.

―――

The next days were eventful. The police were summoned to take the pistoleros into custody, Marcos melting back into the jungle before their arrival. Ricardo had taken a few men up the path where Hernandez had last been seen. He reported finding small spots of blood and some scraps of cloth, but nothing else. No further search was undertaken.

The pistoleros were broken. They directed the police to the cave that had been their staging ground and to a mass grave containing the remains of twenty-six men. The village pitched in to re-inter the lost dead of Acteal in the churchyard. The people ate together that night and a new tradition was created. The second of November would hereafter be the occasion of the Feast of the Heroes of the Revolution.

Ted saw little of Bailey. She remained indoors in huddled conference with Magdalena. Whenever he visited, she would be distant. She rarely spoke. It seemed to him that his presence upset her. On occasion she would begin to cry without apparent reason.

On some days, she acted almost normal, although she seldom smiled. And when she did, it was that old, sad smile.

Magdalena made no comment about Bailey's state and gave no hint of what they discussed in their time together. When Ted asked how she was doing and whether she would recover, Magdalena would reply, "All in God's good time. We will see."

―――

Five days later Ricardo reappeared in Acteal, driving his motorcycle as fast and recklessly as ever. He was excited and shouted for Ted before his vehicle came to a stop.

"Ted, Ted. We've won!"

"What do you mean? Has there been a battle?" Ted asked. He had been half-dressed and was buttoning his shirt as he met Ricardo in the street. A group of villagers had already gathered.

"No, the government has surrendered! They want peace with us! Read this." Ricardo was waving a newspaper in the air, finally thrusting the two-day-old copy into Ted's hands. The headline was in bold print.

November 5, 2001

SUBCOMANDANTE MARCOS INVITED
TO ADDRESS MEXICAN GOVERNMENT

MEXICO CITY: In a surprise move, President Vicente Fox has invited Subcomandante Marcos, leader of the Zapatista forces in Chiapas, to attend Mexico City to address a joint session of the Mexican National Assembly. This unprecedented offer may signal the end to the seven-year civil war in southern Mexico in which hundreds of opponents of the government have been killed and imprisoned. Observers have speculated that the invitation is related to the recent raid on Acteal by members of the Red Mask, a government-sponsored paramilitary death squad. The attack, the second in four years on the little village, was thwarted by the Zapatista National Army.

The issues in the dispute have included the right of the native Mayans to the return of the land taken from them over a number of generations and their right to a living wage under the North American Free Trade Agreement.

There has been no confirmation as to whether Marcos will accept this offer. A spokesman for the Zapatistas has stated that there are preconditions to Marcos' attendance, which have been communicated to the President.

Experts in Mexican affairs have described these developments as potentially the most significant political event in that country since Pancho Villa and Emiliano Zapata captured Mexico City in 1914.

The news travelled through the village within minutes. The population took to the street, all talking and laughing together. There were cheers and smiles. A guitar was produced, along with bottles of posh. An impromptu street party began that lasted long into the night. New tunes were played for the first time. The defeat of Hernandez and the Red Mask was now legend and had been immortalized in song. Ted sang as loudly as any. He was no longer an outsider and he had learned to sing.

CHAPTER 51

THE NEXT DAY MAGDALENA SENT word for Ted to attend Rosa's home. On his arrival he found both her and Bailey sitting in the house, brewing tea and waiting for him. Bailey was dressed neatly and was without her straw hat. Her hair had grown and her head was covered in short brown curls. Ted noted the improvement in her appearance and dared to hope that her depression had passed.

"Sit down, Ted. I need to speak to you." Bailey was staring at him. Her voice was firm and clear. There was no sign of tears. "I would like Magdalena to stay. Some of this will be difficult."

"Of course, anything you like," Ted said.

She averted her gaze and looked down at her hands. "Ted, I haven't been truthful with you. There were reasons. Some of the time I was just lying to you. I've been deceiving people all my life—it's become second nature to me. And there were times that I couldn't bear the pain. I want to set that straight now, to tell you everything."

Bailey launched into a narrative of her life for the past four years, from her relationship with Ernesto, to the Acteal massacre, to the events on the Day of the Dead. She left nothing out. She told him of the deal with Fuentes, leading to Ted's escape from jail, of her pretended sexual liaison with Marcos, and the cause of the whip marks on Abelardo's back.

"He saved my life, and afterwards visited me in the hospital. I never even thanked him." For the first time that day her eyes shone with tears.

"It's all right," Ted said. "He understood. He told me so."

She spoke at length of the baby she had given up for adoption. She said it was her greatest regret.

"I never should have done it," she said. "If I'd kept the baby, perhaps everything would have turned out differently. But after she was gone, it was too late to change my mind. It was probably for the best. I wouldn't have been a good mother."

"Shhh, don't say that child," said Magdalena, taking her hand.

"Thank you, Mother, but it's true. We both know it."

Half an hour later she sighed. "Now you know everything." There was silence in the room.

"So where do we go from here?" Ted asked.

As if this were a cue, Magdalena rose and excused herself. "This is something the two of you should discuss alone. I will be outside if you need me." She gave Ted a reassuring touch on the shoulder as she passed. He found the gesture odd—he was not the one in need of her sympathy.

Bailey waited until the door had shut behind her. "I'm going with Magdalena, Ted, back to the convent."

Ted was not surprised. The nuns had cared for her before. It made sense for her to return there now. "How long will you be staying?" he asked.

"I'm not just staying there," she said. "I'm going as a novice. I'm becoming one of them."

He felt like he had been kicked in the pit of his stomach, but at some level Ted was not surprised. The whole conversation had been ominous; he had felt that something bad was coming. This explained Magdalena's solicitous gesture. He had been hoping against all reason that things would play out differently, that the future would find them together. His fantasy was crushed in the instant it took her to say the words.

He must have been quiet for a long time.

"Ted, you heard me? I'm going to become a nun."

He did not think to argue with her. This was not a casual decision. The pieces all fell into place. This had been a long time coming.

"When did you decide?" he asked.

"I've been thinking about it for a while, but I felt that I really knew that night in the graveyard after everything was over. When Hernandez held me captive and I thought we were all going to die, I began to pray. I prayed to God not to let Acteal happen all over again, to stop this thing. In return I offered to do anything He wanted of me. He heard me, and my prayers were answered.

Since then it has been clear to me what I must do. Magdalena is not sure I am doing the right thing. But this is my decision. This is all my doing."

"I see." It was all Ted could bring himself to say.

"Don't be angry, Ted. Don't you see it could never work between us. I'm not well. Oh sure, I can be okay for days or even weeks. But then . . . you've seen what happens. What kind of life would that be? We would spend our lives fighting my demons. This is better, for both of us."

Ted could think of nothing that would dissuade her. What was more, he knew that she was right. He had imagined what life would be like with Bailey, but in doing so had been forced to ignore the fall-out of her shattered life. She had merely exposed his dream for the fantasy it was.

"What happens now?" he asked. "When do you start?"

"I already have. Magdalena has been giving me instruction. We leave for San Cristobal tomorrow."

"Will I see you again?" he asked.

"I hope so. We are not cloistered. I hope one day to return to work in Acteal. But for the next while, I can see no one. Novices must spend a year in contemplation and prayer before they become members of the order. I hope to take my vows in time to celebrate the Day of the Dead next year.

"And what about you, Ted? I know that this is very sudden, but what will you do now?"

It had been only minutes since her revelation, but in his eyes she had already changed. Her actions, her words, the way she held herself—she had become a nun.

"It is time to leave," Ted said. "One of Marcos' conditions for the meeting in Mexico City was that all charges against you and me be dropped and our passports returned. I hoped that we would leave together. There is nothing for me here now. I'll go home, home to Canada. I hope one day we'll meet again." Forcing himself to smile was one the hardest things he had ever done.

Bailey rose from her chair and kissed him. It was a warm and loving kiss, but like one from a sister. She was already moving on.

"Goodbye, Ted."

"Goodbye, Bailey."

264

CHAPTER 52

THERE WAS NOTHING LEFT but for Ted to say his goodbyes. He met with Rosa and Miguel. There were tears; Rosa kissed him for the first time. She was at peace. The death of her family had been avenged and her husband rested in the Acteal churchyard. She smiled more often now, and doted on Miguel. She made it clear that there would be no more soldiering for the boy without her permission. Ted made promises to return next year, to celebrate the Day of the Dead and participate in the Feast of the Heroes of the Revolution.

Magdalena came to his house before she and Bailey left for the convent the next morning.

"I'm sorry that I couldn't tell you sooner," said Magdalena, "but the decision was hers to make. She wanted to tell you herself."

"I understand. Is this a wise thing for her?"

"Only time will tell. I do not know if she has the calling. That is why all novitiates must wait a year before taking their vows and joining the order. In that time she will learn to know herself. It is a serious decision, and she may decide that the life of a nun is not for her. In the meantime, the convent is the best place. She has many wounds to heal."

Ted did not answer. There would be enough time to ponder the possibilities in the months ahead.

"Magdalena, one thing still bothers me. Bailey's daughter, is there anything that can be done? Should I make inquiries? The social services agencies may be able to tell us something."

"I have already looked into it," said Magdalena. "The baby has been adopted into a good home. She appears happy and is thriving. When Bailey is ready to know, I will tell her. Her new parents named the girl 'Donata.' Bailey will like that."

"Thank you for everything, Magdalena. I will be back here next year for the celebrations and will see you then. Please don't tell Bailey. I will see her then, whatever her decision."

"Come here," said Magdalena. She seized Ted by the shoulders and hugged him. "You are a good man and you are always welcome here. Yes, come back next year and see us. Strange and wonderful things happen in the world every day."

Ted's last meeting was with Miguel. He arranged a time when he and the boy could be alone and without distractions. Ted's decision had not been made easily, but once made it seemed right. They were in the main room of their little house.

"Sit down, Miguel. There is something we need to talk about."

"What is it?" Miguel asked.

"I am leaving Acteal. I'm going back to Canada."

"Si, I know this."

"I would like you to come with me, Miguel. Not just to visit, but to live with me. I can arrange a visa; you will go to school, and we can be together."

A puzzled expression came across Miguel's face. It was a moment before he responded. "Ted, we are compadres. I love you like my father. But I cannot go to Canada. I am Zapatista—my place is here. Rosa, she needs my help. Without me she has no one."

Ted had not expected this. He had spent a lot of time thinking about whether he should ask Miguel to come to Canada, whether the boy would fit in, whether their relationship could survive civilization. The one possibility he had not considered was that Miguel might turn him down. His momentary hurt from the rejection was replaced by understanding. Miguel was like Bailey—he knew his place in the world, knew where he belonged and what was expected of him. He knew his course. Ted did not argue with him. Instead he reached into his knapsack and took out the watch he had taken off months before.

"This is for you. This is to remember me by."

Miguel took the timepiece reverently. He examined it closely before slipping it on his slim wrist. "Thank you. I will wear this always. I will learn to tell time so I can use it."

"Yes, and you are going to have to learn to read and write as well, because I will be sending you letters, and I want you to write back." Ted was fighting back tears.

"*Si*, the nuns will teach me. I will write."

"And I will be back next year for the celebrations," Ted said. He embraced the boy. "I'm going to miss you."

"*Si*, compadre, next year."

———

The day came for Ted to leave for Mexico City. Ricardo was to take him on his motorcycle as far as San Cristobal and Ted would take a bus the rest of the way. From there he would catch an overnight flight to Vancouver.

A number of the villagers gathered to see him off. "You should not go now, Ted," Ricardo said. "There will be glorious times in Mexico City. You should come with us."

"It's tempting, Ricardo, but I have commitments. There are things that I have put off too long. I will watch you on television."

"Yes, I will be the dashing young revolutionary surrounded by the beautiful women," Ricardo said. He straightened his shoulders and became serious. He motioned for people to gather around. He raised his voice so that all could hear.

"Marcos would be here himself to say goodbye, but he is busy preparing to meet with *el Presidente*. That meeting is critical to the outcome of our struggle and the welfare of our people. He sends his regards, and this." Ricardo pulled a small velvet package from his pack. In it was a star, made of finely hammered silver, attached to a purple ribbon. On it were engraved the words "*Tierra y Libertad.*"

"This is the Zapatista medal for bravery, and as well it makes you an officer in the People's Army of Chiapas."

"I am honoured, Ricardo. Tell Marcos that I will wear it with pride."

They embraced. "Till next year, compadre."

"Yes, until next year."

A motorcycle bearing a helmeted rider roared up to where they stood. It sprayed gravel as it came to a skidding stop.

"I thought you were taking me to the bus, Ricardo," Ted said.

"There has been a change of drivers. I hope you don't mind," Ricardo said with a shrug. "He insisted."

The motorcycle driver made an exaggerated display of checking the time on his gold watch. "Come, Ted. It is time to go. Don't worry, I am a good driver."

CHAPTER 53

AT THE AIRPORT TED WAS MET by a senior official of the Mexican government. With smiles and elaborate apologies, the man presented Ted with the wallet and passport that had been taken from him months before. Everything was there, except that the American currency had been replaced with a bundle of pesos. The man extended his regrets on behalf of the Mexican Customs Service and promised there would be an investigation into the border incident. Ted no longer cared—it seemed like an event that had happened a long time ago and to someone else.

In the midst of the Mexican's act of contrition, Ted smiled and took the man's hand. "Thank you. Thank you for everything," Ted said. He meant every word.

He walked away, leaving the official bearing a stunned expression. Ted smiled to himself all the way onto the plane.

The Air Canada flight departed Mexico City after midnight, arriving in Vancouver at dawn. Ted relaxed in the first-class cabin and accepted a cocktail from the pretty flight attendant. He sat back in his seat. He would rather have been riding a bus with Bailey.

Ted thought back to the parable Rosa had shared with him—life was like water in a stream. It was true. Some people not only understood it, they were living it. Miguel was following his course—he would be a Zapatista and save Mexico for the campesinos if he could. Bailey knew her course. She would do the only thing that was right for her, and work as a nun. Perhaps in time . . .

Ted as well had a course to follow. It was waiting for him back in Canada. There was no use to complain that the course was difficult or that he would have preferred some other. All he could do, all anyone could do, was to meet their destiny as best they could. In the end, as Rosa said, they would all end up in the sea. It helped the world make sense.

Ted opened a copy of the English-language *Mexico City News*. A small story on the inside pages caught his eye:

EL JAGUAR RETURNS

SAN CRISTOBAL, CHIAPAS: Sources near the mountainous town of San Cristobal near the Larandon rain forest have confirmed sightings of jaguars. The largest of the beasts is reported to be over eight feet long and weigh in excess of three hundred pounds. This is the first confirmed jaguar presence in Southern Mexico in over twenty years.

Experts claim that the jaguar became extinct in Mexico as a result of the loss of natural habitat. Mayan folklore connects the absence of the beast, the largest cat in the Americas, to an oppressive political system and the persecution of the campesinos. The return of the predator is seen by some residents of Chiapas province as one more milestone in their fight for freedom and social equality.

Biologists believe that the unexpected sightings are related to new methods of farming, more friendly to the environment, now practised by the farmers in the high mountains.

Jaguars have been known to hunt and kill humans, sometimes stalking their victims for weeks before attacking. There are unconfirmed reports of a fatal mauling in early November. Authorities have refused to comment on the matter except to state that it is under investigation.

Ted lay his head back and closed his eyes. In the moments before he fell asleep, he thought back to the screams in the night, the rustling in the bushes, the presence in the forest. Had the jaguar been stalking him as well? He knew the answer.

ABOUT THE AUTHOR

NORM CUDDY was born in Manitoba, where he graduated from U of M with a Law degree in 1974. He and his wife, Rose, moved to Halfmoon Bay, BC, in 2007, and Norm continued to practise law in both Winnipeg and Vancouver until 2015. In his free time, Norm loved to write fiction, and one of his many passions was sailing, frequently navigating the beautiful coastal waters of BC with Rose. Norm passed away at his home on June 6, 2016. Several months later, Rose found the completed manuscript for *Return of the Jaguar* on a drive in his desk.